Goliath at Sunset

Jonathan Brandow

Goliath at Sunset, by Jonathan Brandow

Library of Congress Cataloging-in-Publication Data: Brandow, Jonathan

1. Shipyard 2. Working class literature 3. Labor Unions 4. Boston history 5. Militant trade union 6. Racism

Cover art by Marc Nelson.

Interior Map by Maya Feinberg

Book design & formatting by Matthew Tallon

ISBN: 979-8-9898025-8-6

For information about the book and to request copies, email:

hardballpress@gmail.com

This is a book of fiction. Any resemblance of characters to any persons living or dead, or any entities active or inactive, is coincidental.

To the Shipbuilders of Local 5, whose characters
and experiences inspired *Goliath At Sunset*.

"Brandow is unflinching in his depiction of the abuses the laborers suffer and of the complexities that come with working for justice... A thought-provoking portrayal of worker abuse and labor organizing." — Kirkus

"Jon Brandow hits a home-run with his compelling and absorbing tale of the struggle for workers' rights in a Massachusetts shipyard. The book is simply marvelous and so completely absorbing I did not want to even pause in reading it." — Bill Fletcher, Jr., author of *The Man Who Changed Colors* and *The Man Who Fell From the Sky*

"Brandow weaves a telling text, capturing diverse voices, youthful energy, and a shipyard's vocabulary and slang. Even if the reader is not a welder, the workplace's cadence and challenges, along with the pride in craft, shine through. For an authentic working-class novel, one can't go wrong with *Goliath at Sunset*." — Mike Matejka, Power at Work

"Perhaps the greatest strength of the novel lies in making clear that what matters is not just the outcome of a particular battle – for win or lose, it is transitory. Rather what matters is what we take away from each organizing effort, and how to integrate that into one's own life." — Kurt Stand, Portside.

"At a moment when working people are once again told to accept less, stay quiet, or blame one another, *Goliath at Sunset* reminds readers what happens when workers stand alone—and what becomes possible when they do not. It is a novel that respects labor, understands its flaws, and affirms its essential role in the fight for dignity on the job and beyond." — Matt Alley, Blue Collar Writer

"Jon Brandow's novel creatively illustrates the subtilties of union struggles in the workplace—important reading for both up-and-coming labor activists as well as seasoned organizers." — Rand Wilson, Organizer at CHIPS Communities United

"Brandow does not slip into easy good guys vs bad guys tropes. What makes the story seem very real is Brandow's ability to slip into the headsets of all the players and show them as fully believable characters. And of course, his own experience as a shipyard welder and union steward gives the depictions an authenticity that could never be matched by an outsider." — Tess Ewing, Past President USW Local 8751

The Shipyard

Despite the stabbing pain that shot up and down her spine, Theresa Shea worked the assembly line at Cambrian Electronics for nineteen years. Most of the two hundred and fifty employees were women. A third of them were island Portuguese with little or no English.

"They are good people," Theresa told her son, Michael. She gushed to him about Domingas, who covered for her when her back acted up. "I'm so grateful. I'd really like to ask her for dinner."

Mike shrugged. "Okay."

Theresa shook her head. "I can't, Mikey. She's one of those mixed breed Portagees. People in our building would hurt her walkin' in the door. Wouldn't let me forget it."

*****

Soon after Mike graduated high school, Theresa told him that her union was planning to strike come spring. "We just need more money," she said, "and a little respect, too."

The day after the picket lines were breached, she sat him down in their kitchen. "The union's calling everyone down to the factory to keep out the scabs, Mikey. I'm going in there."

Michael Shea said, "You're gonna hurt your back again, Ma."

"No one will get hurt. The union's got our side under control and the cops will go easy on us women. Besides, Domingas promised to stick with me on the strike line."

*****

The picket captain spotted the scab van and blasted an air horn warning. The pickets linked arms, but the cops pulled out truncheons and jabbed at bellies and arms. Domingas tried to hold on, but Theresa was thrust away from the crowd and fell. Domingas lunged and draped her body over her friend. She futilely battled the truncheons. Two cops clubbed wildly at the women and pushed Domingas away. One of them kicked Theresa twice. Her ribs crunched. She went dark.

She lay in Cambridge City Hospital for a month before the pneumonia set in. Shea watched her struggle for breath. She locked feeble eyes on him and said, "You can do more. Find the world." Unable to move, barely able to talk, she breathed painfully for another week and then died. Shea shook with fury. *Why didn't I go to the line with her?*

*****

Shea got a condolence note from his Aunt Bridget in Sturbridge. She had come out some fifteen years before, proclaiming her reality to the collective disgust of her East Cambridge neighbors. Even Theresa distanced herself to protect her young son, whether from Bridget's sexuality or taunts from the project, Shea never knew. Bridget cursed them all and walked away. She had been Shea's lifeline to the outside, taking him to see Williams and Jensen at Fenway, the zoos in Franklin Park and up in Stoneham. No one told him why she was gone. No one told him where she was.

At the funeral, it seemed to him that the entire contingent of black Portuguese women from the plant came to mourn.

Afterward, a gold-skinned woman with a kindly middle-aged face and flowing black hair approached him.

"I am Domingas, your mother's friend at work," she said quietly. She reached out to Shea and hugged him. The feel of her startled him. He had never before touched a colored woman, even a light one like her.

Domingas whispered to him, "Your mother told me you were a good son. The last day on the picket line she tells me that she wants a different life for you. I told her there is work at the shipyard in Quincy. So much even the black Portuguese like me get the jobs. But the place is also difficult for many who work there. Your mother thought a good person like you would be of value. To them and yourself."

Shea said, "I guess my mom would have said something like that."

That afternoon Shea looked through the small apartment. He wanted to keep what came down from his nan: a velvet parlor chair, a light veneer hutch with cut glass doors, and a lacquered cabinet inlaid with carved and brightly painted Oriental figures. In the closet he found a sequin purse that held a handful of silver dollars and about five hundred in small bills. He understood that this was savings his mother had meant to use to get them out of the project.

His mom had believed in something strongly enough to stand up and die. He wanted to know how that felt.

*****

In his teens, Shea headed out on Saturdays with his crew from Roosevelt Towers, the bunch of them eager to brandish their white, Irish honor—again—to the other side of town. They hopped the bus from their low-rise East Cambridge project, disembarking to bust bottles in the Sears parking lot below Porter Square, then heading north to lay in wait for black kids from Rindge Towers.

They cornered a broad-shouldered guy coming out of a mom and pop just a few blocks from Rindge. They chased him down and pushed him to the ground. His groceries scattered. Juice and bruised fruit leaked through his torn shopping bags. Shea and four other kids stood in a circle, waiting for him to move. He was big, but he was scared.

"C'mon, you motherfuckers," he breathed. An angry reddish scar ran from his sideburn to the line of his jaw. He tugged at his doo-rag to recoup some dignity.

One of Shea's friends pulled out a leather-wrapped sap. "Tough nigger, hunh?" He waved the sap.

Shea looked down at their victim, who looked him back in the eye.

Shea said, "Forget this shit. Let's go." He put his hands in his pockets.

"Whatta you, fuckin' nuts? He's about to shit his pants."

Shea started toward home, ignoring calls to come back and have some fun.

He stopped at the kiosk in Harvard Square and stared at the dozens of racked newspapers from around the world, at the browsers who were so much more interested in foreign events than in anyone like his mother.

Well-dressed women drifted by wearing flesh-tone stockings, their blouses clasped with little round collar pins. Scattered among them, college kids glanced at Shea without seeing. From the looks of their biceps curled around books, not one had ever been in a street fight. It seemed to Shea that all of them exuded an insolence he had never experienced in East Cambridge.

Domingas and her friends at the funeral had tried to save his mom. He was convinced that none of these people would have lifted a finger.

Shea was one of those kids that the cops never caught, so there was no sheet to get in the way of his 1-A status.

His first-ever plane flight took him to Da Nang in '69, a year that the war killed twelve thousand Americans. The unfairness of it clawed at him every day, being forced to kill incomprehensibly strange little people worse off than he was, watching the guys who protected him die. When the grunts in his platoon talked about what they'd been through, Shea felt greedy, almost lucky. No one was proud of it, but he knew it wasn't his fault or theirs. Whites and blacks rockin' in the same boat.

*****

Back home he told people he'd been in logistics, never saw combat. He just wanted to leave the war behind. But at night he was up with the sweats, on the lookout for death.

His anger felt righteous. At the cops giving anyone who got in their way a lesson they didn't deserve. At commie war protesters. At the VFW or the Legion, so fucking eager to pimp for LBJ and then Nixon, sending off another batch of guys to get shot up for nothing.

He sat and drank for hours over at the Plough and Stars just a stone's throw from Central Square, then headed over to the Cantab Lounge to scout for tipsy young women. Once a week he stopped into Brookline Lunch with the old gang, where they got meal tickets punched for plates of meatloaf, mashed and peas. Like old times, they told each other. But Shea saw that the Square had begun to turn over to communal houses and professors in search of cheap properties with old chestnut woodwork, driving the old people out. Then a modern dance center and shops selling Frye boots and Birkenstocks popped up just a couple blocks to the north. He knew that no one from Roosevelt Towers would belong there much longer.

*****

He was back from the war on the night that Sean Malley got clubbed over the head by Cambridge cops after throwing a brick through a store window. They dragged Malley into a police wagon and beat him some more. A police captain arrived and ordered the patrolmen to take the kid to Cambridge City Hospital. Three hours later a guard spotted Malley unconscious in a jail cell. He was finally driven to the hospital, dead on arrival.

Malley was a few years younger than Shea, who knew him from Roosevelt. Together they tossed down shots a few times. At the end of every one of those evenings, Malley wound up on the floor. Shea was certain that on the night the kid was killed he'd been too drunk to even stand up by himself. In fact, as far as everyone Shea knew was concerned, Malley was just clubbed to death for throwing a brick through a window—plain as day. Eighteen years old and a sick waste, just like the dead eighteen-year-olds he fought with in Nam.

*****

During five nights of rioting that followed Malley's killing, young whites from Roosevelt set cars on fire, broke more windows and spray-painted walls with *Pigs Suck* graffiti.

Samuel Andrews had driven from Rindge Towers to watch it all with friends from the safety of a nearby building. He left on his scooter and was chased down by three Cambridge police cruisers. He crashed and the cops descended. Andrews wrenched himself loose but lost his right eye.

Project mothers, black and white, demanded a City Council hearing to protest Malley's death and Andrews' lost eye. Within days a community group calling itself Tough Times plastered handbills for the meeting around Cambridge.

Shea urged his Roosevelt gang to go with him to the meeting. At the last minute they headed to the courtyard at the front of the project to get stoned instead. Shea yelled, "How come you shitkickers can't get behind anything that means anything?" He stalked off to the hearing alone.

*****

City hall chambers were foul with cigar stink and Lysol. Two organizers in their late twenties huddled in the center balcony section with a dozen or so teenagers, black and white mixed. They'd hung two placards—*Justice for Sean* and *Justice for Samuel*—over the balcony. An orange batik banner in the middle announced *Tough Times*.

A separate smattering of somber black teens spread out on fixed seats to one side of the balcony, their legs propped up on the row in front of them. They nodded back when the black kids around the *Tough Times* banner turned sideways to catch their attention.

Dozens of white teenagers sauntered in and sat downstairs in a group, their arms folded in front of their jackets. They cast about the room with jutted chins and leaned over to whisper to each other.

Shea was shocked to see so many black faces. Sure they were there for their guy, Samuel Andrews, but to protest the death of a white kid, too.

"Look at that," Shea motioned to a couple of his gang who had finally filtered in to take seats around him, "They got balls comin' here now. Good for them." He gave the black kids a thumbs up.

One of his crew clucked in disgust. "Just niggers," he said. "Fuck 'em." He jabbed two middle fingers at the balcony. The others nodded. Though Shea acquiesced without a word, a wave of unease passed through his gut.

Fuck that, he decided. No reason for that kid to lose an eye any more than Malley bein' murdered. Bein' here with the blacks is the right thing to do. Fuckin' cops.

Around him, two hundred impatient project moms screamed at a hapless row of City Council people at a long, ornately carved table up front. "*Stop stalling! Damn them po-leeces!*"

Saundra Granger, the Council's only reformer, stood up to speak. "We're here tonight to declare an emergency and have the mayor take command of this killer police department!"

Hundreds of voices from the balcony chanted "*Justice! Justice!*"

Councilwoman Granger pointed at the other members. "When cops attack black kids, I say fire them and indict! And when they kill Sean Malley, I say the same thing!" The citizens of the Cambridge projects came to their feet.

At a signal from one of the Tough Times organizers, a dozen black women in purple robes stood up in the front rows to one side of the podium. A middle-aged woman sounded a pitch pipe. The room hushed uncertainly. A young woman sang:

If he's black, or if he's white,
Six to one is just not right!

Without warning a blast of harmony soared over the room:

If he's black, or if he's white
Six to one is just not right!

By the middle of the chorus, the entire room overtook the choir melody, clapping and stamping rhythmically:

If-he's-black-or-if-he's-white!
Six-to-one-is-just-not-right!

Shea rose with them, chanting and yelling until the entire City Council—save Saundra Granger—stalked out. The singing and shouting continued, quieting slowly until the choir closed with a harmonized hush.

One of the Tough Times organizers shouted from the front of the balcony, "Please sign the petition Tough Times is bringing around!" From his seat Shea saw a long reddish scar running from the speaker's cheekbone to his jaw line.

When the Tough Times people clambered down the balcony stairs with their banners, Shea was waiting and held out his hand.

"Mike Shea."

The Tough Times guy took his hand. "I'm Robert. I remember you."

*****

The two of them walked around Fresh Pond while white couples strolling the path watched them uneasily.

Robert wanted to know what had changed. Shea said, "There was that thing near Rindge when my crew knocked you down, right after my mom's funeral. Then Nam, living and dying with guys like you."

"I didn't join up," Robert said. "Not like these brothers from Rindge, got shot into little pieces for nothin'. I hired in at the shipyard in Quincy but left early a few times to work with these young kids you see here. That was worth more to me than any job. So I didn't make it past the Shipworks probation. But that's okay. I was made for this gig with Tough Times."

"Maybe I could fit in," Shea said, but Robert didn't think so. "You'd be stuck arguin' your whole life with the same people been dragging you down. They ain't gonna change. Shipyard might be a fit for you, though. It's a different world. Black people, all kinds of whites, West Indians, Puerto Ricans. All in one big pen trying to figure out how to live with each other."

Late that night, Shea sat in his nan's chair thinking about his mom and Bridget and Robert. About Domingas and courage. Each had glimpsed something deep down that was right and important. Each had turned a face to the sun. Shea ached to find a sun of his own. To turn toward it and bathe in the glow.

NIGHTS

3

Shea took a chair in the large waiting room at the General Shipworks employment office .

In one corner, three white kids angled their seats toward each other and whispered an animated conversation about the other people in the room. One of the kids had dirty yellow hair that trailed over his T-shirt. A rolled-up *Rolling Stone* stuck out of his back pocket. His shirt announced *Sex & Drugs Only—No Rock'n'Roll.* He flicked a brown and white pack of EZ Wider double widths back and forth on his desktop, then shifted in his chair to look at a tall, composed West Indian who leaned in a doorway, his dreadlocks partly covered by a green, black and red striped tam. The white kid swiveled back to the others, rolling his eyes.

Dreadlocks stared ahead. Just once he glanced over and let his lips blow out a quiet "Ppuhhh."

Next to one of the empty seats in the front row, a large applicant filed his nails, inspecting the three white kids with half-closed eyes. Shea thought he looked like the people Aunt Bridget had pointed out to him at the zoo in the city. "Puerto Rican or Dominican," she'd told him. "Good family folks."

The yellow-haired kid mugged to the others in the corner and the three of them turned to stare.

"Hey, man." the big man said mildly. The white kids looked away and restarted their wordless conversation, shaking their heads at each other. The Puerto Rican assessed them for a moment, then returned to his nails.

The seats filled with job hopefuls, all men. Most were in their early to mid-twenties, mixed white and black, a few more Latinos. A small cluster of black guys had come in together and were quietly filling out forms at a long table to one side of the chairs.

The place reminded Shea of high school. Gray and black floor tiles framed by grimy grout. Cloudy metal frame windows set high on the wall. Rows of skewed desk chairs. Lots of authority types patrolling the halls.

A company personnel rep wearing glasses and a navy-blue tie populated with tiny battleships emerged from an office in front of the main room. He looked down at his clipboard.

"William Roark?"

The yellow-haired kid got up. "It's Billy." He followed the rep into his office.

The *Quincy Patriot Ledger* sports section made its way around the room; the business pages swirled in a heap on the floor. Shea counted thirty-three people waiting, plus a couple secretaries. Aside from the group of black guys whispering over their applications, no one spoke.

Billy emerged from the office with the personnel officer.

"Okay," the rep said, "we'll let you know."

Billy said, "Sure."

The rep turned and faced the chairs. Billy shot the finger to his back and screamed a soundless "Fuck you!" One of the guys he'd been sitting with in the corner chair giggled briefly and nudged the third one.

"Okay," the rep murmured to no one in particular. He glanced at his watch, then consulted his clipboard again with visible regret.

"Michael Shea," he announced and looked up at the room. Shea raised his hand. "Come this way."

Shea followed him into his office and took a seat in a hard metal chair in front of a cluttered desk.

"My name is Mathewson," the man said. He ran a pen along the margin of the top sheet on the pile in front of him.

Shea broke into the silence. "I'm really interested in becoming a welder."

"Do tell." Mathewson checked his watch again.

A loud, sustained buzzer shook the thin office walls. Shea looked at the big-faced clock on the cinder block exterior wall. Eleven exactly.

Outside the window, a herd of coveralled men stampeded across Howard Street, clutching hard hats or chucking them underhand past the pavement and onto a grassy hill opposite. The helmets rolled up against a brick building with painted-over windows and hollows between the bricks where mortar had fallen out. Most of the men ran past their helmets into a building directly across from the main gate. A sign above the windows announced *Ziyad's Grill*. Others ducked through unadvertised doorways further up the hill. One had a line out the door.

Mathewson snapped his fingers and Shea jerked back to attention. The hiring officer was standing and straightening the papers on his desk. "Okay," he said. "You got some construction experience. Demo, anyway. And you're a vet. I'm gonna make you a welder trainee. Second shift, three-thirty to midnight. You'll come out of school as a welder third class. Five-forty-one an hour. Wait until you hear from us about a physical in a week or so. If you still have two arms, two legs, two eyes and pass the drug test, you'll get a notice to start right after your security clearance goes through." Mathewson stood and said, "That'll do it." He glanced at his watch again.

Shea asked, "You think I can get assigned to day shift?"

Mathewson was halfway to the door before he stopped and turned to face Shea.

"We have three shifts around the clock and you work the one we tell you. The whistle blows again at eleven-thirty, which is when I need to be back from lunch. So get going." Shea walked out of the office with Mathewson on his heels.

4

Shea spotted a small group of hard-hatted black men talking and munching fries from white paper bags. A metal placard hung over a nearby bench: *Bus 42-Shipyard*. Under their feet, the MTA rumbled its way back to Boston.

Shea approached cautiously.

"Is this where I get the bus to the shipyard?" he asked.

One of the hardhats stopped eating. He was the shortest and oldest of the group; he had dark skin on a broad flat face topped by wooly steel gray hair. He lifted a backpack from the floor and threw it over one shoulder, then turned to the others.

"I told you this is new meat coming," he said, flashing a gold eyetooth, "Pay up!" The others guffawed and held out their bags. The old man took one fry from each, put one in his mouth and stuffed the others in his bag. "C'mere boy," he motioned to Shea, who hesitated. The old man beckoned again. "I ain't gonna hurt you. Jeez!" Shea stepped closer.

"Least not with all these white folks around here!" the man slapped his thigh. The others laughed. The station was bustling but there were no other black men in sight.

"Okay, that's enough," the old guy held up his hand to the others, "We scarin' this boy." He pointed at Shea. "What's your name?"

"Shea. Mike."

"Well alright, Shea Mike, I'm Elijah Cottaway. They call me Cotty. And these guys," he fanned the back of his hand

16

across the others, "are the shipyard's finest. This is Byron Joseph. This here's Rodney Joseph. They all Josephs, these West Indies guys. And that sorry kid on the end is Pretty Boy. That's what we call him, anyway. His name's Luther."

The three nodded in turn. Byron and Rodney looked Shea in the eye. Pretty Boy smiled, keeping his dark liquid eyes down and away.

"Look out, Cotty," Byron said in a Caribbean lilt, "Bus man comin' right at you." Cotty hopped on the curb as the bus pulled up toward the group and swerved away at the last second. The door swung open with a whoosh of decompressing air.

"What the hell's the matter with you, driver?" Cotty demanded.

The uniformed driver leaned over toward the open door. "Wanna ride, Cotty? Get in and siddown. Stay out there and I'll do us all a favor and squash ya."

"You sorry motherfucker," Cotty laughed. "You ain't nuthin'!" He put his change in the box and headed toward the rear of the bus.

The rest climbed aboard behind Cotty. A dozen other black men materialized from hideouts around the station and clambered up the bus steps. All were in their twenties, decades younger than Cotty. The men made beelines for specific seats as if their names were engraved on them. The bus smelled of burnt leather and smoke.

Shea sat directly behind Cotty. Aside from the driver, Shea was the only white guy on the bus.

Cotty threw his arm over the rear of his seat and looked back at Shea. "Now," he said, "what is on your mind, young man?"

Shea said, "Well, for one thing, I don't know where we catch the bus back at midnight."

"Hey, this guy got some sense!" Cotty crowed to the bus. "Good question. It's by the north gate, boy. We don't go by there on the way in, so ask somebody to point you in the right direction later. You make sure you catch us, cause after that midnight bus it's awful lonely here 'til morning." Cotty drew himself up. "And that's what an old man can do for you. I ain't worried about helping out a good white kid, neither. I ain't like some down here." He waved his hand through the air.

"Hey, man," said Byron, "we ain't the ones make for any problem in this shipyard."

"Don't need you to tell me that," Cotty answered sharply. "I'm the one been born here." He turned to Shea. "You know what he's talkin' about?"

Shea asked, "Company problems?"

"Got them, too," Cotty allowed. "But what Byron means is white boys. Twenty or thirty of 'em to every one of us down here, but seems like that still too many black folks. Like God almighty give them rights to this job."

Shea cleared his throat. "Well," he began hesitantly, "if white guys are making problems for you, where are they?"

Cotty looked at him hard and decided it was just an honest question. "There's plenty of white guys in the yard, mostly on day shift. Most of them live down this way since their families move from the city. Others still in Southie and Dorchester. And a few from Fall River or even Rhode Island. Most all of the white guys work on days."

Rodney spoke for the first time. "Good for them fellas, then. Three-thirty to midnight shift much better for me, man."

"Night work don't make you safe in this place, you island hopper," Cotty retorted.

Byron frowned. Rodney turned his face to the window and pursed his lips. Byron mumbled something too quick for Shea to pick up.

But Cotty heard and dismissed it with a wave before his face softened. "Look," he said to Shea. "I ain't tellin' you how to see the world, but I learn some things from it. My granddaddy born in slave times, worked himself up to be a damn shipwright in the Wilmington yards in Carolina, first black man after freedom to do it. Chased outta the city by that cracker revolt in ninety-eight, lucky to make it out with his life and his family. Came north to work the Chester shipyards south of Philly. One yard for whites, one for blacks."

"Two yards by race?" Byron asked incredulously.

"That's right," Cotty said. "Right next to each other, owned by the same company. Granddaddy just gritted his teeth and done it."

Byron said, "Must be the black people here would not let them into our yard so the whites go off and start their own!" There was a hush, then the rear of the bus broke out in laughter. Shea wasn't sure whether to join in.

Cotty held up a hand. "But listen! Union come by Philly after the second world war—this very same Shipbuilders Union we got! They had an organizer determined to integrate those two yards. My grandaddy was the first to sign on, got to organizin' himself. He was set to take out that Jim Crow and they done it. He welded there 'til the whole place shut down years later. Now that's a man I got to live up to!" Cotty dug into his backpack and pulled out a thumbed over copy of *Black Reconstruction* and two tabloids—*Muhammed Speaks* and *The Bay State Banner*, Boston's black bi-weekly. "Time for my education," he said to Pretty Boy. "You might try it sometime."

"Hey," Pretty Boy spoke to Shea from the rear seat, his soft voice NatKingCole smooth against Cotty's gruffness and the West Indians' patter. Pretty Boy's languid stare fixed a little closer to Shea's eyes, but still, it seemed, focused elsewhere. "It's the truth, man. You listen to Cotty. He tell it straight."

The bus stopped abruptly. Cotty said, "Here we are, boy. First day. Eyes and ears open."

*****

Hauner pointed without interest at lunch pails as the hardhats filed past. A sign on the brick wall behind the guard shack warned against incoming cameras. The guard trainee, Thibodeaux, leaned on the door jamb, listening to Hauner repeat, "Open 'em up, guys, open 'em up," as the hardhats streamed by. If anyone bothered to offer a pail, Hauner scanned it without looking. He issued loud, raspy commands now and again to placate his chief in the office off the rear of the shack. And every few minutes he stole a look at Thibodeaux. He wondered if the guy was aware of the instructions Hauner had received to make sure none of the hardhats in the line went batshit on the first colored security guard in the yard's eighty-year history.

Hauner surveyed the line more closely for photo IDs. A week ago he had quietly passed the word that visiting Navy brass had recently watched a bunch of hardhats parade through the gate without a single badge challenge. Within a week the Navy had threatened to pull its crummy frigate overhaul job from the yard. Anxious about future defense contracts, the front office in Omaha had made it very clear that things had to tighten up.

Ever since, the second shift rush between the five-minute whistle and the final one at three-thirty was the worst time to jam through the gate. Hauner tried to get at least a glimpse of every badge but the hardhats crowding by the guard shack were ready to jostle through to beat out the countdown to the time clocks.

From the way Hauner was staring, it was clear to Shea that the guy half-stepping right in front of him wasn't familiar. "Hold it, fella," the guard's voice hardened as he barred the gate with his arm. "Show the badge."

The queue stiffened before someone called from the rear. "Keep it movin'—got a clock to punch!" The hardhats fidgeted impatiently before another one of them burst out, "What the fuck, Hauner?" followed by an approving grumble from the line.

The stranger fingered his badge, obscuring his face photo and ID. Hauner's arm shot out and touched plastic, but the guy backhanded the guard's knuckles before his fingers could close.

The stranger wore a butterscotch hard hat—a shipfitter. He spent half his days measuring steel plates and the other half pounding heavy wedges with a sledgehammer to fair up the pieces. Hauner had to think about the muscle behind that. Maybe the guy was a regular at the Turret Shop gate. Or a snitch from up front sent out to test security.

The fitter leaned back a little. His arms were loose at his sides. "Keep your fuckin' hands off me," he said to the guard. The line behind the fitter quieted. There was a snigger from the rear and Hauner reddened. He assessed the reach to the fitter's badge and considered a second try.

Thibodeaux pushed himself away from the door jamb and took a step toward the gate. "Problem, Eddie?"

The fitter kept his eyes on Hauner. "He's your gorilla squad backup?"

Thibodeaux shouldered past Hauner. "What you say, fitter?"

The fitter addressed Hauner. "You in charge? Or would that be this *African-American* gentleman?" He flicked his own badge. "This what you lookin' for—*Eddie*?"

Hauner cleared his throat and jerked his head toward the yard. He puffed one cheek tightly, then blew it out. "Fact is," he breathed, "I don't give a shit." He sucked in through his teeth and waved the shipfitter through. "And I'm the one in charge." He turned to the impatient line of hardhats with palms up. "What an asshole," he muttered, then called down the line, "Keep it movin'! Show the badge, no exceptions!" He motioned to Thibodeaux. "Move back to the door."

Shea walked through the gate past a poster tacked to a plywood easel. On it, a cross-eyed grizzly wore a high Soviet style military cap while it growled at the passing crowd and clenched a red hammer and sickle above the warning *Don't Feed the Bear*. Far beyond, the Goliath crane glimmered three hundred feet up in the afternoon sun, straddling two shipbuilding basins. To the right, the hull of an enormous tanker was propped on thick wooden chocks in one of the drydocks, cloaked under a high steel superstructure. The ship announced itself at the bow in white paint: 41 HULL. A sign with an arrow pointing rightward showed the way to the welding school, several hundred yards from the steel cage hulking over the basin. Shea headed toward the school, fidgeted nervously at the door for a few seconds, and entered.

5

"Kee-rist," complained a trainee in a flannel shirt, "It's fulla shit."

A rail-thin older man in a short-brimmed blue and gray striped cap scooped a piece of metal from the floor. He held it up, turning the sawed edge toward a fluorescent light in the ceiling. The shiny cross section was shot through with elliptical black flecks the size of a pen point.

"Crank up your machine," the skinny guy said. "Five more amps to burn out that crap, ten if you can handle it." The trainee mumbled, "Thanks, Jimmy," and trudged toward a row of welding booths.

The classroom was a barrage of noises, the steady clank of metal on metal competing against huge skillets of crackling bacon. The staccato synched with a painful white glare and molten spatter that popped and sprayed from the booths. The pulsing roar of an industrial air mover filled the background.

The room held four long rows of people sitting at high-sided metal booths. At each booth, a trainee wearing a fiberglass hood held a welding torch in thick leather mittens. A foot-long metal wand about the thickness of a straw jutted out at right angles. The trainees banged at metal plates with pointy hammers when they weren't welding or flipped up their shields like a visor on a suit of armor and tried to talk above the clatter.

23

Jimmy the instructor lifted a pack of cigarettes from his shirt pocket and jerked one up, then snatched it with his teeth. He fished a book of matches from his pants and folded down a single one with the same hand, closing the cover behind it. He flicked the match and held the book up to his cigarette, dragging deeply, then coughing. He followed the kid in the flannel shirt down the aisle and ducked into his booth.

"Gimme your stinger," Jimmy said, pointing at the welding torch in the kid's hand. "Now lower your shield and watch how I stay with the puddle." He laid his cigarette on a steel tabletop that was welded into the booth and crusted with hardened metal spatter. He spun his cap around so that the brim covered the nape of his neck and positioned the headband of his welding shield around his forehead. "Watch your eyes," he said without moving his own to see who was looking. The booth disappeared in a painful burst of white light.

Shea turned away and followed a sign down the aisle, where a classroom was filling with second shift new hires like himself. He spotted the big Puerto Rican from the employment office, who stuck out his hand and said, "Moises Ramos." The yellow-haired kid who had shot the finger to the company rep the day of his interview introduced himself as Billy the Kid. He gave Shea his story—wife, two kids, Harley.

"I guess I got over on that shithead what interviewed me after all, hunh?" Billy said. "Thought I was a goner."

Shea nodded. "I thought you were, too."

A clump of golden-skinned men with not quite African features sat together, conversing in an indecipherable language full of shushing J sounds. Shea recognized them as what his mom had called "mixed breed" Portagees from Cape Verde, like Domingas. Twice a bearded white trainee said something to the group in a language somewhat similar to what the golden men spoke, yet not quite the same. Billy followed Shea's gaze to the Cape Verdeans and said, "Your affirmative action dollars at work."

Shea said, "Whatta they done to you?"

"Nuthin'," said Billy. "Just sayin'."

Three or four women sat together in the back. One with dark curly hair waved across the room to a cute blond who stood and headed over to join the others. Shea watched her, lifting his eyebrows.

"That's Diane O'Keefe," Billy nodded toward the blond. "So she's gonna be a welder, too? Have a hard time seein' that happen." He paused. "I fucked her once in high school."

Shea said, "Yeah?" He took in the girl again.

"Yeah, wicked good lay, too." Billy hadn't taken his eyes off her. "Haven't seen her since graduation." His voice rose, "Hey, Keefer!" She raised her hand at him without much enthusiasm.

A buzzer sounded. A white man of about forty-five with powerful manicured hands strode into the classroom. A tall, well-built black man walked in behind him, placed his hands on his hips and stared slowly around the room of would-be second shift welders. Both men wore white hard hats and clean, blue General Shipworks jackets.

The white one pushed a stick of gum around his teeth. "My name's Dick DiGuardio. I'm superintendent of training and apprentice programs for this shipyard. For the next eight weeks you work for me. You come in on time and weld and I won't even know your name. That's what you want. We're paying you just to learn, so don't waste our money or I'll be very unhappy and so won't the General." DiGuardio tapped the General Shipworks logo on the breast of his jacket, his eyes dead serious, then took a step back. He nodded at the tall black guy. "After you graduate from the welding school I'll turn you over to this man—Charley Johnson, superintendent of the welding department."

Johnson concluded his careful review of the trainees. He said, "For now you're on probation. You'll get a copy of the union contract but you have zero protection for thirty days. None. That means you screw around once, you're gone. You miss work once, you're gone. Late once, you're gone." He looked around for effect. "If DiGuardio here tells me something about you I don't like, you're gone. Matter of fact, if I just want you gone, you're gone." He let that sink in. "After thirty days you can read to me from your union contract and we'll see how far that goes if you screw up." Johnson looked around the hushed room one more time, turned and walked out.

"Holy shit," murmured a trainee from the back of the room. "What they do, grab him and his brown bag from some stoop in Roxbury?"

DiGuardio searched the room for the offender, then gave up and pointed to the skinny instructor in the striped cap. "This is Jimmy O'Donnell. You may have seen him with the first shift on your way in. He came in early today to help them out, but he'll be with you every day. You listen to Jimmy and you'll have a job in production in four or five weeks." He straightened. "Any questions?"

Silence.

"Good. You all got your ID numbers at the physical, right? Remember it. Jimmy punched in your cards for you today and he'll give 'em to you when I'm done." The silence deepened. DiGuardio started out, then spun on his heel. The new hires hadn't moved. "By the way, you let anyone else punch in your timecard after today, you're outta here. Got it?" His eyes swept the rows, commanding a response. The new hires nodded uneasily. "Good," said DiGuardio. "I'll be back. Count on it." He disappeared through the door.

"Shithead," whispered a voice behind Shea after DiGuardio had gone. "What's he care? They told me down at unemployment that the feds are paying them to train us, long as they bring in enough colored guys."

Shea swung around. A kid with bloodshot eyes held out his hand. "Rick Rochelli. They call me Roach." He pointed to his red, teary eyes and smiled weakly. "I know. I look stoned but I'm really not."

When they returned to the classroom Jimmy was smoking at the big metal desk up front. He laid a set of tools and some steel plate on the desk and held up a torch. "This is your stinger. You plug this socket on the end into the welding cable." He grabbed a welding rod with his other hand and screwed it onto the stinger. "When you touch the bare tip of the welding rod to steel, you make the electrical connection, then break it off just enough to create a gap. Like a spark plug but much stronger. Now, sooner or later, what happens to your average spark plug?"

The trainees looked around at each other.

"C'mon," Jimmy said, "What do I got here, a bunch of girls?"

Keefer put up her hand.

"Okay, you got me," Jimmy smiled.

"It corrodes, burns up," Keefer said. An appreciative murmur rippled through the rows of trainees.

"Right," Jimmy continued. "So the wire core of the welding rod and your steel plate melt together into a puddle." Jimmy ran his fingers along the length of the rod. "You keep moving the rod into that charged arc and lead that puddle. When the wire stub is down to a couple inches, you snap it away. The connection breaks. Then knock off the slag with your hammer. That's it."

The class looked baffled. Jimmy had been through it before. "Don't worry. When you see it, you'll know. Just grab me if you have any trouble. And believe me, you will."

In his booth, Shea held his torch with both hands and shook his head to flip his shield down. In the darkness he scraped the rod and his arc flamed up. It buzzed and spit like the electrodes in a Frankenstein movie. Molten globs popped up from his weld, singeing his arms and shoulders.

"That's on account of jumps in the heat," Jimmy explained over his shoulder, "Out on the boats they're welding and cranking the machines all the time. Makes the power level fly all over." He leaned in to look more closely at Shea's weld. "Not bad for a beginner. You'll do okay." He moved down the line.

At the end of the night, Jimmy assembled the trainees and suggested that they all head across the street to Habib's Supply next to Ziyad's Grill the following afternoon to pick up some leather sleeves to protect their arms. The company would deduct the cost from payroll.

"Fuckin' Arabs got it made," Billy whispered in line at the time clock, "I heard Habib and that guy Ziyad are cousins."

"Why are we paying for that stuff ourselves?" asked Roach. "That should be on the company, right?"

Shea nodded. "Goddam right."

*****

After the midnight whistle, Shea followed Jimmy's directions to the South gate, where he saw a bus idling on the far side of the street with "Quincy Terminus" on its marquee. Most of the group that had ridden with him from the station that afternoon straggled onto the bus a few minutes later and plopped in their seats. Their eyes closed almost immediately.

28

Cotty was the last one to board. Shea watched him drag down the aisle. "Hey, how you doin'?" Cotty asked.

"Good," Shea said. "I've got a few questions. Got an earful tonight at the school."

Cotty held up a finger. "First lesson. Don't push a man to talk at midnight after a shift on the boats." He nestled low in his seat, then continued, almost to himself. "Good, he say, yeah, that's nice." He peered up at Shea without moving his sunken head. "Boy, you don't know nuthin'. Not yet, anyways." He shut his eyes.

In a few minutes Shea leaned back as well. His sore, closed eyes followed a dancing yellow-green puddle across the welding school's monotonous practice plates.

"Quincy Center!" the bus driver called. Shea awoke with a start.

The station lights shone outside the bus. The others had already roused themselves. Shea pulled himself up to join them as they stumbled off the bus, heads down, lids heavy. Together they transferred onto the inbound branch of the MTA, a bunch of dirty, fogged-out zombies drifting through the empty, fluorescent station at twelve-thirty in the morning to catch the last train back to the city.

6

A pot-bellied guy in his mid-forties and a green hard hat worked his way down the aisle of booths, passing out cards as he went. When he got to Shea, he held out his hand and said, "My name's Darby. Take care of me and I'll take care of you." Shea looked at the card in the man's hand. Below the heading "Blue Star Ticket" there was a list of candidates for delegate to the annual convention of the national union. The name Leo Darburton was circled in red magic marker. Darby's finger tapped the circle. "That's me," he said, "number eight on the ballot."

Shea looked up from his chair. "You're with the union? Where ya been?"

Darby said, "I'm the night shift steward. Have been for twelve years, elected four times over." Shea noticed the badge pinned on his jacket: *Shipbuilders Local 8 Steward.*

Shea asked, "So you're a welding steward?"

"Sorta," Darby told him. "There's sixteen department stewards, one for every trade. On top of them are the Official Board guys—Stan Rashford the president and his officers. I'm a steward with a different setup. I take care of everybody on second shift, all trades. The other stewards are all day guys. They just represent the men in their trade."

"Not women?"

"Well, yeah," Darby backed off. "Of course them, too. But there's only women welders, no other trades. Company just hired them in because of the affirmative action."

"One steward to deal with every guy in every trade on second shift," Shea said. "How can that work? Place this big, doesn't seem like nearly enough representation. My mom's shop had stewards all over. For everybody."

Darby's affability disappeared. "You one of those commies sneakin' in with the new hires and suddenly got a better way to do things? No? Then think twice before you open your goddam trap. Lotta bad stuff can happen to guys too busy mouthing off to think about what they're doing in the yard. Or saying." He walked on, skipping Billy and the following three booths before extending a hand with the election card in it to Roach. Darby looked back over his shoulder at Shea, then waved at Jimmy, who was peering into trainee booths as he walked down the aisle.

"Hey, man." Billy tugged at Shea's sleeve. "You ask too many questions, that union guy's gonna cut off your balls—ignore your grievances, keep you on night shift 'til you die."

"Are you kiddin?" Roach sidled up as soon as Darby moved down the row beyond him. "That guy don't have a clue. He couldn't give nobody trouble."

"He don't seem real bright," Shea said. "Pretty sure of himself, though."

Billy hunched into his booth and picked up his slag hammer. He let its pointed tip bounce listlessly on the spatter that covered his welding table.

Roach turned to Shea. "Damn right. I grew up around here listenin' to stories about the yard. Everybody knows the union's a fuckin' waste of dues money, but there's no choice." Roach walked back to his booth, tearing Darby's slate card into little pieces and letting them flutter to the floor.

Jimmy came over to Shea, took off his cap and wiped at the sweat high on his balding forehead. When he leaned in to talk, Shea could see scars from hot slag that mottled the whites of his eyes.

Jimmy gestured vaguely toward Darby's back. "My uncle, Big Jim O'Donnell, organized the union here. Got himself elected the first president of the local, too, though he was always a shipfitter at heart. Bear of a guy. He had a shit-fit when I took the instructor's job and lost my seniority 'cause instructors are management. Then he got the company to give us rights to move back into the union when the yard goes down and they don't need instructors. That day's gonna come again, always does."

"That's hard to imagine with the buildup they got going now," said Shea.

Jimmy shook his head slowly. "Big Jim knew enough to think what's next. Groomed Stan Rashford to take his place when the time came. Stan was just a kid then, completely in awe, gave my uncle his best." Jimmy pulled on his cigarette. "Hell of a guy, Big Jim. I'll never forget him." Jimmy told Shea how Big Jim clutched his throat and keeled over with a heart attack in a bilge tank many summers ago. He had crawled through four compartments to reach the next fitter, who took one look and lit out for help on the deck. It took two hours to get Big Jim through the access holes and strapped up to a body cradle hung from a crane. He was dead before he reached the main gate.

"Stan's been in charge ever since." Jimmy sighed. "At least Big Jim knew enough to die in the yard." He crossed himself. "Doubled my aunt's insurance claim."

*****

At midnight Shea ran for the bus, holding his leathers over his head to keep out the cold drizzle. The temperature had fought its way above freezing during daylight, then started to fall after the seven-thirty dinner whistle.

"Thousand men on nights and one lazy steward!" Cotty said when Shea mentioned Darby's visit.

"But you elected him."

"No sir!" Cotty snorted, "Day shift votes for the night steward, too! And they got three or four times as many guys as on nights so they really the ones choosing our steward for us. Ain't that some shit? That Darby in tight with the union and those guys tell everybody in the day shops to go with him. Well, second shift is mostly all black boat welders and we know that guy ain't nuthin! And I'll tell him a thing or two, he ever come crawlin' around in any tank of mine. But I ain't holdin' my breath on that."

"Hey Cotty," Byron called out sarcastically, "just you give the man a call, he supposed to come right away."

"I give up on that shit, Byron." Cotty was really angry. "I screamed for him when that cracker whitehat Pody threatened my job last summer. Darby couldn't find the time to see me 'til I got suspended and on the outside lookin' in. Useless, trashy, no-good motherfucker."

Shea was dumbfounded. "What kinda union is that?"

Pretty Boy leaned forward and nestled his chin on the rail at the top of Shea's seat. "You call for Darby when you get out on the boats." Shea had to strain to hear him. "You'll see. He won't get off his ass, not even for a white guy."

The three black men leaned back in their seats and chuckled unhappily. The conversation died. The bus moved slowly through the dark, wet Quincy streets. The rain turned to sleet.

"Looka this shit," Cotty said glumly. "Damn boat be a sheet of ice by tomorrow afternoon."

*****

Night after night at the welding school, Jimmy coached the new hires to keep their arcs tight to the steel. He pushed

33

them to practice vertical and overhead welds. "Can't turn the ship upside down every night just so's you get a tit weld on the flat," he warned, then nodded to the small group of female trainees. "Scuse me."

"Arc hot and tight," Jimmy never got tired of telling them. "Burn that shit out before it burns you. And speaking of burns, remember this: There's gonna be times that a gas pocket blows that hot metal right back at you. If you're workin' a flat weld, that glob will roll right back at you, drop inside your boot. If it does, you just let it burn. It's gonna hurt. Really bad. But if you untie your laces and go after it, that lava works its way down to the bottom of your shoe, burns through the sole of your foot to the bone. That happens, it digs in deeper, you'll be screamin' for your mother and off your feet for a couple months."

After four weeks the school began to thin out. The first to pass the x-ray test on their welding plates was the group of Cape Verdeans. They were coached by a slightly older Portuguese islander named Manny who was fluent in both Creole and English. He came up to the welding school two or three times a week and spoke to the Cape Verdeans in the classroom. Like Jimmy, he wore a yellow instructor's helmet. When the group headed out for the boats, they were assigned to a single crew. Manny went with them.

Roach was one of the next to move out to the yard. "The school's a fuckin' joke," he told Shea one night during dinner break at Ziyad's. "They clean the steel, give you a nice shiny plate to lay in the weld for your test. Out on the boat, it's all junk. Rust. Big gaps between the joints. Damn weld just blows back in your face, just like Jimmy told us."

Just before Christmas, Shea watched anxiously as the mechanical hacksaw sliced through his final overhead test plate.

"This one's a go," Jimmy said with satisfaction. "Grind it flat and stamp it with your number. Let's get it to the lab for x-ray." The next day Shea was told to report to 41 hull under the high steel superstructure.

7

Shea looked over his shoulder as he descended the ladder. He saw that the maintenance guys still hadn't bothered to replace the burned-out light bulbs he'd reported to Griswold three days before. He'd also called for Darby to get on the electricians but hadn't received a response.

Twenty minutes later he was still tracking down cables, drenched with sweat, his palms wet inside leather mitts. His boots were damp with greasy water that had rained into the tank from access holes or dripped between unfinished seams. The thick, heavy air sealed in a film of smoke.

Up on the tank's sidewall, the brass coupling of a welding line glimmered in a tangle of cable. There was no ladder anywhere close to it. Shea frogged his way up several rows of stiffeners. He was only a reach away from it, twenty feet from the floor of the ship. He grabbed at the line. An electric jolt rocked him through the rubber sheath. His hard hat clattered against the sidewalls on its way to the bottom of the hull. He tottered, instinctively clutching at the closest L-stiffener.

The lip of the stiffener bit reassuringly into his fingers. He steadied, still buzzing from his head through his chest and his arms. Slowly, the tank came back into focus. He took a deep breath. In ten minutes, the tingle narrowed to his left arm. He looked down to the bottom of the hull and thought of Big Jim, dead in the tank. How long would it have taken someone to find him if he'd fallen? He shivered.

He spotted the cable and hard hat, then eased himself down to the floor of the hull. Dragging the cable out of the tank, he made his way under its weight to his job. The tool room ventilation guys had already positioned an air vac by his gear to suck in his smoke.

Shea looked over his job for the night. Pin butts. Connecting L stiffeners near the bottom of the curved hull, rusty, five or six inches high, sparks storming at his face, clawing under his leathers. Pin butts near the floor of hull demanded upside down welds that practically guaranteed spatter burns all over the arms and chest. Griswold routinely assigned them to the Cape Verdeans, who never complained.

Billy burned wire below him. Anticipating a shower of sparks from Shea, he had rigged up a green fiberglass blanket a few feet above his job. Smoke curled around the blanket's edges and drifted up toward Shea. "Hey, Billy," he called down, "pull that sucker hose closer, will you?"

Billy's gloved hand thrust out from under the blanket and waved before pulling in the hose.

*****

From his perch on the staging planks by his welding gear, Roach took a pull on his thermos cup. He set his coffee on the plank and climbed up a short, fixed ladder toward Shea's welding arc. He approached the white glare with one hand in front of his face, and called, "Hey, Shea—take a look!"

Shea broke his arc and flipped up his shield. Roach pointed to a shadowed figure struggling at the access patch. Their foreman Griswold thrashed, rocked back once, and finally broke past the logjam of hoses, heaving his bulk inside. He lurched a step, then caught himself. "Fuckin'-A-Right," he said proudly and straightened. He picked up

37

his whitehat and put it on, then pulled a cigarette from his red lumberjack coat. The fingers of his other hand raked at his beard while he adjusted to the dim yellow glow of the tank and looked around for his welders. He leaned heavily against the bulkhead.

The senior guys on the crew had tipped Shea off. "Just act surprised when you see him. Keeps him happy when he thinks he put one over on you."

Shea had learned that once Griswold managed to heave himself into the tank, he wasn't about to leave again soon. The whitehat would settle in and expound on whatever came to mind. It was his way of extending some break time to the welders he felt deserved it.

Griswold took a seat on the stiffener by Shea, catching his breath. When he puffed at his cigarette his last two fingers twitched and leapt with pleasure. With the thumb of his other hand, he picked at a nostril. Satisfied, he waved Roach back over with the butt. "I've been watching you guys," he said after Roach had settled in next to Shea, "And I got no real complaint. For new guys."

Griswold dragged on the cigarette and his fingers twitched again. He assessed the butt and stubbed it out on the stiffener, then flicked it away from his thumb. "Now here's the story. This boat's gettin' hot and Rosa wants to see some serious smoke. I'm puttin' the senior people in the tight spots tomorrow. Today I need some real work done on the flat welds around the bulkheads. I need a hundred and fifty feet of plate sealed up tonight and goin' forward. From each of you."

Roach shook his head. "I'm not tryin' to be smart, Bobby, but look at this shit. Those gaps need two, maybe three passes. That's more like three or four hundred feet of stick weld."

Griswold took off his hard hat and lit another cigarette. His hair was flat with sweat, despite the cold. The filter disappeared into his beard. "Did I tell you guys that I came down from Maine for this program?" he asked.

Jesus, Shea thought, only a million times.

Griswold dragged again on the cigarette. His fingers twitched with delight. "I worked ten years at Woolwich Shipbuilding. Best goddam yard in the country. People kill to work there." He leaned forward and sucked. The end of his cigarette glowed red and crept toward his mouth. "Up there we worked bonus for every foot of weld. Make your quota, the rest is gravy. So when a guy finds himself in a situation like this, what's he do? Sometimes he just cranks up the heat and puts the weld in faster. Maybe he uses bigger wire, lays down more metal. But welding wire comes just so thick." Griswold held two fingers apart to show them what he meant. "So sometimes, when he's really up against the wall, he sticks some welding rods flat in the gaps, just pours the metal over them. Kick up the heat, it all smooths out and looks real pretty. When the pressure was on, that's what they did." The whitehat settled back, hugging his elbows. "Right now, the pressure is on."

"Are you shittin' me?" Shea couldn't help himself. "Goddam boat could break apart after launch."

Griswold's gaze back was steady. "Sluggin' the weld, we called it."

"I heard about that shit," Roach forced a laugh. "And *that's* what you want us to do?"

Griswold stood and dusted himself off. "I'm not tellin' you to do a fuckin' thing. Just make sure this tank is done by the end of the week—however you need to. You deliver, you can coast for a night."

Griswold plunked on his white hat and lumbered toward the access patch. He thrust off his right leg and launched himself through the hole into the final minutes of late afternoon light. His exit was so smooth and powerful that Shea questioned whether his clumsy entry had been staged just to warn them of his arrival.

Roach looked at Shea. "Well, what are you gonna do?"

"Work like a bastard, I guess."

"Yeah, but I ain't gonna do that slug thing. QC catches that and it's all over." Roach stuck out his thumb at the access patch. "You don't think he's gonna back us up when we're caught, do you? I can see it now. Slug the weld? He's never heard of it."

"I know." Shea stretched the fingers of his right hand and twitched the last two, mimicking the whitehat. "He ain't tellin' us to do a fuckin' thing, right?"

Roach shook his head.

Shea cocked an eyebrow at him. "Maybe we oughta run it by the rest of the crew, tell 'em what's coming, right?"

Roach looked at his watch, "Let's stay in for lunch, then. They'll be at the toolboxes." He stood and walked back to his gear.

Shea got on his knees and picked up his stinger. He twisted in a wire and set it above his weld, then jerked down his mask into darkness. In a minute the tank flickered with harsh, playing shadows thrown by twin arcs of welding light. Smoke that escaped the suckers billowed up until it was trapped by the solid plate that sealed the welders off from the tank above. The smoke hung in a dark gray cloud, then slowly settled low in the tank.

8

When the lunch whistle sounded Shea and Roach headed for the muster area, where they found most of the crew already eating on their toolboxes. Byron, the only English-speaking black on the crew, was outside getting dinner at Ziyad's. He never ate at the muster area. "Not with this crew, anyway," he had told Shea on the bus. "Minority is one thing, outnumbered another." Shea was struck by the small number of black American or West Indian welders on Griswold's crew. From what he could tell they were about half of the second shift department.

Farrell, a white guy from Taunton, sat off by himself. He wasn't on Griswold's crew and not exactly a welder. He was a marker who sported yellow stripes on his brown hard hat. Marking made Farrell one of a half dozen guys in the department who were free to roam the basins and shops without challenge, checking blueprints of the ships then painting the required dimensions of weld on each joint. The markers never welded.

Farrell was wired to the job by the welding steward, Charney. The other welders—at least white welders from Southie, Dorchester or the South Shore, where the union's old guard had its tightest connections—ached to become markers like Farrell, or pipe welders or lead men; to get into one of the soft shops or the specialty jobs that transformed a shipyard brownhat into something more than a grunt and earned a few extra dollars. Though only a privileged few were ever allowed inside such circles, their fantasies promised a leg up and over the shipyard walls. Every one of the markers was white.

Between mouthfuls of fish salad, Farrell bragged about women he harassed with his pool buds at Big Dan's, a New Bedford bar with a skanky reputation that stretched to the Irish end of his Taunton hometown a half hour away. "Bitch goes in there lookin' for it and we give her what she wants." His marking partner, Cochrane, chortled.

"Guess you need a gang to get pumped," Shea said.

Farrell threw him a dead-eye stare.

*****

Except for a couple of white Portagees from New Bedford and Fall River who could understand some of the Cape Verdean Creole, the rest of the crew actively kept its distance.

"Too bad," Shea commented to Roach over his thermos of coffee. "Seem like nice guys. They're harmless."

Roach shook his head. "They just make it harder for everybody by pounding away like they do every night. Even the other black guys don't like them being here."

"I guess it's just what they know," said Shea.

Oliveira, the Portagee lead man on the crew, pulled two plastic jars out of his toolbox. His wrists peeked out from his denim jacket as he extended the jars to the new guys. "Brought in too much," he said. "You get a deal here—half price." He took the lid off one of the jars and hiked it up toward their noses. "Half buck apiece."

Roach waved his hand and gestured toward his lunch pail. Shea reached out and sniffed at the jar.

"Portagee fish salad," Oliveira announced. "Gonna clear you right out."

The pepper sauce was oily with crushed greens covering cold white flesh and potatoes. Shea took the fork that Oliveira offered and tried some. His eyes watered. "That is hot!" he gasped and waited for it to settle while Oliveira led the others in a short laugh. Shea sat down on his toolbox.

"I like that stuff," Farrell said when Shea's color returned to normal, "But those niggers really wolf it down." He stuck his thumb over his shoulder at the cluster of Cape Verdeans.

"They no niggers, Farrell," Oliveira corrected. He was white Portuguese raised in the Azores. "Look at them. Almost white."

Farrell shrugged. "Whatever. Niggers are niggers, far as I'm concerned."

Shea said, "They haven't bothered you, Farrell. What's your problem?"

Farrell leaned toward Shea, knitting his eyebrows. "Maybe the fuckin' problem is *yours*. And maybe I'm gonna turn that pretty little nose to mush if you don't shut up when I talk."

The tank silenced.

"Y'know, Farrell," Shea said. "I realized the other day that those guys are on pin butts every single night, bustin' their asses on the worst job the crew has. The rest of us get put on pin butts maybe once every week or two, but that's cause the Cape Verdeans take up the slack. So give 'em a break."

Farrell said, "You're so fucking self righteous, Shea. Take it to Griswold if it's too much for you to live with." Next to him, Cochrane smirked, "Tough guy."

Shea forced himself to inhale slowly, drawing himself up and leaning toward Farrell, whose snarl was close enough to reek of oily fish. "You're right, Farrell, I should."

"And fuck every white guy on the crew? Sure, go ahead."

"Make your move, Farrell," Shea said quietly, "or leave those guys alone."

They glowered at each other before Farrell spat out a surprised, "Christ—you're really a nigger lover!"

"Look at it this way," Shea said, "I just don't like you."

Roach cut through the silence. "Hey, knock it off!"

Farrell stared at Shea for a moment longer, then leaned back and began forking up his fish salad again, his eyes fixed on Shea.

"Griswold wants us to slug the welds in the bottom of the tank," Roach announced to the group.

"Ain't the first time," Farrell said, moving on, "You're just new and he's tryin' to get over on you. He's bluffing."

"What's Griswold telling the Cape Verdean guys about this?" Shea said to Oliveira. "Any idea?"

"Ain't him, it's Pete Rosa." Oliveira named the welding department general foreman for the second shift. "He tells them he'll send them back to Cape Verde if they don't work harder."

"*Harder*?" exclaimed Roach, "those guys are killin' us already." He saw Shea giving him the eye and protested. "Hey, they are!"

Farrell nodded vigorously and saluted Roach with his fork.

"Well," Oliveira said, "Rosa's tellin' them that's how he made it when he started here in the Fifties. Welded until the tears came every night to his eyes. Now he's the first Cape Verdean general foreman in the yard. Says they gotta come up the same way."

"Yeah," Farrell said, "didn't tell 'em he was cryin' all the way to the fuckin' bank with the cash the General gave him to bring them all over here, did he?"

Oliveira said, "All I know is Pete Rosa got big respect in Scituate. All the Cape Verdeans live there. He tells 'em what to do, they gonna listen. He made it big here and he knows the families. He's got their green cards. They can't go work anywhere else without them."

Shea said, "He keeps their cards? He got no right to do that. It's like keeping them slaves. No wonder they never complain. You should tell someone."

Oliveira looked down. "Not me. I'm the lead man on the crew, Shea. Gotta protect my spot with Rosa and Griswold."

"Shit," said Shea, "Somebody oughta do it."

"Jesus Christ," said Roach, "can't you mind your own business?"

"Yeah," Farrell chimed in, "why dontcha?"

*****

"Hey, Shea," Griswold beckoned at the end of the shift, "I hear you got a problem with the way I assign jobs." He took off his hard hat and held it up. "Know what this is?"

"It's a white hat."

"The white hat means I make the assignments on this crew. However I want."

"All I said was that the Cape Verdeans catch pin butts every single night. Don't seem right."

Griswold said, "No one seems worried about that 'cept you. But since you are, I'll do you a favor. Until I tell you otherwise, you're on pin butt duty. Every night, so it's not all on your friends from the islands." He put his white hat back on. "Damn shame when one of our own don't know when to keep his mouth shut."

*****

Shea pulled a beer from the fridge and spread out on his skeletal rear porch. He allowed himself a cigarette. He was dog-tired when he got home after one in the morning, but he kept thinking about his mom. About Robert. About Sean Malley and the City Council meeting, the crowd rising together.

9

The next afternoon Shea scouted the sidewalk outside Ziyad's for Manny Amado. He spotted a glossy yellow instructor's helmet on the grass-covered hill across the street and headed into the bar. Manny was leaning over the pinball—too heavy on the flippers. "Yeah, I remember you from the school," Manny told him. "My guys really liked you."

Shea explained about the green cards.

Manny said, "Rosa must have them scared shitless. They didn't say a word to me." He slapped his hand on the side of the pinball machine. It tilted and he frowned. "Damn."

"The tilt or Rosa?"

Manny sighed. "Whichever. Okay, I'll check your story out with the guys. If it's true I'll definitely have a few things to say to Mister Pete Rosa about it." He flexed the flippers twice. "On the side that is, nothing official. I got a job to keep, too."

*****

"Jesus," Roach scolded Shea, "you go any faster you'll take a header on the ice, break your fuckin' neck." They were on a nightly walk across no-man's land to the shithouse. The waterfront wind chewed at their faces. Roach said, "I can't believe you told Manny Amado about that green card business. You just looking to get fired?"

47

Shea shrugged. Hell, he didn't understand half the things he did himself.

The shithouse was heated with gasping steam pipes. It had a line of stalls, some with working doors, a couple with latches. Newspapers and *Hustler* magazines were strewn around the toilets and window ledges.

Inside, hardhats leaned on asbestos wrapped pipes and let the heat penetrate while they shot the breeze. Lured by the promise of heat, hardhats young and old, of all colors and every trade, flocked to share the warm pipes.

The place was plastered with graffiti, almost always signed *Quitewhite* in a dozen anonymous scrawls. Much of it targeted the meager population of women welders in the yard, usually by name, though *Niggers Suck White Man's Cock* was by far the most popular theme. Yet blacks and whites hung in the shithouse together, warming and sometimes trading jokes. Though no one mentioned the graffiti it was always in view.

Byron finally brought the issue into the open. "Ain't none of you concerned with this filth?" he asked a cluster of white workers warming up. "Not one man in here got balls to say this is wrong and disgusting to any decent person?" It made no difference to him if the return silence was stony or ashamed—it was silence.

Byron cast his eyes from face to face. "Not wasting my time calling Darby. Who comes in early tomorrow with me to corner one of those Board members?"

No one.

He corralled the bus riders after work. "You comin' Cotty? Pretty Boy?"

Pretty Boy nodded but Cotty was more enthusiastic. "Damn right!"

Shea said, "You askin' me, too?"

Byron took that in. "Damn right, boy," he said.

*****

Manny mounted the steps to the white clapboard house and rang the doorbell. Pete Rosa opened the door. "Itching for that white hat already?"

"Not exactly, Pete. Still thinking on that. But I do have something else. About the guys."

Pete sat him down in the parlor. A side table waited with coffee from the islands, fried plaintains and *donetes*.

Manny said, "Look, Pete, I owe you, like everyone else, and I'm grateful. But I hear that you're holding the crew's green cards. They're not complaining. This came from somewhere else."

Rosa poured two cups of coffee. "If they're not complaining, what business is it of yours—or anybody?"

"With all due respect, holding the cards is a risk. For you, but also for those poor guys if this ever comes out. They'd probably get sent back, right? And then the families get hurt, too. And I don't know where that would put you."

"I'm a citizen. Nothing could happen." Rosa stared over his coffee cup at his visitor. "You're outta line, Manny."

"Due respect, Pete, let's look at this. Holding someone's green card is just not legal. It's a federal thing. How do you think the company would take that with the bids they got out on defense work? And no matter how it comes out, your wife and kids would be embarrassed—for no reason at all."

"C'mon, Manny. I'm trying to make sure that a group of Cape Verdean kids don't embarrass the whole community by running off if they're not up to the job."

"You really think a single one of those guys would humiliate their families like that?"

Rosa took a sip of his coffee. "Okay, maybe you're right about that much. They'd come to me first." He set down his cup, folded his arms across his chest. "So tell me, who brought this to you?"

"Pete, you don't want to know."

10

Shea surveyed the men across from the shipyard gate. "Which one's Charney?"

Cotty pointed. "Over there in front of Ziyad's, with the Trustee button on his chest and the name on his hard hat. Kevin Charney. Was day steward for welders. Moved up to the Board. That's when Townsend got elected to fill his spot. First black steward."

Byron led the others over. He loomed over Charney. "Hey! When you gonna have the company clean out this graffiti? Catch this Quitewhite and bring him up on charges, get him fired?"

"Your business is with Darby. He handles second shift welders."

Byron edged up to the steward. "This is no second shift issue, man. That shithouse is there twenty-four hours. What's the matter with you?"

"It's not in the contract," Charney said, "so it's none of my business."

Cotty said, "Now look. We all know who does this stuff. Let's see—who walks around the yard whenever and wherever, has all kinds of stuff to draw and paint with and hates black people? And women? You got any ideas in that pea brain of yours?"

Charney stared back.

"Farrell and his marker boys, that's who!" Cotty spat out, "You wire them to those tit jobs, they run around wherever they want at election time to promote you—and now you protect them. They probably behind those stories about Klan trash bein' passed round the yard, too!"

Cotty stomped away. After taking Charney's measure, Byron followed. Shea held back until he had Charney alone. "What *is* the matter with you?" he demanded, "That shit should make anyone who believes in a union angry as hell."

Charney said, "Be careful what you say, mister. I got you in my sights."

Shea clucked in disgust and caught up with the others. Byron was asking, "What about Charley Johnson? Take it to him?"

Cotty said, "Not me, I'm sick of that oreo and he knows it. And no West Indian guy gonna qualify with him either, so forget about that, Byron. Anyway, he won't touch no race issue with this company. Let's you and me go in early tomorrow, meet up with Townsend at the gate."

11

"And you didn't come to me first because..." Kenny Townsend let the question hang, "You thought Charney would jump on this? Cause now he's such a good friend to the black man you don't need the black steward?"

Cotty said, "We thought Charney might want to get the graffiti cleaned up and keep his boys outta trouble."

"Still shoulda come to me."

Byron said, "So now we are here. What's the next step?"

"No next step," said Townsend. "There's no constituency to make a big deal of this, least not on days. And this the wrong time to turn off white welders."

"Why is that?"

"'Cause I filed for a special union meeting to get the welders more stewards, just like I promised. There's a new issue of *Hot Slag* about it out tomorrow. And equal steward representation is something that white welders will get behind, long as you don't scare 'em off."

Cotty said, "So racist crap all over these walls and we keep our mouth shut?"

"For now," said Townsend, "I'm goin' for some real power."

*****

Shea was at a table of welders at Ziyad's close to the whistle. They had just gulped down the last of their coffee

53

when Farrell barreled up to them with his hands clenched. "Think you're fuckin' Jesus Christ come to save us? We were doin' just fine before you showed up."

Shea tried to stay low key. "Just trying to look at what we might be able to get done together, Farrell. You got somethin' against clean bathrooms?"

"You act like the rest of us can't make out for ourselves."

"Well, we're not all in that sweet marker pipeline of yours, are we?"

Farrell took a step toward Shea. "Y'know, Shea, mouth off to the wrong guy and you're gonna find yourself on the wrong end of a wedge storm. Or maybe you'll just run into some other markers who don't got my patience."

Shea said, "Why don't you go jerk off in the shithouse? Paint the walls with your Quitewhite."

"Yeah? I knew a guy once, turned on his own, got his hands dirty with the wrong kind. Didn't turn out so good for him."

Roach jumped between them. "You know what? Nobody really wants to watch you guys go at it."

The five-minute warning whistle blew. The rest of the crew rose and walked out the door. Shea and Roach followed.

*****

"What's on your mind, Farrell?"

"Not much, Pete. Just thought you might want to know who dimed you out on the green cards."

"And what? Then I owe you?"

Farrell shrugged. "Might be worth something, sure."

Rosa stared at the marker. "You know, Farrell, you're not only racist, you're an asshole. You snitch on one of your own union guys and think a black Cape Verdean boss is gonna trust you?"

"You guys ain't black, Pete."

Rosa snorted. "Anyways, I already know who it was. Those kids don't keep nothin' from me. It's the new guy from the city."

"Shea? And you're gonna nail him?"

"See, Farrell, you just don't know me. I'm not gonna touch him. Don't like what he did, but you think I'm gonna go for him after he sticks his neck out for my kids? Add stupid to that list I gave you."

*****

Before the second shift whistle the next day, the Cape Verdeans crowded around Shea at his toolbox before the start of the shift. "Thank you," Joao said. He pulled out his green card for Shea to see. Tony and Pedro, and then the others gathered closer and clapped Shea on the back.

From the far end of the muster area, Griswold and Farrell watched with narrowed eyes.

12

With a start, Lonny realized that an incoming second shift welder had made his way over the deck and was just outside her access patch. A bundle of folded leaflets stuck out from the top of her wire can. A second stack of them lay at her feet. She picked up the papers from the tank floor, stuffed them in the breast of her jacket and stuck her head into the fresh, sweet air. The five-minute whistle blew. She jumped out of the tank, calling to get the welder's attention.

"Hey there!" Her gravelly voice echoed from an access patch in the sidewall. She climbed out and scanned the area for whitehats. Shea was alone with her on the deck skirt overlooking the last of the cargo holds.

The woman was husky, mid to late thirties, Shea guessed. She reached back through the access patch and pulled out a metal can of welding wire by its shoulder strap. The can clanked against the edge of the access hole and a sheaf of folded papers fell out and scattered. Lonny scooped them up and reinserted them between the welding wire and tools in the can. Her round Irish face was heavily freckled, as was the hand that slipped under her coat and held out another of the stapled sheets of paper. "Have a good read in the shithouse," she said.

Shea looked around for whitehats.

"Don't be a wus," Lonny said. "This is important information I'm givin' you here. Just be smart about it." She hefted her wire box up and over her shoulder, pausing once more to make certain she hadn't been seen. "Took me all night to write this up and get it printed, so it's damn well worth your time to read it." She pushed the papers into his hand and started to move toward the stairway off the boat. She turned around once. "Keep it out of sight when you're in the open."

Shea looked at the flyer. The masthead said *Hot Slag*. The headlined first page demanded *Union Democracy Now!* Shea folded the paper and stuffed it in his back pocket as he walked on to his muster area. He grabbed his gear from his toolbox, took the flyer from his pocket and sat down on the box. He skimmed the lead article. Roach looked over Shea's shoulder and then nudged him when Griswold walked in and noticed.

"Hey, Shea," the whitehat said, "read that shit on your own time. I don't wanna see it in here."

Shea looked at his watch. "This is still my time."

"And it's my shipyard." Griswold snatched the paper. The three-thirty whistle sounded and he smiled wickedly. "And now it's my time, too."

"Jesus Christ, Bobby," Roach said to Griswold, "they got copies all over the yard. He'll just pick up another one in the shithouse."

Griswold handed the newsletter back to Shea. "Just keep it out of sight then. I don't need Rosa breathin' all over me. And get back on those pin butts you started yesterday. Fuckin' day shift let them go."

"Okay," said Shea. "But I got a right to read what I want on my time."

Griswold screwed up his face. "Slow learner, Shea? Not gonna wise up 'til it hurts." He turned to give out the other assignments.

*****

At dinner break Shea dragged Roach out to Ziyad's, where he corralled Byron and Cotty. "Where's Pretty Boy?" he asked. Cotty cocked his head toward the bar, where Pretty Boy was making time with a young black woman Shea hadn't seen before. Little Z was pouring out ginger brandy for them, straight up.

"Oh yes, man," Byron said after glancing at the newsletter. "Lonny and some of those other white girls on first shift turn this thing out. It's some good readin', too."

"Like what?"

"They used it to push Townsend for steward when he was standing alone, then move on to this call we have now for more stewards. But they also cry out when a job not safe for a man to work. Last year we finishing some little barge work and the company spray epoxy paint before the seams are welded. Turns out this paint render a rash on the skin and the body with cancer. Lonny the one did the research. She call it out in *Hot Slag* and force the company to grind it all off."

"So you know her?"

Byron nodded. "Every man in the yard knows Lonny one way or the other. She is one powerful woman. Got her way of making someone feel like she really listen to them—at least before she tell them the truth of her opinion."

Cotty chuckled. "Her sometimes inflexible opinion."

Shea said, "But you both like her?"

"Man," said Byron, "that woman is a hurricane, but in a good way. Honest, strong heart, but also knows how to speak to the boys that's not so brave as her."

"So, what's the democracy issue all about?"

Cotty smacked the lead story with the back of his hand. "I already told you. Here on nights alone we got twice the welders to every other trade put together, right? Well, only one steward for fourteen hundred welders, days and nights.

And more hired in every day! Pipefitters and sheet metal and riggers got the same one steward each, and there ain't but two hundred guys apiece in those departments. It don't add up."

Pretty Boy had joined the table, alone except for his brandy. He took a gulp while he considered Cotty and then said, "You so down on the union, I don't know why you care how many stewards you got."

"Damn boy, I got rights. Equal representation! And remember that whitehat Pody suspended me last year. I know good as anyone we need a real steward."

"Hey, I ain't arguing." Pretty Boy held up his glass.

"Hunh," said Byron. "I say the union itself hold up the issue. Contract don't limit no welding stewards. So now the union see Townsend in there and they scared that we gonna elect another black man. That's why they so opposed."

Shea didn't hide his surprise. "How do you know what the contract says?"

"Hey, man. Maybe a lot you don't know about me." Byron allowed himself a smug twitch of the lips. "Regardless, this union and this company will gang together to stop any move by Lonny and Townsend to demand a welder's right to more stewards."

"That's the truth!" Cotty exclaimed, "More welder stewards means black stewards, and more black stewards is the end for that do-nothing crew."

Roach chipped in, "I hear Townsend is supposed to be some hot shit. Guess even the white guys on day shift like him."

"Look here!" Cotty shot a stubby finger toward Roach. "Townsend don't need your approval!" He would have kept going except for Byron's touch on his arm.

"This Roach man okay, Cotty. You take it easy on him."

"Alright, then," Cotty allowed. He scratched the top of his head with one finger. "Now, lemme tell you about Townsend. Young kid. Smart."

Byron protested. "Cotty, the man almost forty, you know."

"Whatever, then. He got brains enough to take on the union and that joker Rashford and the old steward Charney put up against him. He don't take sides with the company every time you turn around. And he ain't fooled by that Steppin' Fetchit Charley Johnson in the welding office. Now that is one sad motherfucker. Anyways, I don't always agree with the man, but Townsend is a fighter. And he do make them mad, the way he strut around with that two-tone hair of his and all."

Shea was intrigued. "Not sure that two-tone hair is what I'm looking for in a steward, Cotty."

"Look, that boy is quick on his feet. Listen to this." Cotty was getting excited again. "Just before he was elected, Townsend gets a job on the main deck. He been out partyin' all night, so he finds a grate, right out in the open. He kneels over and goes to sleep. Face down on his knees, broad daylight, right on the main deck. Bosses walkin' by every couple minutes, but that boy ain't movin'. He is *a-sleep*, I tell you. Finally, one of these whitehats comes up and nudges Townsend with his toe. 'Get up!', he says, and Townsend jumps up, all pissed off.

"'Whatchoo mean, 'Get up', man?', he says, and I mean right in that whitehat's face. 'I been a half hour lookin' through that grate for a line and I just spotted one. Now you kick me and I lose it! Shee-it!' And he storms off.

"Whitehat just left standin' there with his mouth open!" Cotty laughed out loud and clapped Shea on the shoulder. "Motherfucker didn't even touch him. They do want to get him somethin' bad, though."

Shea was lost. "Cotty, what's he really been able to do for the guys?" The question hung in front of them all.

"Well, he can't get much done by himself, I admit it," the old man said at last. "They just won't let him. Point is, he smart and he make them all stupid crazy. And he tries to do us proud. That's the best you can ask for around here."

*****

At home after midnight, Shea pored over the newsletter again. He checked his contract. Just like Byron had said, it permitted one steward for each two hundred hardhats in a department. Despite that, the union by-laws capped the number at a single steward for each.

He couldn't let that go. How could it be possible that the union—not the company—limited the number of stewards, the front-line protection guys had on the job? Shea realized that Byron was right; it really was a black and white issue. The only truly affected department, the only one that qualified under the contract for additional stewards, was welding—the only department with a significant number of black votes.

13

Townsend's end-run campaign had focused an unusual amount of effort on the heavily black night welder vote. With help from Lonny and her *Hot Slag* circle, he had turned out second shift and surprised everyone by winning the election.

She held her breath for a week while Townsend settled into the job, then gave him a push she described to others as gentle.

"No time to dawdle, Kenny," she told him. "What about that change to the by-laws you promised—more welding stewards?"

Townsend gave her a comrade-in-arms smile. "Been waiting on you to show up and harass me, Lonny. Just been feelin' out my territory. But I'm ready."

"What we need is special union meeting to vote on the increase. The department's up to fourteen hundred now and still growing. We're due at least six more steward slots."

"Six it is. I'll file for the meeting. You and *Hot Slag* do your stuff."

Over the next week Shea came in early to help distribute *"Union Democracy Now!"* bulletins to second shift. Lonny met him inside the yard to replenish his stack and update him daily about the upcoming union meeting. "It's all in the turnout," she insisted when he asked how to know who to recruit for the vote. "Don't matter who. The vote's by voice or divide the house. No one in the welding department's gonna go to the hall and stand up to vote 'no' on this thing. So beat those bushes!"

Shea took it to his crew and anyone else he knew who would listen, urging them to show up at the hall the following Tuesday. At first the welders didn't see why they should go through the aggravation of a trip to the union hall just to get a few more stewards like Darby. "But they won't be like Darby if you have better choices, and more of them," Shea told the doubters dozens of times each day. "Doesn't that make sense?" He was met with some nods, but more shrugs.

*****

Ziyad glanced up from the grill when Shea, now a regular, came in. Little Z let the bottle linger over Shea's glass just a hair longer and whispered about who to watch out for in the union hierarchy. Shea used the perch at his table to talk. "It's just democracy," he kept saying. "Isn't that what it's supposed to be about?" Besides, he pointed out, could it really be an accident that the welders were not only the most under-represented department but also the most harassed? The brownhats agreed more readily with that. To the black guys and a few whites he trusted, Shea repeated Byron's thinking, that the union's limit was directed against minority welders and the black stewards they were almost sure to elect.

Pretty Boy's new friend Patty came by and listened. "Sounds nice," she said, watching Shea closely and smiling. When he smiled back her eyes opened wider. "But tell me, Mr. Shea. That what you say to your white friends, too?"

When he tried it out on Roach he got a warning. "You gotta be careful with that. Focus on more representation. Keep the color out of it or you'll lose 'em."

*****

The issue was distant from most workers in other trades, though some of them mulled over the implications suspiciously. "Cant'cha find anything better to do than go against the union, for chrissakes?" one long-term fitter wanted to know. Eventually most welders gave Shea a sympathetic ear, and an impressive number of them vowed to make it to the hall for the vote. Cotty, Pretty Boy and Byron promised to take the early shuttle from Quincy Station for the two o'clock second shift meeting. They assured Shea that they could herd over the other bus riders, too. Byron thought he could entice Rodney with the promise of a free beer afterward. Pretty Boy promised to escort Patty. "She still at the welding school, just up from Lenoir County in North Carolina," he told the gang on the bus, "and she is something." Shea was surprised how often his thoughts wandered to her.

14

Stan Rashford pointed his gavel at each of the seated workers around the hall, moving his lips as he counted heads. Six union officials sat at tables on either side of his podium.

A full row of the young Cape Verdeans sat toward the rear of the room. Shea took a seat a couple rows away, next to Roach. Joao gave him the high sign while the others looked out over thirty rows of empty chairs and waited. Shea's insides growled anxiously.

"Don't even know what they're votin' on," someone wearing a union badge grumbled, glaring at the Cape Verdeans.

Roach looked to Shea for assurance. "They do, right?" Shea peered down the row of them sitting erect and formal in their greasy work clothes. They leaned forward and smiled at him and straightened back up.

"Don't worry, they get it," Shea said.

A few dozen welders filtered in, along with a handful of hardhats from other trades. Cotty and Byron sat by themselves in a corner, quiet and watchful. A row behind them, Pretty Boy was talking intently to Patty. The rest of the bus riders were no-shows. Aside from Billy, Roach and the Cape Verdeans, no one from Shea's crew had arrived.

Shea caught Cotty's eye. The old man came over and leaned into his ear. "This is okay. You got more than forty guys here. That's more'n they ever get for a second shift meeting."

Shea looked over at Patty and said, "I see Luther got his new girl here."

"Just focus on business at hand," Cotty told him,

Rashford banged his gavel and abruptly announced, "No quorum, no meeting." He turned away from the podium toward the union hall office.

"Hold it!" Shea stood. "You can have the meeting. You know we're all here to vote on the steward issue."

Rashford continued toward his office. "Need fifty for a quorum, same as the first shift meeting," he called without turning. "Don't got it."

Shea persisted. "What kind of bullshit is that? There's three times as many guys on first shift. Besides, there's fifty here including you guys up front. Count 'em."

Rashford looked over his shoulder. His expression made it clear that he wasn't accustomed to floor debates with second shift. "We don't count the officers until the first shift meeting. No quorum."

Cotty stood, agitation written all over his face. "Why you blocking this vote? Even black welders got a right for the stewards that's in the contract."

"This has nothing to do with black and white, Cotty. The quorum is fifty, always been."

Patty jumped up without warning. "You afraid of us? Afraid of black people and the vote we deserve? Your day comin'!" Her voice was like a low rumble of thunder. Next to her, Pretty Boy shrank into his seat. Rashford ignored her.

Shea called out, "Take a vote without a full meeting and put it toward the first shift count!"

Rashford took a step back into the room and searched Shea's face. His blue eyes were hard under the forelock of white hair that fell over his forehead. "I know you?"

Shea stood his ground. "Michael Shea. Welder."

Rashford turned away again. His officers had already left for the back office. His voice trailed behind him. "You don't know the rules, son. Go read 'em. You want to vote, come back to the first shift meeting. You got the right to do that—on your own nickel during your work shift." He vanished into his office, leaving the welders to stare at the vacated podium. A murmur started among them. A few got up and shouted angrily for Rashford. Their yells soon petered out. The welders settled back down in their seats and then, one by one, got up again to leave.

"This sucks," Shea said finally. "I'm comin' back tonight when they have the first shift meeting."

Roach said, "Yeah? I'm not givin' up a couple hours pay just to screw around with these assholes."

Cotty, Pretty Boy and Patty joined them. "I'll make it," said Cotty. "Get signed out at dinner." Pretty Boy was non-committal.

Shea looked at Patty. She said, "I'm thirty days plus one now. Still in the school but off probation. They can't do nuthin' about it if I come back later to vote."

15

Shea found Griswold and held out his timecard just before the seven-thirty dinner whistle. Griswold said, "I'll sign you out, but if you're goin' back to that meeting like I heard, you might find yourself with a lost time chit tomorrow."

"Look, Bobby, I got no lost time and I'm hardly ever off my job. You can't nail me just cause it's a union meeting."

Griswold talked while he marked down job codes and signed the card. "You think I'm bustin' your balls? I'm not. Just don't set yourself up for some whitehat to build a name for himself."

He handed the card back to Shea. "You the next steward?"

Billy the Kid broke in. "Nope that's me." He held out his card. "Sign me out, too."

The whitehat grimaced. "Look who's the big union guy."

Shea was grateful for the company. He hadn't expected that Billy would give up a few bucks to go to the hall. Together they ran out the gate and jogged up Howard Street to the first shift meeting.

*****

The parking lot was jammed with big cars and milling men. Shea pushed through the glass doors and found himself at the rear of a standing room only crowd. A varnished pine tongue and groove chair rail surrounded the room. Above

68

the wood, the walls were painted sea blue and decorated with old photos of men at work and ships that were launched from the yard's basins as far back as the early nineteen hundreds. Nautical nets hung from the ceilings.

Cotty and Patty were standing at the back near the door. Cotty pulled Shea by the arm and said, "Come with me." He led Shea toward a cluster of white old timers in the middle of the room, listening to a large gray-haired guy in the middle. "You watch and listen," Cotty said as they got close.

"Hey McKinnon," he addressed the man, "I figure you either owe Rashford one or come to your senses. Otherwise I wouldn't be seein' you this long before you punch in for third shift."

"Cotty, you come round to insult me again?" The bigger man smiled. "Maybe I owe Stan, but you know me. When you're right you're right. Can't think of a single reason to be against equal representation—less it makes you into a steward, of course, you little bastard." He guffawed at his own joke.

"Good man, McKinnon" Cotty said, "Let's me and you catch up after fishing season, match up lies about what we pulled in." McKinnon offered a thumbs up.

Cotty led Shea away. "That's John McKinnon, third shift crane man. Been here longer than dirt. Straight shooter more or less. If he's here with a couple guys from other trades, that's a good sign for us."

Shea nodded and Cotty headed back toward Patty. He elbowed his way down to one side of the hall and moved to get a better view. The five hundred empty folding chairs he had counted that afternoon were all occupied. The room was a din of voices in dozens of conversations. Looking at the crowd of showered and combed men in button-down sports shirts, Shea felt suddenly conspicuous. Except for Darby, no one else was dressed in work clothes.

Blotchy white cloths had been laid over the two tables flanking the podium at the front of the room. Rashford stood behind the lectern and looked at his watch.

From the afternoon session, Shea knew that the middle-aged men lounging at the front tables were Rashford's officers. Each of them, and Rashford, wore a round badge with the title of a union office in large blue letters.

One of the officers was busy counting the assembly. Periodically, the others waved to an acquaintance in the crowd or pointed a greeting. Several times they snapped their fingers at a chair on the main floor. When they did, one man or another scurried up to incline his head and receive some tidbit of apparently confidential intelligence that was followed by a slap on the back.

The first three or four rows of folding chairs seemed to be reserved for lower-level union officials of various ranks sporting smaller badges that said "Steward" or "Alternate."

Shea had trouble connecting the freshly shaven men on the floor with the grimy workers who filed in and out of the gates alongside him every day. If this crowd was representative of day shift, it was very different from the shipyard he knew. It was hugely white men, many older than forty, some in their fifties, all loudly enjoying themselves. Well-groomed and self-consciously dignified. No one seemed drunk or high. Most wore pressed chinos and polished loafers.

It occurred to Shea that many white day shift guys lived close to the shipyard and could easily make it back for union meetings at night. The much smaller number of first shift black workers probably lived in the city and were not likely to make the extra round trip in the evening.

Despite that, a clump of excited young black men engaged with each other in the rear of the room. Shea didn't recognize any of them and assumed they were first shifters.

One of them, tall and skinny, was talking and gesticulating forcefully. Some young whites, including several women, listened around the fringes. Shea picked out Lonny and tried unsuccessfully to catch her eye. When the talkative black guy turned slightly, Shea saw that his hair was natural and kinky on one side, peroxided to a light red on the other. He wore hound's tooth pants and a union badge. From Cotty's description, it had to be Kenny Townsend, the welding steward.

A few older blacks were seated in small groups throughout the hall, talking quietly among themselves. Several times one or another of the badged white men from the front rows ambled over and flashed a smile as he shook hands or playfully punched one of the black men on the shoulder and received a quiet hello in response. Then the official would spot someone else, wave to him and move in that direction.

Shea was delighted to see a half dozen welders he had met at the school and then lost in the shipyard abyss after their class had moved on to production. From their street clothes he guessed that they had lucked out and gotten first shift as their initial assignment. He waved across the room to Keefer, the training school's heart throb. She waved back. Her brightly colored nails flashed and Shea felt a wave of disconcerted excitement. In his head, he heard Billy the Kid boast he had fucked her in high school.

Next to Keefer, Shea spotted Moises Ramos, whose trim bulk spread across two seats. Billy saw Ramos at the same time and scooted over to sit with him. Shea was surprised at the apparent connection between the two and, though he wasn't exactly sure why, that Ramos had taken enough interest in this union issue to attend.

Rashford banged the gavel and the room hushed. "I call this meeting to order. This is a special session convened by petition to discuss a by-law change—and that issue only."

From behind his chair a burly officer said, "Mr. President, I move to vote on the question."

Rashford responded on cue, "Our recording secretary Frank Salvucci has moved the question."

"Yeah, let's eat," someone seconded from the front row.

Townsend advanced swiftly down the center aisle, one arm upraised as he shouted and twisted to face the chair and the audience. "What question? Where's the discussion? How 'bout some *de-mo-cracy*? That's what we're here for!" He was greeted with cheers from the back of the room and some mild clapping from the middle seats. The small groups of older black workers leaned forward in their chairs.

Shea saw that a large number of younger white workers had jammed into the room from the parking lot. The standing room area was suddenly packed and about evenly divided between young blacks and whites.

Townsend must have been really beating the bushes to turn out the young guys, he thought. Wants to make his case in front of a crowd.

Scattered voices from the front rows called out, "The question! Move the question!" Rashford hit the gavel twice, loudly. "The question is moved. All those in favor of the amendment to the by-laws, say aye!"

Townsend shouted to the young crowd in the rear seats, "That's us!" and was rewarded with a lusty "Aye!" that boomed from the groups of welders at the rear of the hall.

Someone in the back of the room started chanting "Aye-Aye, Aye-Aye-Aye!" Billy took it up and Shea joined in while Ramos clapped. The beat quickly resounded around the hall. In the front rows, the stewards and alternates screwed around in their chairs to look.

Rashford leaned into his microphone and blasted out the chanting. "All those opposed!"

"*No!*" Opposition to the amendment was strong from the badged men in the front rows, but not, it seemed from many of the older whites in the middle of the room who seemed content to be spectators. The ayes were clearly in the majority.

Townsend had the same thought. "We did it! Wow!" He raised two fists above his head then shook his hair and yelped, "Yeah!"

"Mister Townsend," Rashford warned, "you will sit down or I'll have the Sergeant at Arms eject you." Townsend slammed backwards to a seat. He turned his face down and murmured something to the welder seated next to him. A titter rippled from the nearby chairs.

Rashford glared at the steward. He gripped the front of the lectern. He picked up his gavel and banged it once, then looked out over the rows of faces. The room quieted. Rashford pressed his mouth to the microphone. "The nays have it. The motion fails!"

There was a long, stunned silence.

Lonny stepped out of the rear of the crowd and pointed at Rashford. "You sleazy bastard!" she screamed.

A small black woman with a *Workers Unite!* button pinned to her blouse hopped onto the seat of her chair and shouted, working her fists in the air. "Fascist motherfucker! *Fascist!*"

Salvucci gestured at two men with union badges pinned to their sweaters. They strode quickly in her direction. One of them called out, "We got it, Frank!" He pulled at the small woman's hips from the rear while the other pushed her shoulders down decisively from the front. She disappeared wordlessly below the crowd.

A young white guy wearing the same *Workers Unite!* pin stood up and screamed, "You company lackey!" He rushed over and flailed wildly. Before Shea could tell whether he was trying to free the black woman or hit her assailants, Salvucci was on him and clamped a very large hand over his face.

Another officer yelled, "Show that commie, Frank!" Salvucci's fingers whitened, squeezing at the kid's cheekbones and eyes, pushing his head back until it faced the ceiling. Salvucci's hand wrenched clockwise. The kid spun off balance and downward. He thudded against the metal-edged back support of a folding chair and he sagged to the floor. In the clearing made by his fall, Shea could see the other two union officers pressing the small black woman's shoulders from behind so that she was doubled over in her chair. She was trying to yell but scarcely able to pull air into her lungs.

"That young woman is right!" Shea jerked toward the sound. Cotty paced down the aisle from the back of the room with Patty on his heels. "This is some racist shit like I never seen! You and this board are filth of the earth, Stan Rashford! Beat on this company, not us!"

Rashford pointed the gavel. "You know better than this, Cotty." He turned to Salvucci and said, "Eject him, Frank." Salvucci left the white kid on the floor and hustled down the rows. He grabbed Cotty by the collar and pushed him toward the exit. Cotty feinted, swung around and planted a furious knee in Salvucci's crotch. They both went down. Shea and Patty rushed in from opposite directions. They met over Cotty and exchanged a look, then smiled at each other without restraint.

"Don't let me break in now," Cotty said to them both, "but jus' help me up." He glanced down at Salvucci. "Who cryin' now, Big Frank?"

Kevin Charney stood up from his seat at the front of the room. "Move to adjourn Mr. President."

Rashford's auctioneering staccato was quick. "All-those-in-favor-all-those-opposed-ayes-have-it-meeting-adjourned!" He smashed the gavel on the table one last time and walked out.

Townsend was on his feet. "You cocksucker!"

In his nicely fit shirt, Charney's chest looked like it had once bulged with muscle. He addressed the rear of the room in a booming voice. "I was the daytime welding steward here for ten years. Any steward that thinks he's gotta have more help isn't doing his job, *Mister* Townsend!"

Townsend ignored him and ran down the aisle at Rashford. He only made it halfway before Lonny sprang out of her row and grabbed him around the middle. The momentum spun them both around, crashing into chairs. They locked in a standoff embrace.

Townsend yelled into her face. "Lemme go, Lonny! I swear I'll lay you out, too!" He tried to push away, his reedy arms working like a madman in a straight jacket. Lonny enveloped him, gasping between huffs.

"Hey Kenny, you know I'm with you. But this ain't gonna do nuthin'..... Go home, willya? We'll talk about it tomorrow."

Townsend pushed back to free himself. The crowd was on its feet watching. Shea saw Ramos get up from his chair, move to the aisle and walk at a measured pace toward Townsend and Lonny.

When he got there the whole room went silent. Townsend and Lonny froze in front of his mass. Ramos stood motionless. Shea moved down the aisle toward him, listening intently.

"Don't fight with the womens," Ramos said quietly to Townsend. "Not worthy." Then he turned to Lonny and said, "This man is here for all of us. Better you show him respect."

Townsend and Lonny dropped their arms. "Yes," she said, "we should calm down. Regroup. This isn't the end."

Townsend shook his head and sagged. "It is for me. No more. I quit."

Shea said, "Don't worry, man. You'll figure it out tomorrow."

Townsend almost found his footing but tripped over himself, grabbing a onto a chair. He put one leg up on it and hung his head, breathing heavily. "No, I mean I really quit." He took a big breath, then unpinned his steward's badge and threw it toward Rashford's lectern. It clinked off the union emblem on the front and fell to the floor. His eyes were wet. He gave his head several vigorous shakes and came up clear-eyed.

"Hey!" He raised his voice to take in the few remaining welders at the back of the room, "Anybody for a quick one at Ziyad's?"

16

"He the best thing ever happened to this union, and he gone," Cotty mourned, "And they ain't lettin' no black man take that steward spot again. Not never." He stared at the ground. No matter how many ways Shea asked, "What now?" he couldn't get a response.

Shea found Lonny inside the yard near the access patch where he'd met her. They agreed to talk over a beer during second shift dinner.

He sat beside her on the grass across from Ziyad's. The floodlights from the security shack at the gate cut through the dusk. Dozens of second shift welders drifted by, waving to Lonny or calling out a greeting.

"They seem to like you," Shea said.

"I been around for a while. I make friends. But you don't see the rest."

"Like what?"

"Like the porn that gets taped to my tool box. The creep calls into my tank. The whispers from Rashford's guys—lez this, commie that. It doesn't stop. And I got it easy. You get into this full throttle and they'll come after you like a man. Threats. Corner-shoved in a tank. Wedges dropped from the deck. It's no game."

"And Rashford's behind all this stuff?"

"He creates the mood, let's them know who's pissed him off. And the guys that follow him read the message."

Shea said, "I get more impressed every time I see you."

"Their favors and connections give them clout. Nobody wants to lose that if it's all they got goin'. So we gotta build the momentum, win a few things. Gotta find guys the others respect, maybe even connected to the system somehow but with a low bullshit threshold. Guys you don't know yet, like Richie Millis the rigger or Fat Sal from the tool room—even Johnno McKinnon, old school crane operator on graveyard shift. Guys with an open mind. They listen, they offer information, and they get around the yard. Kinda like the markers do for Salvucci and Charney, but quietly, on the good guy side. They talk to the unwired hardhats who never speak up but know in their gut something's wrong, that they're gettin' the shaft but they might not want to be seen with any of us."

She sipped at her drink. "But when something big comes up—like Townsend's election or this call for more stewards, those quiet guys show up—like those older white guys last night that you woulda thought were Rashford's but didn't vote at all. McKinnon was there last night with them. I saw Cotty drag you over. They're in that yard right now, maybe not sayin' they support us, but tellin' people who weren't there what a fraud the vote was. In the end they're our friends. Or could be."

Shea hung on her words.

"Getting out *Hot Slag* is important, but people are afraid to take it at the gate, so we mainly pass it around on the inside." Lonny gnawed at the inside of her mouth. "Kind of cuts back our impact, but they're afraid of the union seeing them take it. The company, too. That's another reason why we need people like Richie and Fat Sal. They're like walking newsletters."

"Then there's the radicals," said Shea.

"Hell, yeah. A few months ago they had people from outside the yard handing out leaflets at the gates that called for revolution in the tanks. Now, maybe I'd like revolution in the tanks, too, whatever that means. But I know when to keep my mouth shut and when to open it wide. And I know what to say without scarin' people any more than they already are."

"So how come you didn't run for steward instead of Townsend?"

"This department needs a black steward. Plus, I like girls, and you can guess how that would play around here. I'm not someone who's gonna hide who I am."

"You remind me of my Aunt Bridget, all spit-in-the-eye attitude for bullshit and people who insult her."

The warning whistle blew. Shea thanked Lonny for coming down to see him at night. He headed back through the gate.

*****

He hadn't been welding more than ten minutes when he heard someone behind him. He broke his arc and lifted his shield. Griswold was standing by his job, smoking. The whitehat gestured with his cigarette. "Personally, I don't give a flyin' fuck who your friends are. But you start hangin' out with a red like Cheryl Lonergan and her lezzie buddies and you got some real trouble comin' from the front office. Just a little advice is all."

"Who? I lost ya."

"Don't fuck with me. Cheryl Lonergan. Lonny."

Griswold flicked away his cigarette and climbed out of the tank without effort.

17

Shea poked his head in Rashford's open office door. "Darby said you wanted to see me."

Rashford looked up from his desk and beckoned Shea to a chair. "Come on in, Mike."

Kevin Charney sat at one end of Rashford's desk. Frank Salvucci perched on a stool in the corner. Shea spread out his knees, placed his hands on them and leaned back.

Rashford said, "You seem like a smart guy." He lifted his eyebrows theatrically. "Why hast thou forsaken me?"

Shea said, "Why am I here?"

"You mean how did you come to my attention? You try to save Kenny Townsend from himself, you give me shit at a public meeting, you hand out that *Hot Slag* rag. And you're a tough guy from East Cambridge who must know there's better ways to operate. That's a mix that makes me look."

Shea cleared his throat to speak, but Rashford touched a finger to his own lips and shook his head slightly. "And I think you got ambition."

Shea stared at the union president.

Rashford said, "Well, Michael, we'll just forget that last meeting. That was Townsend's mess. Between us, just an honest disagreement among friends, let's say."

Rashford shuffled some papers on his desk and picked up the latest issue of the newsletter. "You've seen where these people are going?" He laid the *Hot Slag* on the desk so that it faced Shea.

The headline announced a reform ticket for the special election to replace Kenny Townsend with Lucien Bly as the candidate.

"You could do alright against that coon, hunh, Shea?" Salvucci suggested from the corner.

Shea said, "You're an idiot, you know that?"

Rashford closed his eyes briefly. "Frank, will you excuse us?"

With a nasty look at Shea, Salvucci climbed off his stool and left.

"And close the door," Rashford ordered. He waited for it to click shut before turning back to Shea.

"Yeah, I seen that." Shea gestured toward the flyer, "And yeah, I talk to them, help them out." He drummed on the arms of his chair. "Guess they wanted to find somebody black to run."

Rashford said, "I got six thousand Local 8 members, almost a third welders. More of them are my friends than you'd like to think." He tapped the newsletter. "Maybe you want to run yourself. Maybe Bly's not sitting quite right with you. Yeah?" He pointed at Shea. "It's not smart gettin' mixed up with the bunch that puts outs that newsletter. They're all reds out to destroy the yard."

Shea drew up. "Y'know, Stan, I hear you helped put it together when the union meant something in this shipyard, and I respect that. That newsletter's got something to say, though."

Rashford said, "Does it now?" He looked at Shea placidly. "Have you given any thought to a slate? Maybe my help is yours for the askin'."

Shea frowned. Rashford nodded at Charney, who held out a sheet of paper with a short list of names.

Shea hesitated, then took the sheet and browsed the list. He had run into a few of them. Young white welders, mostly Vietnam vets. Should be his kind of people.

Rashford watched Shea's expression. "I thought you'd like those guys," he said, sounding almost fatherly. "They're all on my team. You could lead a ticket with them and win. With my help, of course."

Shea felt a tingle of excitement at the idea. But goddam if he'd let himself be bought. "That train's left the station. Maybe Bly wouldn't have been my choice, but I made a commitment for this time around."

"Well, there's something to loyalty—long as it's not misplaced. But I don't ask twice." He turned to Charney. "Kevin, nothing to stop you from sitting on the Official Board and taking on the steward slot one more time. Looks like Shea here don't want to step up so it's you against Bly."

*****

While the small group of activists around *Hot Slag* had been intent on recruiting another black candidate to replace Townsend, Shea didn't like the idea of choosing a guy just because he wasn't white. But he didn't argue. He'd pushed Cotty to go for the post, but the older man refused to consider it.

Lonny's search had narrowed to Elroy Washington. Elroy's low-key demeanor had won him unusually good relations with the mill's cohort of older whites. And blacks throughout the department respected his steady style.

"I don't think so, Lonny," Elroy told her, "I got five years seniority on any other black welder, not to say I work the auto-welder in the Stiff Mill. That's an extra fifty cents an hour and the breathing room to stroll in the gate at the last minute. I'll go with your pick a hundred percent but I ain't fool enough to risk what I got."

"Elroy, you could actually win, get blacks and whites behind you. No one else can do that."

"Look, Charley Johnson put me on the machine first week he was super. I know damn well he got his own agenda—get us in line with a couple favors while he pisses off white guys who think they got some eternal rights to the tit jobs in the welding department. They don't seem to see all the marking and pipe welding slots that they owned for years and still do. Now I'm supposed to run for steward and get on Charley's wrong side, throw all that away?"

*****

Finally, Lucien Bly's name had surfaced. Or rather, Bly surfaced it himself to mixed reviews, reckoning to anyone who'd listen that all they needed was a steward with enough balls to face down the company as well as the union. When Byron heard that he sniffed, "I do not prefer to call out the name of any flimsy self-promoter among my black American brethren."

When Lonny checked Bly out with Townsend, the former steward was reluctant to venture an opinion. He seemed content to weld away in the tanks, biding his time until he heard about the job application he'd made to the firefighters.

"Kenny, you had a right to get out, and I understand why, but you also got a responsibility. You built your name as a fighter for the welders, and what you say—or don't— about a replacement will mean something."

"I'm not about to blackball anyone," he said. "Especially not a brother. I got no objection to Lucien, long as he keeps himself straight. But that's your job, not mine."

83

Lonny herself was an obvious choice for the steward position. But what she had told Shea was accurate—fair or not, she was a lightning rod for the worst prejudices and suspicions of the hardhats, and not only because she was a woman, though that didn't help.

"I told you, I'm tolerated cause I know how to play most of these guys," she said to Shea. "But electing me to some position of authority? The same woman they see on the shithouse walls suckin' some cartoon dick? The lez?" She laughed bitterly. "No way."

*****

Lucien Bly spent most of his time at the yard running his mouth. "Can't tell what's worse," he complained, "company assholes or those shithead union guys." To Lonny and Shea, Bly's general hostility to authority initially seemed like it could be presented to the welders as evidence of his willingness to get tough. But as the campaign wore on, it became clear that most hardhats thought of him as a blowhard. The one night that Bly visited second shift during the dinner break, Shea heard him mouth off.

"Like I been sayin'," Bly told a group of welders gobbling fish and chips from paper bags, "this union ain't worth payin' dues. Those guys up at the hall are in the company pocket."

Shea thought he was trying to help when he asked, "So what will you do that's different, Lucien?"

"Still workin' on that," Bly said loudly. "But I'm smart enough to get over on them and this company too. Anyway, how could it be worse?" He pulled a flask from his back pocket and took a swig. "I been around. Trust me."

Even Bly's familiarity with large numbers of welders turned out to be a mixed blessing.

"Of course he knows everybody, he's into everybody's shit all the damn time," Lonny reported hearing more than once. Worse, she told Shea that Bly's own crew complained that he didn't pull his weight on the job. If a man didn't do his work, and do it right, someone else had to take up the slack.

*****

The campaign began with a blizzard of flyers. A small army of insurgent leafleteers smothered the gates first thing in the morning, assaulting the hardhats' shuffling entry like cutthroat street hawkers. In the afternoon Lonny flagged down Shea on her way out.

"I need a real distribution for night shift, too, Mike. No way Bly can win without that. The guys will take the flyers cause it's an election. Think you could put it together?"

"Sure. Don't give it a second thought."

Though they took Shea's leaflets, few welders commented on the campaign as they went past the gate. Shea doubted that many of them read the handouts or paid much attention to the campaign. And when he wandered into the shithouse to stir up support and chanced upon election discussions already in progress, conversation tended to grind to a halt.

Bly's obvious deficits made him wonder—next time, why not me? The thought made him feel eager, like he was on the right track. But just for a minute. He was still a short-timer. And none of that time on first shift, where the vast bulk of welders and everyone else worked.

*****

Patty pulled him aside at dinner break, the first time they'd spoken since trading that long smile at the union meeting.

"I passed my test and left the school," she said. "They movin' me to day shift and I wanted to talk to you before I go on tomorrow." He struggled to unwind her rural southern accent. He said, "Sorry to see you go. I was hoping we might hang out a little after you got out of school."

She gave him a look. "This ain't really no social call. I came to let you know that Bly's gonna lose. Not half of the black welders I talk to votin' for him."

Shea wasn't surprised, but the certainty in her voice weighed on him.

"That makes it pretty tough math for him," he said. "Why are you tellin' *me*?"

Patty twisted her lips. "Cotty and Luther tell me you almost the perfect white man," she said, "so why not?" And when he didn't respond, "Is that really so?"

"Not sure what you mean. But I *am* a white man who wants to know you better."

"Guess you missed your time, then. Different shifts don't leave much space to socialize."

*****

Before long, Shea's band of night shift leafleteers dropped away until he was left with a stack of flyers at the gates and a skeleton crew. Lonny told him that when she woke up early to hand out leaflets, more often than not she found herself standing there without the candidate anywhere to be seen.

At lunch she found him holed up with a shot glass in Ziyad's, or huddling with friends in the parking lot, toking furtively on a fat joint. One time he showed up to hand out flyers at six in the morning with some serious alcohol on his breath. Lonny got up in his face. "You're supposed to be an example of the fight, not the poster boy for why we're always losing."

"Hey girl, you worry too much."

*****

Rashford's loyalists smelled blood. They sought out older first shift welders in the largely white shops, men with whom they had traded favors over the years. On a second front they hailed down groups of young South Shore guys on the gangways. Inevitably, there were one or two in any crowd of white kids who owed this officer or that one his job through a father or uncle.

Rashford's guys nodded sagely: "Yeah, so and so's kid, the old man's a great guy." Then they launched into scathing attacks on Bly and Lonny, the puppet and his dyke commie mastermind. They pressed for Charney's all-American slate. Vote the White Ticket, they implored, though the inside slate name never appeared on any flyer.

Lonny and Shea had targeted the department's disgruntled young whites as the reachable swing vote, but not even their core of black welder sympathizers turned out. Charney ran away with the election.

18

"What a jerk!" Lonny lashed out to anyone who would listen. The welders were startled by her fury at Bly's loss, which she rapidly turned on herself and Townsend. "How could I have let this happen? I spent two years building the democracy campaign with Kenny Townsend, who does nothing when it's stolen from us, then walks off like a frustrated little boy. Then our candidate destroys our reputation. Damn them both!"

The election result was bad enough. But when she crawled into the tank the morning after, she knew something more was off. The bulkhead configuration seemed familiar, though it wasn't until coffee that recognition gripped her.

In the identical tank on 41 hull, almost a year ago, Farrell put down his paint bucket and approached her. "Lemme show you how good it can be," he boasted. Lonny turned away wordlessly and he grabbed at her. "You got nowhere to go, lez," he said, "If you didn't want it, you wouldn't be in the shipyard." They were alone in the tank. Help was a long shot away and the treacherous crawl to the access patch even longer.

"Yeah, Marty, let's do it," Lonny told him, licking her lips ridiculously. Maybe it was just her numb terror talking, but she hoped that a fool like Farrell would buy it.

Farrell tugged at his zipper. It snagged and he looked down. Lonny grabbed her slag hammer from a stiffener shelf and slammed it broadside against his helmet. She made for

88

the access patch, glancing back only once. Farrell was woozy though still on his feet. When she stuck her head through the patch her whitehat was in sight. The first and only time she was glad to see him.

She didn't report the incident to anyone, though she warned the other yard women about Farrell. Not one of them was surprised. Farrell moved to second shift on assignment a few days later.

After coffee this morning, she thought of leaving mid-day, even if it did mean a chit. She could ask for a job in a different tank just to tamp down the shivers from the year before, but decided against it. Hey, she had to deal with it all, and she would. She knew about stuffing things in a box.

*****

Lonny had lived with Margo and her younger brother Stephen in Providence at the turn of the decade, happy to waitress at the Brigham's downtown, chatting up her regulars and meeting new people at the counter every day. She loved being with Margo and Stephen at Christmas, joyfully fermenting brandied peaches in a mason jar for months before the holiday, then dishing it over vanilla ice cream she'd brought home from Brigham's. On the big day the three of them sat and gorged in front of the worn fireplace in their old rental house. It felt like a real tradition. A family.

Then Stephen got caught in the next to last draft and ended up as roadkill in a B-52 runway accident during Linebacker, the final operation of the war. Lonny tried hard to get past it with parties and booze. None of it worked. Margo finally got fed up and left, and eventually her friends at Brigham's could no longer cover. She lost the job and signed on to drive a cab at night. Solitary suited her until she became dimly aware that the life she had molded shrank her world day by day.

She applied to General Shipworks just to get out of Providence. No experience needed, they told her. She became the first of the young women in the shipyard's initial wave of affirmative action hiring. Well, relatively young. When she mustered in, there was less than a handful of women, all of them leftovers from the second world war who had pretty much blended into the bulkheads.

These days, with a few years on the job, she thought of herself as a bridge for the crop of really young yard women who came along in the years after she'd started. She'd watched them hire in straight out of high school and recognized the confusion and fear on their faces as they wandered through the thicket of men, rules and scary graffiti that stared at them from the walls of the ships. The new women made her feel she had a real purpose being there. She became convinced that every time she mouthed back to some guy or made a stink over porn photos taped to her toolbox, the odds improved for somebody else to have a reasonable chance in the place. She learned to get through it and without intending to, made a name for herself.

Not that the crap ever stopped. Look at Farrell.

But it was worth it to get past all the junk. Where else was she going to make this kind of money without some insufferable dose of pretense? Fact was, Lonny had no intention of hiding, and this was the one place where most people didn't make an issue of who she was, at least not out loud. Not as long as she carried her weight on the job. Which she did. So, for as long as it lasted, this was okay.

Enough, she decided. Better to plan for the next round. Her thoughts went to Shea and the next steward election. The guy was smart and tough. He had a good head, good sense of justice. Knew how to get along with white vets and the black guys. And now that she thought about it, he'd poked around with some questions about the process.

She had a feeling he wouldn't much mind.

19

"Come on day shift," Lonny urged Shea. "You've done enough time to qualify for rotation. And you'll be well-known enough to run when the slot opens up."

Shea thought it felt right. By his second February on nights, he had learned the rhythms of the shift, the ship's nooks and crannies. He used his break time to lug his thermos to distant tanks, calmly urging resistance to the union's old guard and company abuses alike. He could feel the support from passing welders he barely knew.

He explored the idea of running for steward with a few of the guys. Roach called the news to Billy the Kid in the next tank through an unpatched rat hole.

Billy started talking trash before he appeared from the other side of the bulkhead. "Hey, *I* was gonna run for steward."

Roach yelled back, "Gonna read the fucking contract first?"

"I'm just shittin' ya. Shea's the man."

Outside at dinner, Cotty's response was more measured. Shea had hoped for a satisfied grunt and a slap of support, but Cotty only said that it sounded alright and then lapsed into a pensive silence. Mourning, perhaps, over Townsend's loss or Bly's embarrassing performance.

"Told you," Cotty said. "Those union guys ain't lettin' no black man take that steward spot again. Not never."

On the bus ride back to the station after the shift, Cotty announced that he and Byron had talked it around. Everyone was solidly behind Shea's run. Shea got his slap of support. Cotty's counsel tallied with Lonny's: "Get your ass on first shift. You can't win by staying on nights." And then, quietly, "I'll be sorry to see you go."

Shea said, "I won't disappear on you."

"You watch out, though. You in the company crosshairs now, not only Rashford. You got support, but there's guys that hate what you tryin' to stand for. A lot. Gonna weigh on you. So watch your back and take care of your head at the same time."

*****

He was determined to leave second shift with an edge of support that no candidate who had spent his time on first shift alone could match. To seal it, he would see through the winter on nights.

He broke into Griswold's pep talks at the weekly company safety meetings to highlight a specific problem. He spent coffee breaks preaching on the issue to as many welders as would listen. Each week he restarted the drill.

At first, Griswold thought Shea was joking. But the whitehat's eyes narrowed when he realized what Shea was doing. "Back to the fuckin' job," he announced to his crew, then balled the week's lesson between his big hands.

"What about the staging, Bobby?" Shea asked with an innocent look. "Or the suckers? Or the ice on the deck?"

Griswold faced his palm forbiddingly toward Shea. "Back to work!"

Sometimes he was able to squeeze new staging planks from Griswold, or an air sucker to reduce the smoke in a tank. More often Griswold merely tensed up and sulked. He no longer came by Shea's tank to chat.

Shea began to circulate among nearby crews at lunch, scouting out instigators for other safety meetings. Within a month, crews on every deck level of the boat were berating whitehats about the same problem at the same time each week. From there it was a short step to wandering the tanks at break in search of welders working on unsecured ladders or missing staging planks, instructing them on their rights if he discovered anyone taking undue risks on the company's behalf.

He arrived earlier at Ziyad's, leaving for the gate just before the whistle. Welders came by with questions about their safety rights on the job. Little Z was thrilled at the additional traffic, glad to put that extra splash into Shea's shot glass before he went in.

*****

Shea heard the complaints about the high narrow tank in front of the engine room on the first day that Griswold assigned half of the crew to it. The tank was smoky, stuffed full of welders from multiple crews, most of them without air suckers. On the second day, Shea and a few others were added to the gang in the tank. All morning a smoky fog built until their lungs were bursting and the bulkheads were obscured by choking gray clouds.

Shea found an excuse to go to the tool room at the start of the shift, where he called into the back for Fat Sal, whose union jurisdiction included the shipboard ventilation men. When Sal checked with his guys, they confirmed that the access patch into the tank simply wasn't large enough to shove in a six inch round vacuum hose for every welder. Less than half of them had one.

"Look," Fat Sal told Shea, "You gotta get Griswold to cut another patch just to snake in the suckers. It's the only way."

By lunch, welders emerged from the tank with burning lungs and eyes. They pleaded with Griswold, who assured them that he would do everything he could to get more air in there.

"That's bullshit," Shea faced the whitehat toe-to-toe. "You got an easy solution. Take some of the welders out. Or get the burners down here to cut another patch."

"If I slow down this job I won't have one. And you think Charley Johnson is gonna let me cut a piece outta the ship at this point? You got your head up your ass."

After Griswold left, the crew huddled in a corner with their lunch boxes. Roach couldn't stop coughing. "Alright," he announced, "I've had enough."

The rest of the crew chewed on their sandwiches noncommittally. Although there were two boats under construction and the shipyard was a frenzy of activity, the union contract was up in a few months. The revolution in Iran had already sparked shithouse rumors of threats to the General's backlog of LNG tankers, undercutting the union's position. Though it was just talk, Shea could feel the welders retreating into their shells, fearful of making waves about a smoky tank in the face of that kind of uncertainty.

After lunch, Shea was exhorting the guys to walk out to protest the smoke when Griswold popped up from behind a bulkhead and motioned him to the deck. Topside, the whitehat grabbed a phone rigged to the deck rail. When he got off, he said to Shea, "Get off my boat. You're outta the yard as of now. The guards will meet you on the runway. And be at Industrial Relations first thing in the morning."

Griswold started to walk Shea off the ship. In the tank Roach called to the others, "Let's go!" The crew stopped welding, climbed out of the tank and headed together toward the shithouse to relieve an extended collective case of the runs.

*****

When Shea arrived at the administration building the next morning, Charley Johnson was already there conferring with a suited labor relations man. Shea was shown to a seat in a small, windowless conference room cluttered with blueprints. He stared at photos of old ships on the walls.

The doorknob jiggled and Kevin Charney walked in. "I'd as soon let you hang, mister," Charney said straight off. "You risked the job of every man you pulled out of that tank. You should've called me if it was so bad."

"And what?" Shea countered, "put in a complaint that you and the grievance committee would get to after everybody was dead?"

"It would've covered your ass. Now you got nothin'. I'm just gonna try to save your job."

Charley Johnson came in with a suit from the front office. Both men nodded at Charney.

Charney asked Shea, "You know Charley Johnson the welding super?" He gestured toward the other man. "And this is Irv Hershfeld, the company industrial relations director."

Hershfeld was tall with a pencil mustache and a mop of blow-dried curls. He stared directly at Shea. "No one with your level of short time in the yard should already be known to me, much less sitting in this office. This is your first and last warning."

Charney said to Shea, "You made this bed for yourself."

Hershfeld added, "You have a ten-day suspension, Mr. Shea. You have Mr. Charney to thank for your job. Consider yourself lucky. Next time you're done."

Johnson rose from his chair and left without speaking.

*****

The crew's diarrhea hit once or twice a day until the end of Shea's suspension. On the day before his return to work, the ship super directed a burner to fire up his acetylene torch and gouge a large hole in the deck. Fat Sal told one of his vent guys to lug a dozen additional suckers over to the boat. The vent man inserted the hoses into the tank, then laid out additional sections that ran back to two roaring air movers. He wrapped duct tape around the hose connections until the suction was strong.

The next morning, Shea checked back into the yard. By the time he got onto the boat, Griswold had assigned the rest of his welders. "Get on over to that tank," he ordered Shea. "Finish it this time, and no more fucking around or you're out the door."

Shea dropped down the ladder into the tank. A dozen additional welders had been assigned there to make up for time lost to the disruption. Each of them had a vacuum hose by his job to suck out the smoke. The welders stopped work and clanked their slag hammers against the steel in applause.

"Hey, Shea!" Roach called from one of the far stiffeners in the bilge, "look, you can see me!"

The tank was unclouded by smoke.

20

"I'm tellin' ya, every three years. Count on it." Johnno McKinnon lifted his coffee and eyed Richie the rigger and the other crane operator at his table. "The yard's burstin' at the seams, contract's due next month. Guaranteed the pre-contract speedup's in gear."

"Yeah," Richie said, "over in the South Yard I never seen this kind of smoke on graveyard shift. Never seen this many guys crowd into Ziyad's when third shift gets out."

McKinnon nodded. "Remember in seventy-one? We had that Navy oiler overhaul. The General was crazy to get it done before any strike come up. Put on the lead paint before the hull seams were even welded, then threw every welder on board. Told them to lay in the wire right over the paint 'stead of the other way round." He sipped his coffee and chewed off some egg and muffin. "Pretty soon we had welders pukin' all over, headaches and pain in their knees. We all knew it was the lead paint. With the strike comin' on the union was of course big-time with threats to grind it all off. But suddenly Rashford and Pennock come to a settlement. I was all ready to walk but no strike and work on the lead paint continued. Welders kept getting sick, but then Rashford told us the union gave a little on the paint and won real big on the contract."

McKinnon pulled a piece of bacon out from his muffin. "I been clockin' the ambulance calls overnight for the last couple weeks." He swallowed. "They've tripled. Gotta be worse on first and second shifts."

*****

Ziyad listened to the third shift old-timers munching and slurping. Watched his regulars at their tables, the black guys leaning carefully on the metal frame around the glass plate on the pinball machine, always respectful. He got that he was just a hand and an arm filling coffee cups and putting burgers together for these guys. For the last twenty years, that is, thank you very much.

He had nothing against any of them. They were his bread and butter, some of them friends of a sort. He understood them.

He could still taste the bitterness of his own labor in the old country, hand-mixing concrete with a shovel and hoe in a trough nine hours a day, struggling up four flights to the top of an unfinished apartment building under the weight of three-foot stacks of floor tiles strapped to his back with a wooden L brace, bent over like a hunched old woman at the *souk*. Working past quit-time without pay because Alphonso the Tunisian told him he had to. The fear of what it meant to say "No."

So despite the words, he heard their mood, the pitch of the voices, the expressions on the faces at the tables with every rush of hardhats on every shift.

All of these guys were scared shitless.

21

John McKinnon wasn't itching for a strike. But he could almost see the small mouth bass leaping into his net. Could almost taste that sucker crisp from the fire. Oh, he'd hang around at the gate the first day and play at pushing back against the cops, let the union guys know that he was with them. He'd stay away from the front of the line. He was getting too old for that stuff. Time to just leave it to the pros and the radicals. And then, after a day or two of that, he'd just take off.

Janice had been on him to get away to Sebago just to hook up with the O'Briens from the old block in Jamaica Plain. Ernie and Liz would be up at their cabin near the lake for the last two weeks in July. McKinnon had no doubt of that. But no matter how he said it, or how many times, Janice could never get it through her head that he was done hanging around with the two of them. He'd got outta Jamaica Plain to plain get the fuck out, period.

No way he was doin' two weeks in Maine listening to Ernie and Liz bitch about the spics taking over JP, not to mention Liz reminding him on the QT about that one damn time at the motel with her that he wished to God had never happened. McKinnon had no intention of letting himself in for two weeks of that when Sebago bass were just a couple hours further north.

Fuck the O'Briens' cabin. Ernie and Liz would understand. Well, Ernie would, anyway. McKinnon would just rent a trailer and hitch on the boat. Janice would have a better time of it that way, too. Maybe he could even hint around and John Junior would come up for a weekend. They could spend the day on the lake.

McKinnon took a swallow of coffee and leaned against the leg of his crane. He stuck one hand in his pants. They were getting tight. Even a little tug like that around the pocket made him want to pee.

Stick around for picket duty and forty bucks a week? Let the rest of them slug it out. McKinnon knew the General. If the guys go out, the summer would be over before the strike ended. The company would lose face otherwise. That went for both sides.

He had nothing against the union, always showed those guys the respect they deserved. And they respected him back, the top seniority crane operator in the yard. And maybe they were right, maybe they needed to throw a strike at the General once every few years to keep things honest. But like McKinnon always said to the kids in the yard, you never make back the money you lose.

He saw it coming as far back as March. He'd been through the clumsy square-off many a time. Watched both sides move to the center of the ring with their gloves on and up, ready to sneak a quick kick to the balls if they had the chance. This one had all the earmarks.

They're even close to floating out the second tanker on sea trials, McKinnon thought, more than a month ahead of schedule. So they press that advantage, tighten the screws. The whitehats are everywhere, all the time. From his cab at the top of the crane all he had to do any morning was lean over and look. They were all over the place. Not that they'd ever bother him. But Christ, he felt bad for those poor bastards down below.

Most of the guys waited until the strike was staring them in the face to work up a little savings. Not John McKinnon. By then it was too late, and they had you begging for overtime to sock away something extra. He started early, as soon as the weather began to clear and the signs were unmistakable.

First, he poked around the War Room looking for the shift superintendent. "Hey Tom," he'd say to Kelly, "I got a few bills comin' due, so anytime you got it, I'm game. I could sure use a piece of that overtime."

Kelly would say, "Sure, Johnno, I'll see what I can do" and began to feed it to him even before the speedup got cranked. By the time the General really got in motion and beefed up third shift they were counting on him regular. For the last month or two, McKinnon didn't even have to ask. They just come to him.

And okay for weekends, too, as long as Kelly threw in a Sunday here and there. That double time was sweet. Kelly was the kind of guy that understood that without a word between them.

Yeah, Sebago sounded just fine. With the little bundle McKinnon had now, he might even stay up there three weeks or so.

Now that the contract deadline was on them, he wasn't the only one lapping up overtime. All over the yard the steel trades were working two, three hours extra on the boats, and he'd heard that even in the shops they were sucking up all they wanted. There was so much OT that second shift began to look as crowded as days. The whole place jammed up with hardhats working and whitehats keeping watch on the welders making smoke.

Back in the winter, third shift had been down to maybe a couple hundred guys, mostly steel trades—welders and fitters, a few burners. Cozy and quiet, the way McKinnon liked it and had worked it for years. In April, though, the graveyard shift sprang to life. Whole crews of welders and fitters stayed over from second shift, turning the graveyard shift busy and black. Dickie DiGuardio had even put on a third shift class at the school.

McKinnon watched them all from the cab of his crane. Seemed like half of them were so new to the yard that they drifted in circles like blind men, unable to find their way around the basins or even back to their jobs.

It wasn't right, shoving young kids like that into production without a clue. And it just ruined the solid, contented feeling McKinnon had always loved at the top of his crane. Looking out over his eerie, luminous night world, secure in his command post at the edge of the walls of darkness.

What was funny, McKinnon thought, was that the union hadn't told anybody to stop working overtime. He woulda thought that they'd want to jam up the company's schedule this late in the game. But those guys knew what they were doing, so why worry about it? John McKinnon went back a long way with Stan Rashford, better believe it. Knew him when he was still a pup on the tools in the pipe shop. Straight as an arrow. If there was a problem, Stan would have said so and fixed it long before now.

McKinnon rolled his tongue around his lower gums and plowed out a few gritty specks of coffee. He spit and looked in his cup with distaste, swished around the dregs and tossed it.

He placed his foot squarely on the first rung of the crane ladder. Above his head a metal safety cage encased the rungs. McKinnon peered up through the open tunnel it formed. Seventy-five rungs to the cab. Wish I was back on the Goliath, he thought, sure could use that elevator. Almost sixty years old and still climbin' a boom crane. I should talk to Stan about that.

McKinnon started up the ladder. It occurred to him that maybe he should scout out one of the smaller lakes, north of Sebago, without the crowds. Course, if he was gonna do that, it would make sense to go up alone for a few days and scout out the area, then drive back and get Janice. Then do the three weeks. Nice.

He plodded up the ladder, unable to decide whether to tie up new lures or just use the old spoons in his tackle box.

22

Kelly waited impatiently in the War Room. He'd told Hauner in the guard shack to have Pete Rosa call him as soon as Rosa got to the gate. Five minutes later he called Hauner again to find out if Rosa had got past him. The guard swore up and down the general foreman hadn't clocked out. If Hauner wasn't lying, and with that stupid prick Kelly could never be certain, then that Cape Verdean bastard Rosa was sure takin' his time before leaving for the night.

"I'm the goddam shift super," Kelly said out loud to himself. "Thinks he can avoid me? Fuckin' welding department, no concept of shift coordination. Well, whaddya expect from a bunch of niggers?"

Kelly looked at the swirl of papers on his desk. His anger welled up.

The phone rang.

Rosa was on the line, sounding a little impatient himself. "Whattya want?" he demanded, "I'm on my way out, for chrissakes."

What Kelly wanted was a detailed status on the two hot units in main assembly. He needed them fully welded, in the basin and tacked in place by the end of third shift. If they weren't sittin' there ready to marry to the keel when the general manager showed up at seven-thirty, somebody's ass would be in a sling and it wasn't gonna be Kelly's.

"They'll be ready," Rosa assured him, "I got good crews on them right now."

"When can I have 'em?"

"Hold on." Rosa did some quick calculations. "I can promise them both set to move by six-forty-five."

Kelly's voice tightened. "Well, when can I get the first one to the fuckin' basin? Not just 'ready to move'!"

Rosa worked to keep his tone airy. "Just told you, Tom, I'll start the move at six-forty-five."

"Not good enough. Where's my time to get them lifted and set down in the basin? Faired up and tacked?" Kelly's yellowed teeth ground in frustration.

"Hey," Rosa said, "my budget tells me to sign off on two welded units for tomorrow morning. That's what I'm gonna do. You got plans to take them somewheres, that's your problem, not the welding department's."

Kelly exploded. "You little shit! How the fuck am I gonna set both those units down in the basin, tacked and in place before seven if you don't even release them to me until six-fucking-forty-five?"

Rosa let the silence linger a moment. "I know my job, Tom, and I'm doing it. You want somethin' different, you talk to my boss. What is it, one AM? Charley must be home in bed right this minute. I'm sure he'd love to hear from you in the middle of the fuckin' night."

Kelly didn't mind the idea of going head-to-head with Charley Johnson any day of the week, but he didn't want to waste time arguing with the general manager afterward. Pennock would shit a brick and call him up to the corner office to let him know about it the same day.

"Fuck it," Kelly said, "I'll piggyback the units. McKinnon's done it before." He slammed down the receiver.

"Great idea, Tom," Rosa said into the dead phone, "you're a fuckin' genius."

*****

Back in the War Room, Kelly examined the penciled notes scrawled on the corners of his pad. He picked an extension number and dialed the #6 basin boom crane. Through the window he could see the floodlit crane. Aviation lights flashed on the cab as it rumbled along its rail track down the length of the drydock. Beyond the basin the Goliath crane loomed, blue and silent, its iron claws clutching a massive white sphere that descended like a regal peg-in-hole toy, with progress so slow as to be almost imperceptible, into the womb of the ship below.

Kelly judged the distance between the sphere and the deck of 42 hull underneath it. The ball would be in place by the middle of the next shift. Anything faster risked banging up against the hull and wounding the pricey insulation that covered the aluminum sphere. He dialed McKinnon's boom crane extension and waited for the connection.

"Yeah?" said McKinnon.

"Johnno? It's Tommy Kelly." Kelly could barely hear McKinnon above the static and the screech of the crane wheels on the track. "How's she humming tonight, okay?"

"Everything's good, Tom."

"Look, Johnno, I got a little problem. Thought you might help me out. I got two units comin' over and I gotta get them both positioned before I leave. Think you could handle it piggyback?" Kelly listened again. "I know, I know, piggyback's tough, but the safety guys'll look the other way." His mouth twitched up. "You're right, Johnno, best fuckin' operator on the East Coast. For you it'll be tit. I'll do the paperwork right now. Tell you what, I'll even give you Richie Millis to do the rigging. I know you like working with the kid."

Kelly hung up and looked at the stack of memo slips on his desk. He lit a cigarette and stuck it in his mouth, letting it dangle. He plucked the top sheet out of the pile and studied it. 42 hull, #3 tank: Customer inspection next AM. Okay. Check with the laborers, make sure it's clean.

Kelly searched his desk pad for another extension number, then picked up the phone and cradled it between his neck and shoulder. Smoke curled into his eyes. He twisted away from it in the harsh fluorescent light. With one hand he dialed the cleaner boss. With the other he crumpled the memo. Two down.

23

A half hour before the units were scheduled to move out of main assembly, Richie strolled over to have a look. The two transporters were already there, spewing a thick oily exhaust that choked the air between the assembly area and the shithouse.

The senior rigger in main assembly flagged Richie over and led him to the units, pointing out the lifting pads on each. Richie stooped over to look. The pads were a foot square and secured to the units with thick layers of shiny weld. Above the weld, each pad was punctured with a circular cut-out about the size of a large fist.

Richie compared the bright yellow numbers painted on the units against his paperwork and summed the registered weights. One hundred sixty-eight tons. McKinnon's boom crane was rated at one-seventy-five. He added the figures again and was satisfied. He checked the placement of the pads to get a sense of how the larger unit might hang in the air once he hooked it to the crane cables through the cutouts in the pads. Tricky lift, but do-able. He signed off on the other rigger's papers and walked back to #6 basin to wait.

Around six, the transporters crept from the South Yard past the Stiff Mill and into sight. In another half hour they had made it to the skirt of McKinnon's crane rail.

Richie initialed another set of transfer papers from the rigger who'd walked the unit from main assembly. He scrambled onto the bed of the lead transporter and pulled himself onto the unit. He hand-signaled McKinnon to lower the boom crane's cables. When they were within reach, Richie grabbed at the cables and attached the U-sockets to the unit.

He saw that the rigger from main assembly was watching him closely from fifty feet out. Guess he don't get to see too many piggyback lifts, Richie thought with a smug smile. He whirled an uplifted hand in a tight circle, then jerked his fist, the signal for McKinnon to test the lifting pads with a quick stop. The crane cables strained and rose. The first unit creaked and went with them. The transporter crawled out from underneath. The suspended unit hung in the air, perfectly balanced.

Richie motioned McKinnon to bring it to the ground with another round of hand signals. He hooked the second unit's lifting pads to the crane, then guided McKinnon to set it on top of the first.

Richie watched for any signs of the units shifting. There were none. He signaled McKinnon to pull both sets of cables taut. "Okay," Richie mumbled to himself and made another small circle with his hand. As one, the units lifted and held.

"Hey," Richie called to the back-up rigger from main assembly, "am I good or what?" He clenched his fist and held it up, snapping his wrist repeatedly. The piggybacked units dropped an inch in synch, then abruptly halted. They held. Richie squinted up at the crane's boom. Lookin' good. From high up in the cab, McKinnon gave a thumbs up.

Richie took off his green hard hat and wiped his forehead with the cotton back of his glove, then popped the helmet back on and whirled his right arm over his head. The crane groaned as the double load moved clear of the basin.

McKinnon watched the units rise. When they passed the storage sheds by the runway next to his rail tracks, he threw a lever and the crane's travel bell rang like an unhinged alarm clock. The crane jogged backward on its rail, carrying the units above the side of the basin.

McKinnon glanced mechanically at the weight gauge on his instrument panel and frowned. On the blink again, no weight at all registering on the gauge. He reviewed the log posted next to the panel. Inspected just last week, so that's gotta be alright. And Millis was a good kid, probably checked the unit weights a dozen times. Besides, in a pinch a crane in the right position could carry half again over its rated tonnage.

He leaned back in the cushioned cab seat and began to swing the boom toward the interior of the basin. He flipped another switch and a horn blared, alerting the welders and fitters working below. At the far end of the basin, all the way down to the water, another set of riggers in green hard hats made ready to guide down the piggyback load.

McKinnon thought about Kelly. Glad to have done him the favor. A piggyback now and then wasn't too much to ask if it was done right. Saved them some time. That couldn't hurt when Rashford went back to Kelly about that transfer to the Goliath.

McKinnon accelerated his rate of travel and inched the crane's boom downward, still swinging it around to bring the piggybacked units into position.

Maybe tyin' up some new lures would be fun after all, he thought. And it might get John Junior interested enough to stay up for a few days. It had been a long time since he'd been out on the water alone with the kid. They should have more of that now that things had eased up between them. He pictured them both on Sebago and savored the thought.

From the land end of the runway, Richie watched the crane jog away from him along the rail. The boom lowered to position but then it kept dropping until it swung almost horizontal over the basin. "Mother of God," he breathed, "he's too low for that weight!"

The riggers in the basin waved wildly. McKinnon saw them and his forehead creased. He leaned toward the full-length glass panels at the front of his cab to see what was going on.

The cabin lurched. A storm of shattered glass blew back at McKinnon from the windshield. A spear of it slashed through his leg and sliced his safety belt. The blood hadn't yet spurted when the cab lurched again and McKinnon hurtled forward.

He never saw the unleashed cable that had ripped away from the lifting pads. It whipped up the boom and through the crane's cab like a viper striking its prey.

The units tumbled toward the basin. One thudded by the crane tracks and sank into the asphalt. The other hit the edge of the basin and thundered off the steel and concrete wall, bounced high and disappeared over the side.

The shipyard shook.

McKinnon shot out of the cab. One leg dangled loosely from his thigh while the other leg and his arms scratched at the sky. The crane's cement block counterweight catapulted after him. The man and the wreckage dropped like stones a hundred feet into the basin, smashing into the unit that lay at the bottom. The yard thundered again.

The gnarled boom tore away from the crane and dove head over heels into the basin, dragging a clutter of cables over the lip and out of sight. After a tottering pause, as if as an afterthought, the crane itself buckled on its wounded girder stilts and collapsed in a slow, sickening heap on the runway.

Then the yard was absolutely still. Third shift hardhats stood speechless at the punch clocks in front of the basin, hands frozen on their timecards.

In the distance, the meat wagon wailed.

24

"Hey Millis, I hear they found his leg."

Richie looked up at Salvucci. "You know, Frank, you are one sick motherfucker." He sucked on his beer.

"Hey, I'm just tellin' you."

"Right." Richie shifted in his chair. "So what ya gonna do about it?"

"Whaddya mean?"

"I mean what're you gonna do now that these motherfuckers have murdered somebody?"

Salvucci held his palms out. "Whoa, Richie. It was the guy's own fault. And wait until they check out the weld on that pad. Or maybe somebody asks why the rigger didn't stop that lift in time—oh, that's *you*, right? You wanna highlight all that?"

"Fuck that shit. I checked the weights. Twice. Those units were under the limit. The goddam company asked him for something that was high risk in bright red letters."

"Maybe."

"Frank, your Grievance Committee's gotta do something. The whole union does."

"Or else what?"

"You're the damn grievance chairman. Figure it out. Or else the guys will be all over you. Everybody. Me. And I'll tell you something else," he said, "We'll be right."

Salvucci lip farted, "You're crazy, mister, you know that?" He leaned down and tapped the Alternate Steward badge on Richie's shirt. "And don't forget, you're wearin' a badge, too."

"That don't make me like you."

"What're you doing in here this time of day, anyway Millis? Talkin' with the company?"

"They shut down third shift after the accident and brought me back in for a debrief. But either you know that, already, Frank or you're a complete moron."

Richie strode out of Ziyad's to the parking lot, muttering under his breath. He yanked at the door of his Chevy several times. He hadn't unlocked it. When he did, it was like a goddam sauna inside. He cranked the windows with such force that he scraped his knuckles on the handle plate.

He rammed the gear shift into reverse, burned rubber pulling out of the lot and drove hell-bent away from the yard toward Wollaston Beach. The car zipped onto the boulevard that ran along the bay. Richie eased off the pedal and tried to relax. He felt the heat rising from the sand and scanned a couple of girls sunning down by the water. He wanted to get interested, but his irritation at Salvucci got in the way. Calm down, Richie told himself. His eyes darted to the other side of the boulevard.

The bathhouse area came up quickly on the left. He slammed on the brakes and pulled across the road to the Greek's food stand. He stared blindly at the illuminated overhead menu board.

The counterman startled him. "Hey, awready, whattya have?"

Richie ordered medium fried clams with bellies to go, then sauntered across the street, picking at them.

He hopped up on a stone wall shading his eyes from the late afternoon sun across the bay. The Goliath stared back from across the water. He sat there, chewing the clams.

Almost seven years and it never stopped. He knew the guys in the yard, good people most of 'em. All they wanted was to be left fuckin' alone. Do the job and go home. But sooner or later it gets impossible to breathe and there's a blowout. Then they say it's your own fault and fuck you up. Like McKinnon. Just went along with the program and got killed for it.

Richie tried to capture just one of the hundred good images of the crane operator he knew he had tucked away somewhere. He came up with the day McKinnon took a bite out of his ass for doping up at work, warned him to straighten out if he wanted to hold on to the best job he'd ever see. Then McKinnon had turned around, put in a word with the rigging steward and the next thing Richie knew he was wearing a union badge that said Alternate. He'd never even thanked the guy.

And is any of this my fault? His chest tightened. *No. Checked twice, He should've said no to Kelly, but no doubt he got pushed.* Big, slow breaths to calm himself down.

He watched the water lap in and wash out. Grubbed for a clam in the greasy carton and came up empty.

He scooted his legs over the stone wall and faced back across the street. His eye was caught by four figures wearing work clothes and sitting at a small table in front of the nearby Beachcomber. Brown hard hats at their feet. He squinted. It was Cheryl Lonergan with a pretty blonde, a black girl and a guy he didn't know. They were passing sheets of paper back and forth.

Another flyer in the works, Richie thought. Good for them.

He slid down onto the pavement and crossed the boulevard to the table. The four welders looked up. Lonny smiled and said, "Hello, Richie. I'm sorry about Johnno."

"Hi, Lonny. Hard at work?"

"We're doing a special newsletter issue on the accident as soon as we can pull it together. And we're gonna do it at the gates this time. I know you were tight with him, Richie. Maybe you can help."

"Yeah, I don't know about that," Richie fingered his Alternate Steward badge.

Lonny pointed at the other three welders. "This is Keefer. Patty. And Shea. He's second shift. Clocked out early to work this up with me. He's in charge of night handout."

Richie shook hands with Shea. He recognized the fury he saw in his own mirrored eyes every morning.

"Well, I might help. I guess I could come in before second shift and meet you at the gate.

Lonny made a note and said, "Thanks."

"Just watch out for yourself. The union's got a whole 'nother take on this, blamin' Johnno himself. And let me know if you decide for sure to go ahead with the flyer."

"I will, Richie," Lonny watched him walk to his car and climb in.

She said to Shea, "He's a good guy."

"You shouldn't have told him about the gates. He's got a badge, probably in with Rashford."

"He's an angry vet with a good heart. And he just lost a friend. I told you, look for the guys with a low bullshit threshold."

25

Shea propped himself up and fumbled for the phone. "Hello?" He tried to make out the clock. Six-twenty-five in the morning. He hadn't gotten home from work until almost one, then an hour or more on his little deck with a few Buds.

"Michael, it's Lonny. We were handing out the flyers and they beat us up. Keefer, me, Patty, Magdalena." She sounded as if she had been crying.

"Are you hurt?"

Lonny said, "I'm okay, I guess. They knocked us over and tore up the flyers."

"Who? The Guards? Or the union?"

"The union. Frank Salvucci and his kid and the rest of them. Rashford's guys. It was a mob scene, pushing and screaming. I'm not really sure what happened."

Shea waited for something more, but it was as if the phone line had gone dead. "Do you still want me to pass out the flyers before second shift?"

"I guess. I just wanted you to know. Be careful. I think maybe they got tipped off. They seemed ready."

"Richie Millis?"

"Not a chance."

Shea checked his front door. Lodged behind the screen was the stack of newsletters that Lonny had left on her way into first shift. He scanned the front page.

WHO MURDERED McKINNON?
One man ordered the speedup.
One man put it in motion.

They had debated the nuances of proposed headlines for hours and finally settled on one after Patty announced, "This man been kilt. Just tell it like it is."

Okay, Shea thought, give it a shot. See if you still got some balls.

*****

By mid-morning Shea had called the second shift welders who had promised to support Townsend's call for equal steward representation and then failed to show for the vote. "Don't tell me you're down for it this time and then punk out," he said bluntly. "Gotta be able to count on you."

He had a dozen promised recruits when he left for work. At the yard he pulled a few more volunteers from the grass in front of Ziyad's.

"Hey man," Pretty Boy lodged a mild protest. "I gotta keep this face clean for the ladies." Cotty slapped him upside the head and Pretty Boy laughed. They were both posted as lookouts.

Shea was only halfway surprised when Richie Millis walked up to Ziyad's a half-hour before the start of second shift. He waved Richie over and showed him one of the flyers, watching him closely while he assured the rigger there was nothing in the handout that pinned things on him or the crane operator. "They're lookin' to blame McKinnon—or maybe the riggers."

Richie nodded. "I went to see McKinnon's old lady last night after I met you. You know, they never told her a fuckin' thing. She had to hear it on the radio. Called the yard hysterical." The weight of it showed in Richie's pinched face. "They were all set to go to Maine for a couple weeks with some friends." He reached for a stack of flyers. "So fuck yeah, I'm with you."

*****

At quarter of three Frank Salvucci's Caddy clunker pulled up to the no parking zone in front of Ziyad's, directly across the street from the main gate. Shea stopped handing out newsletters long enough to make out Kevin Charney and two lower-level union officers inside as well as Big Frank himself.

Shea called, "Richie!" pointed toward the car, then waved with both arms to Cotty on the grass.

The Caddy was quickly surrounded by Cotty, Byron and half a dozen other second shift welders. They leaned against the car, pressing at the doors. Roach deliberated, then jumped up on the hood and bounced a few times, nervously enjoying himself. Byron draped his long frame over the driver side of the hood. He stuck out a wide tongue at Salvucci and left it hanging out as he moved it up Salvucci's face on the other side of the glass.

"It sure is nice of you union fellas to come down and see us on second shift." Cotty poked his head into the driver side window. "We got some grievances to discuss cause we can't never find that no-count Darby. Now, you can come around the corner and talk over these grievances. Or you can come back at some other time."

Salvucci's look from the driver's seat was pure hate.

"On the other hand," Cotty said, "you make a move toward that gate and you got yourself some big trouble this afternoon. Yessir."

"No trouble here," Byron announced. His eyes were fixed on Salvucci. "Not from these boys." He stared through the windshield for a long moment, then stepped away from the Caddy. Without a word, Salvucci gunned the clunker and pulled out.

Byron called after him, "Hey, man! Best you buy a new muffler with that dues money you been stealin'!"

Shea and Richie went back to handing out flyers. Cotty and Byron joined them. Pretty Boy stood watch. To Shea's delight, the second shifters pouring through the gate snapped up the handouts. Richie poked Shea with an elbow. "Don't get too comfortable. Maybe we ain't seen the last of them."

*****

A few minutes before the whistle, Marty Farrell lugged up to the gate with his marking partner Cochrane three steps behind.

With a stack of flyers in one hand, Byron moved quickly in front of Cochrane. The marker scowled and said, "Well, Mister Ja-*mai*-ca. This is *my* message for *you-hoo-hoo.*" He lunged. Byron kept his feet planted and hammer-fisted across Cochrane's jaw. Cochrane dropped to the asphalt.

Richie held up his flyers and called out, "Who murdered Johnno McKinnon? This is *my* message for you!"

Farrell hissed at him, "Commie!"

Richie looked back at him incredulously. "I fought, you stupid prick! Where were *you?*"

Farrell rushed at the flyers cradled in Richie's arm, trying to tear them loose. With his free hand, Richie swung roundhouse and Farrell went down on all fours. His yellow-striped marker's helmet went flying. Before he could look up, Richie was on him, kicking at his ribs and then, when the marker collapsed, at his side. Richie grunted with the impact of each kick. "Don't call me a fucking commie, you faggot!"

Farrell grappled toward the gate on his knees. Richie let him crawl, trailing just behind, mocking and pushing Farrell's butt down repeatedly with the sole of his boot. With every step, Richie pushed him down again, each time more viciously, sweating through his shirt. With every kick Farrell went down, pulled himself to his knees, rocketed forward and flopped flat again on his face, each time a foot or two closer to the guard shack and sanctuary.

When they reached the chain across the asphalt that marked the General's property line, Hauner the guard put up a hand. "Hey, Farrell," he said gravely. "No rowdy behavior on shipyard property." He leaned over and pulled him in.

Shea walked up to Richie and held out his hand. Together they turned around and lifted their intertwined fingers above their heads. Shea called Byron and Cotty over to join them. Dozens of second shift hardhats stood across the street, clapping and whooping.

26

Shea saw right away that Darby was terrified by Farrell's humiliation at the hands—and foot—of Richie the rigger, and by the relaxed way Byron had rousted Salvucci and then Cochrane at the gate. "Where did those guys come from?" Darby wanted to know. "Since when did the commies get tight with hardhats who know how to fight?" Darby launched into a frenzy of actual activity, trolling the gate and even the boats now and then. He avoided the welders, but he went to work on the friendlier tradesmen from the shops.

"Those newsletter people want to dance on the grave of a dead man," he confided. "How do you think the widow feels?" Shea watched Darby gripe about it to a succession of sympathetic pipe fitters and sheet metal men who were more than willing to listen. Never saw the guy put out so much effort, Shea thought.

And it wasn't just Darby.

Rashford's Official Board was suddenly out at the gates before second shift, glad-handing and throwing tidbits of news from the contract talks with the General, reminding the hardhats of favors long past and loyalties due. They swarmed Ziyad's at night—and days, too, according to Richie and Lonny—suckin' up to guys for support that suddenly seemed up in the air.

After the ass-kicking at the gate, the second shift welders chattered like children, busy retelling the story from tank to tank until the embellishments outshone the event.

Something big had happened, though exactly what, no one seemed able to say. Richie and Byron stood out as the ones that scared off Salvucci and Farrell, but Richie insisted to the riggers and fitters that he just provided the muscle, not the brain, that Shea was the one behind it all. And when second shift welders asked Byron about it, he just smiled his slow smile and nodded toward Shea as well.

Like Ziyad, Shea heard the hardhats' fear of the onrushing contract abyss. How were they supposed to feed their kids on forty bucks a week strike pay? Why wouldn't the union tell them what's really going on? And most terrifying, how could they count on Rashford to outsmart the General when Richie Millis and some West Indian and a new guy like Shea can come outta nowhere—and so easily put him on the run?

27

"There's so much work in the yard," Rashford proclaimed into the mike, "the leverage belongs to the union! I say another dollar an hour every year! Strike now!" His words resounded throughout the football stadium. "Tame this goddam company for years to come!"

There was a round of uncertain applause. Rashford knew the drill. Thousands file into the high school stadium. They cram at the entry gate, but once they're in their seats any half-wit can see that most of Local 8 hadn't bothered to turn out. A crowd he could easily manage.

He called for the vote.

A murmur rippled back from the seats. A few hardhats demanded the floor, "Don't rush us!"

"Onto the field!" Rashford yelled over them, "Solid union ayes at the home team goal post," he pointed, "and anyone afraid of a strike, go to the visitor end of the field."

Under the far goal post, a straggle of men huddled, embarrassed at their fear of a strike. At the home team uprights a spirited mob roared "Yes!" and carried the day. Rashford raised both fists over his head. "Tomorrow we stand at the gates—together!"

But a third of the hardhats remained in the stands. They observed without voting or speaking and then turned, round shouldered, heads down, toward the exits. Eleven minutes after the pledge to the flag, the meeting was over. Local 8 was on strike.

*****

When Shea pulled up to the gate before six the next morning, Ziyad and little Z were already unfolding tables they'd pulled out from the storeroom and placed in front of the Grill. Little Z had run extension cords from inside and rented extra Brewmasters, then set them up out front. On Ziyad's instructions he kept the bar shut. He refilled coffees again and again without charge.

Well before seven, the thousands from the stadium, and thousands more who hadn't bothered to come out for the vote, gathered at the gate. A picket line formed and began to circle but quickly melted into the mass.

The company kept its people out of sight. The hardhats debated whether the company would try to break through the lines. Shea thought the General might wait for the pickets to thin out before telling its people to force their way into the yard.

"I called up my whitehat last night," one welder told Shea. "Just let him know that this thing goes past favors or friendship. Never had a problem with the guy, but if he comes through our lines he's fair game."

Roach agreed. "It's about the families now."

Shea detected a note in their voices that was different than Farrell's growled threats against whitehats in winter. He heard a sudden determination in these people who bent and shaped raw steel into ships. Just a day after the farce at the stadium, they'd already stopped gnawing their knuckles.

The strikers spoke to each other in reassuring tones. They moved about the picket lines, relaxed but ready to spring. Though their talk was of Red Sox, their eyes spoke of strikebreaking whitehats and fightback and scabs. Shea was certain that, like the steel on their work benches, these guys would bend the General to their needs, even if it cost them. They had, for this moment, left fear behind.

Just before lunch, a half dozen cruisers pulled up. The sirens whooped briefly to clear a space in front of the gates. A carload of cops climbed out from each car and grouped outside the guard shack. The strikers swarmed around them, swallowing blue uniforms like gum drops.

A lieutenant spoke through a bullhorn. "Disperse now! Right of way through, the gate must remain open!"

Two vans, each filled with more cops, arrived and discharged their cargo. A blue wedge of reinforcements bellied up to the picket line and prodded the massed hardhats in front of the gate, who were crammed too tight to budge. The cops snatched a random handful of them at the center and hustled them off to the side, holding them back by their belts or their collars.

Stan Rashford held up a palm to the cops and motioned to Salvucci, who strolled over to the detainees. Shea saw Salvucci shake his head at the cops. He could make him out mouthing the words "Not them" just before the cops let the guys go.

*****

Ziyad watched from his doorway. He had been there through five contracts and three strikes. Since the failed wildcat of sixty-nine he had filled an order from the secretary up at the hall just before every Christmas—two cases of Jameson's and one of a nice Chianti, all to the station house. Without fail, Rashford called Ziyad just before Christmas Eve to make sure the booze had been delivered. Ziyad once heard him tell Charney that it was a sound investment. One he'd call in on a day just like this.

*****

Rashford moved closer to the police commander and his lieutenants. They looked each other in the eye. Years of unspoken understandings passed between them. Eyes darting, then fixing, the cops listened and nodded. Hardhats on the line pressed their lips tight. Rashford thrust his chin toward various spots in the picket line as he spoke to the cops. Salvucci handed a piece of paper to the commander, who studied it, looked through the crowd, found what he wanted, and looked down at the paper again. And up. Down and up.

Rashford gave the high sign to the other Official Board members. At the signal, the Board jogged to the front of the line. They pushed half-heartedly against the row of police, who took out their clubs and waved them at the Board without conviction. After a brief play-acting minute, the cops fell back. A few of them chuckled.

"Like Sammartino at the goddam Garden," Shea muttered in the middle of the crowd. "Big show."

The union officials turned to the hardhats. "Didja see that?" they rasped to the guys at the front of the crowd, "I gave that cop hell. Fuck 'em all."

"Are you shittin' me?" Shea yelled.

"This ain't right," Richie said. "Somethin' ain't right here."

Rashford was staring at Shea. He pulled the police commander close, his mouth working while his eyes remained fixed. He tugged at the commander's sleeve, nodded toward Shea and swiped the flat of his hand in front of himself to indicate "No." Salvucci twisted up his face and protested. Rashford waved him away.

The cops drove sudden and hard into the line. The commander read to his men from the paper Salvucci had given him. His troops pushed through the hardhat ranks and picked out *Hot Slag* distributors and commies with the *Workers Unite!* buttons. They twisted their arms behind their backs and yanked them to the curb.

Angry voices tumbled out from the crowd of hardhats around Shea.

"That ain't right! They're with us today!"

The cops pushed their captives toward the open doors of the police wagon. Shea surged across the street with a wave of hardhats. The thuds and slap of the scuffle grew heated until a second line of cops pushed them back.

Union officials appeared at the front of the swarm, flanked by a blue entourage. The officials steadied the pickets with a touch on the arm like they might offer the bereaved at the wake of a member. Or they gave pats on the ass, like they were buddies at the Y.

"Hey, take it easy." The officials moved along the edge of the crowd with assurance. "We got things under control. It's okay."

Shea spotted Cotty at the far fringe with Byron and Pretty Boy next to Patty, and there, Elroy with Sonny and Hicks, his machine mate from the Stiff Mill.

"Over here!" Shea called. "With the action!"

Cotty motioned the other guys to stay put as he worked his way over.

"You want me to mix it up here? That like a man what can't swim jumpin' in the ocean with a hundred sharks around." Cotty looked across the street at Rashford. "Seems like you got a guardian angel here," he motioned. "That angel food always white, you know what I mean?"

"What're you sayin', Cotty?"

"Man told the cops to leave you alone. I saw it, plain to the world. What you think that means?"

Shea was speechless as Cotty's words sunk in. "Maybe he's tryin' to make me look bad."

"Or maybe he just smarter than you think, playin' the long game. Let you know there's still a seat for you at his table."

"Fuck him."

Shouts broke out from the gate. Cotty turned toward the noise and shielded his eyes from the sun. "Sonuvabitch. They goin' after Lonny."

*****

Lonny slammed against the edge of the van's open door. Shea tasted the jolt. Her hair quickly rusted with blood. Gloved hands reached for her from the back of the van. She clamped her teeth while the cops spun her, grabbed fistfuls of braid and jerked her inside. The double doors were pushed shut from the outside and the van laid rubber, siren screaming. It happened like lightning, before Shea could move. Hardhats milled in confusion. The cops on the street pulled back.

Rashford legged up on the bed of a pickup and held out his hands for silence. Salvucci lifted a bullhorn in front of the president's face.

Shea's call punched from the crowd. "What the fuck are you doing? Where's Lonny? Who's gonna get her out?"

"We've made a deal with the police," Rashford blared through the bullhorn. "We cut the lines to fifty pickets so the courts won't clear us out due to violence."

Richie yelled, "What violence? Nobody did shit! Get Lonny out!"

"You want your wife and kids to come get you from the slammer? Some of you already got charges." Rashford motioned the bullhorn away. "It's gonna be a long strike, so go home, take it easy." He pointed at Richie. "You think I like doin' this? I'm a fighter. It kills me to hold you guys back, but that's what I gotta do."

Rashford was loose now, back in the saddle. His voice was calm, his baritone soothing. "We'll keep you in touch." He hopped down stiffly from the truck and ducked into Salvucci's Caddy. The big car started to roll to the hall.

As the Caddy disappeared up the hill, the hardhat mood turned ugly. Someone yelled, "What the fuck, we just let them take those kids in the wagon?" followed by a chorus of curses.

*****

The pickets slung their coffees to the ground, then moved across the street into Ziyad's. They banged on the bar and demanded some service.

Ziyad said, "No bar today, fellas, never the first day, you know that. Plenty coffee, and here, on the house." The hardhats banged some more. "Okay, okay, no hard stuff, though, just beer," Ziyad finally told them, and Little Z started to pull out the bottles and cans.

A chorus of protest. "You Arab fuck, we'll just take it!" So Ziyad forced a laugh while his hands trembled. He motioned to Little Z again. The kid ducked behind the bar, brought out the hard stuff and set up clinking stacks of shot glasses on the counter.

Shea sat alone at the bar lost in thought, his face writ large with rage. And with shame that he hadn't been snatched up with Lonny.

"Clean up this garbage, willya?" the hardhats called out to Ziyad. When Little Z moved to empty the trash pails, his father broke out in one of those minor-keyed songs from the old country that always made the hardhats snigger. But inside the traditional Lebanese melody he sang to Little Z in reproving Arabic, "Don't touch their slop , maybe they'll leave before they tear the place apart."

Outside, hardhats shifted from leg to leg on the grassy hill opposite the bar, musing and bickering with increasing fervor as the day worried on. By late afternoon, they began to despair and shook half-empty smoke-green bottles at the gate.

By nightfall they resigned themselves to a cowering strike that they couldn't win without lines and no fight. They tired of waiting for a company assault that never came, knowing that Rashford would bar them from blocking the gates when it did.

"This is fuckin' ridiculous," Richie slurred his words. "Might as well go home."

"Home?" Roach replied. "I'm gonna get a job, take anything I can find. Can't stick around all summer and watch 'em do my work, take the food from my kids." With a last long glance back at the gate, he departed with others, shaken and despondent, to wait until the union called to say it was over.

28

By the end of the first week only a couple hundred hardhats still walked the line. "Fuckin' Rashford. Fuckin' sellout," the dwindling diehards muttered. Lonny made bail and trudged in circles with Shea and the other remaining pickets, six hours a shift.

The company lined up vans across from the gate, each driven by a whitehat ready to plough through the lines. The pickets saw them coming and tensed, their blood racing as it had on that first morning when they had been thousands. They beat on their chests until Rashford came down from the hall.

"You touch a single whitehat and the union won't be able to protect you," he warned, pointing at Lonny. "We got her out, but next time won't be so easy—for her or any of you."

The hardhats stood down. With mixed resignation and anger, they waved away calls from Lonny and Shea to resist. The whitehats rolled through the gates and for the first time since the wildcat of sixty-nine, they signed out stingers and shields from the tool room and they welded.

*****

"Seat taken?"

Jimmy O'Donnell swiveled on his stool. He brightened. "Hey, Stan! Haven't seen you in Sully's for a long time." His

132

face narrowed. "This ain't about business is it? Hope you're not gonna slip me a message for the front office."

Rashford smiled. "Nothin' like that, Jimmy, but I guess the yard's senior yellow hat instructor might just be the perfect go between." He took a seat and leaned in, rubbed his palms over the bar wood. "Not much welding goin' on at the school, I'll bet."

"Guess not. But now that they took the whitehats through, the instructors are next. I think they're givin' us a few days to get used to the idea, but they'll force us to run past your line after that."

Rashford nodded. "Of course. Well, ya gotta do what ya gotta do. But you haven't done it yet so let's share a drink." He signaled the barkeep with two fingers. When the shots arrived Rashford held his up and studied it. "We were both tight as bandits with Big Jim," he said finally. "What would he think of all this?"

Jimmy sipped his whisky. "What Big Jim did thirty-five years ago and what you might do today are two different things, Stan."

"Of course. But that's not an answer. Ever since we called that wildcat in sixty-nine and come back with our tails between our legs, things ain't been the same. Guess we overplayed our hand. Now it seems like the company's always looking for a chance to squeeze somethin' new, and not just at contract."

Jimmy watched Rashford's face in the bar mirror. "Big Jim knew how to do one thing—fight like there's no tomorrow. In his day the union was new. The guys were always ready for a bust-up. They would do whatever he asked. Now? It's different." Jimmy high signed the barkeep for another round. "This one's on me."

Rashford said, "There's something off. I can feel it in the talks. Some things, like the money, are goin' smoother than

I expected. But there's a lot in the background, like the suits got other stuff on their mind. I got my opinion. But I want to hear what *you* think Big Jim would do. Nobody on my team I can really ask."

Jimmy hunched around his glass. "I don't know as much as you think I do, Stan, but I feel somethin' lurking in that big building up front, too. Lotta tension, lotta meetings that no one wants to talk about after. I get the impression they're not even focused on the strike. It's later on that should worry you. But what, or why I don't know."

Jimmy clapped Rashford on the shoulder. "You'll figure it out, Stan." He raised his glass. "And on Big Jim's grave, my lips are sealed. Yours, too, right?" Rashford held up his shot. Their glasses clinked.

29

Lonny dreaded the scene unfolding in front of her. What was she supposed to do—appeal to Frank Salvucci's better angels? There he was, screaming at the scab crossing over from Ziyad's side of the street, one of a trickle of strangers who appeared in the ranks of the foremen and went through the lines. Strikebreakers recruited from the city's cash-starved African-American neighborhoods.

Salvucci got in the scab's face and spit as he passed by. "Nigger-nigger-nigger-nigger!" he yelled, skipping along to the gate with the scab. "We'll get you, nigger!" he yelled and turned to Lonny. "They act like niggers, so that's what I call them." A white scab walked through unmolested.

She said, "You make me sick, you asshole." Salvucci just smirked at her. He was having a party. "Then go tell that nigger scab that I'm so fucking sorry," he laughed. The other pickets stared at their shoes.

When she told Shea the story he said, "Write up a newsletter and call Salvucci out." But every draft they came up with sounded like a defense of the scab. The issue never got published. There was almost no one left on the lines to read it, anyway.

*****

From a distance Lonny caught a glimpse of Slidell, an achingly shy black kid who had worked on her crew for about a year. She was thrilled he showed up to picket and started to wave him over, then whipped back her arm as if she'd been burned. Her chest tightened.

Slidell was walking from further away. Leaving his car out of sight. He was there to cross the lines.

When he was first assigned to Lonny's crew, their whitehat put them in the same tank, day after day. It took Slidell weeks to present her with a wallet-sized photo of his wife and twins at their christening. Lonny exclaimed over the little girls before Slidell wrapped the photo and carefully tucked it away. She told him again that they were all quite beautiful, and Slidell's face lit up.

The two of them settled into an odd friendship characterized by her appetite for conversation and his smiling difficulty engaging it. Now the guy was a scab.

She watched him hunch toward the pickets, starting his run to get through. She moved to head him off before he reached the picket line. She tried to tug him aside. "Talk to me, man. This will never go away once it's done."

Slidell slapped the air in front of her face. Lonny's eyes widened. "Don't waste your breath," he barked. "This union treat me like I don't exist except to take my money. They tear out the heart of that good man Townsend. I been forced out on strike and called nigger on these lines. The damn *company* treat me better'n that!"

And after the longest speech Lonny had ever heard from his mouth, Slidell walked through the gate.

*****

"Patty, this is Mike Shea. From the shipyard."

There was a long silence before she said, "I know where you from, Michael. Don't be stupid. How did you get my number down here?"

"I asked Pretty Boy what had happened to you. He told me you'd gone back to North Carolina until the strike was over."

"And you callin' me to say hello?"

"I'm callin' because you disappeared. We need people up here and you've been a help and a voice when it counts."

He thought the line had gone dead before she responded.

"Look here, Mike Shea. I do what I can. But I don't live and breathe this crusade or whatever it is you and Lonny got goin'. I got kin down here in Lenoir County what I ain't seen in half a year or more. My family's as important as any shipyard, you understand? I be back there when I be back." She waited, but there was no response. "Then again, I hear what's goin' on up there. You want me to come up north to tell that union guy to stop callin' names at black folks comin' through the lines? You got a mess to clean up, and in case you ain't noticed no black folks volunteerin' to do it for you—not Luther, not Cotty, not Elroy, not none of 'em. And not me."

Shea said, "Okay, I get it. I, uh, also thought we might have a drink when you came back. Not at the yard."

"Oh. So this is really about the almost perfect white man thinkin' he needs some black pussy to make it total perfect? Tell you what. When you want me for me, not for some job you got for me, or for some fantasy you got, you ask me then. When you want me for me, you understand?"

Shea said, "I'm sorry."

"And before you make any more moves, you might want to check in with your friend Pretty Boy. Matter of courtesy, you know?" She hung up.

*****

Shea phoned Cotty, who had refused to visit the lines since watching Rashford in action on the first day of the strike. He wanted to know what the old man could tell him about the black scabs.

"It's our snake super, Charley Johnson," Cotty said. "Got himself a list of phone numbers and he just goin' down it. Doin' the white man's work one more time."

"This looks real bad."

"You missin' the point, boy. We take care of Charley Johnson, ain't none of your worry. One day soon could be he'll need a new car. It seem to me, though, that he's digging in some very fertile ground. This company is looking for black men to strike break and there's a reason they easy to find. No-count union racists brought this on themselves."

Two weeks later, the number of black scabs dropped steeply. On Shea's picket line shift, Salvucci himself remarked about it with regret.

Shea called Cotty again.

"I ain't sayin' we done nuthin'," the old man said, "but I did hear Charley Johnson's van got in a real bad accident. Right in his own driveway."

Shea had hoped for action. Now he wasn't so sure. "Not you, right?"

Cotty said, "You more nosy than you oughta be. So we clean up our end. What you gonna do about yours?"

30

Kevin Charney passed the word to the remaining main gate pickets. "The old man's done it again. We got a settlement. Ratification at the stadium on Sunday."

The news was greeted with a ripple of exhausted excitement. Roach calculated it would take three years to make up the money he lost during the strike. After a summer of poorly paid lawn mowing, he argued, "Past time to go back."

Shea glared at him. "This isn't just about the money. Rashford staged a show, not a fight. He let them frighten us off the line, took our self-respect."

After every other strike, the hardhats had walked back through the gates together. But as they filed into the stadium to vote on the contract, Local 8 officers handed out printed sheets that detailed a staggered three-week company schedule for the return to work. The stewards and officials circulated in the crowd. "Just a routine," they insisted. "Some of you go back now, the rest in a week or so."

Shea scoured the list. He called over Lonny. "Those high seniority numbers at the top of the list are scabs. When the rest of us get back in they'll force us to work side by side with those scumballs. And Rashford *agreed* to this."

"Let it go, Mike." Lonny gestured to the men walking in the gate. "They're done."

****

139

When the first wave of hardhats went back to work, the truth of Shea's words sank in.

With animal instinct the hardhats lashed out. Cursing savagely, they hocked phlegm in scab faces and onto their gray scab coveralls. Heavy steel wedges were lobbed toward scabs from the decks of the boats. The wedges clattered down sidewalls, ricocheting madly to terrify scabs who were passing below. The company whisked the scabs from the boats and set them to sweeping the safer floors in the shops.

The hardhats turned on the union officials. Fury overshadowed their fear of Rashford and Salvucci. "You gave the scabs our jobs before we get back in? What kind of assholes are you?" The officials stretched arms over shoulders and said, "Hey, take it easy, you know me."

The hardhats whispered to themselves, "Is that so?"

*****

Fat Sal wasn't sure what to think. He'd looked forward to getting back to his work routine. He had his lead man job overseeing the ventilation guys and equipment repair in the main tool room—informally, of course, 'cause he was also the steward, so naturally no white hard hat for him. And on a normal day, after collecting the week's fares and driving in his van load of Portagees from Fall River, he would stop by Ziyad's for boxes of cow flaps and donuts and then hurry on to the tool room in the center of the yard to plug in his percolators and set out the pastries and mugs and a change box. Then he'd start working the phones to line up bets on the Celts or the Pats. Dangle the promise of winning numbers and arrange the day's drops for his runners. When a guy welshed on a bet Fat Sal wouldn't threaten or even get angry. He just cut off the guy's game and moved on.

He played all the angles, came out on top and still everyone liked him. So he didn't understand when, on the third day after he was back at work, right at the morning whistle, his whitehat called him over and handed him a job assignment, a real one, the first in nine years.

"What is this, a fuckin' joke?" Fat Sal tried hard for a smile.

The whitehat could have bet that he and the other foremen would take the brunt for this front office brainstorm. "No, not a joke, just orders. You want time off the job for union business, you gotta ask me for a pass now. A request. The rest of the time you actually work. Understand, I don't like it, neither."

Fat Sal reached for the phone and dialed the hall. Rashford already knew. "It's across the board," he told Sal. "Fuckin' double-cross. Nuthin' in the contract permits this."

"And nothing rules it out?"

"Not a word either way," Rashford said, "So they claim they got the right. All of a sudden."

Every steward was on the tools now, begging for a pass if they wanted to stretch their legs or even see one of their guys to talk over a grievance. Instead of sitting in shacks with whitehats or roaming the yard, slapping backs and handing out election slate cards, the stewards picked up their tools and worked.

They stood at the gates and called on the hardhats to show their support at a lunchtime rally. At the eleven o'clock whistle, just a handful of Local 8 members tramped around the shipyard in a dreary union parade. The rest ate Portagee fish salad and bathed in the sun on the decks of the hulls. Or they savored a beer on the crabgrass across from Ziyad's, content with the final hint of October warmth.

Later that evening, the hardhats leaned on their rakes, listening to their children rustle in the leaves. They smelled nutmeg and cider from the kitchen and took in the salt air. Beyond the bushes that ringed their little plots of land, the Goliath crane rose high in the twilight. They looked up at the crane and they swelled, just a little. If it were only enough.

DAYS

31

Shea leaned back in the frayed wicker rocker on his rear porch. He looked at the sagging rows of them on the three-decker opposite his rental. He had called the city inspector about the porches a week before. Took a bite outta the guy's ass, too. There was still no sign of shoring them up. Well, those other buildings weren't his fight.

He pushed back on the rocker. He picked at the blackened mildew between the reeds of the chair. The mold had settled deep into the wicker.

I gotta get out of this dump, he said to himself. The South Shore was the logical place to go, but maybe too close to the yard, listening to that damn whistle around the clock.

He thought about buying a house. After all, his kitty was building back up now that he was back to work. And much as he enjoyed his bus rides with Cotty and the guys, leaving night shift was inevitable if he really wanted to run for steward. It would be strange living outside of Cambridge but it made sense.

He scoured the *Globe* real estate section and discovered an aging, overly large Victorian for sale in the Fields Corner section of Dorchester. Lou the agent immediately took him to meet the Krywukaviches, an elderly Lithuanian immigrant couple eager to sell.

Mr. Krywukaviches showed Shea around. The house was generous. It felt good to shake off the constriction of every other place he'd called home. The intricately carved mantle around the living room fireplace was unlike anything he'd seen. He could easily block off and insulate the empty third floor. The apple green exterior clapboard was starting to alligator, but painting was just painting.

After the tour, Lou let Shea know that the Krywukaviches were determined to make a deal with someone white. "Hold the line, so to speak," Lou said. He explained that the neighborhood was sharply divided by Dorchester Avenue— whites on the east and blacks and Latinos on separate blocks on the west. The house was on Dakota Street, right off Geneva Avenue, on the cusp of the dividing line. "Just so you know."

"Is that what it sounds like?" Shea asked, "I don't want to get into anything that smacks of that stuff."

Lou shook his head. "They just need to get away from the Boston weather. Mr. K. told me that that he and his wife had been in the neighborhood for thirty years, that people got along, all types. They want to do the right thing, keep it open and mixed."

A few days later Mr. Krywukaviches called Shea directly and invited him back. The couple seated him at their large, round mahogany table, then plied him with sausages and slivovitz and reminiscences about the old country. They hoped to abandon Fields Corner for Florida and offered Shea a discounted price. Sixteen thousand dollars for the nine-room house.

After several pony glasses of slivovitz, Mr. Krywukaviches led Shea down a steep stairway to the cellar, which was dominated by an octopus-like furnace with sheet metal air ducts skewed out in all directions. The old man showed Shea a custom-built rack of hand-crafted storm windows. Each pane of glass was set in a hardwood frame which Mr. K. had hand-sanded and re-lacquered every spring for the last thirty years.

Mrs. K. begged Shea to keep the mahogany table. Her daughter had scorned it as old-fashioned and would just sell it for cash after the old people left for Florida. It hurt Mrs. K. to think that the table would end up with strangers. Shea should have it.

Fields Corner was less than a half hour north of the shipyard. Shea let himself surrender to the lure of the house. Lou secured him a sympathetic lender at the Shawmut bank branch down the block and Shea bought the place. He moved in with his nan's furniture.

The day after he closed his transfer to first shift came through. Billy and Roach put in to move with him to days. He tried to decide what to say when he ran into Patty.

*****

Around him, the neighborhood was a ratty slum of trash-laden streets lined by three-deckers and once proud single-family homes. There was a handful of nicer houses struggling to gentrify six blocks south of Shea's place. As Lou had suggested, the neighborhood was almost perfectly segregated into a series of shriveling white and more recently settled black and Latino ribbons. Across Geneva Avenue from Dakota Street, a disheveled bar seemed to be entirely frequented by hostile young whites who once lived in the neighborhood but had moved out to points further south in Dorchester and beyond.

Dakota Street itself was still mixed but barely. The parallel streets were almost solidly black for blocks in either direction, then interrupted by a thin swath of white people's homes to the south. The cluttered rows of apartment houses across Geneva Avenue resounded with Spanish conversations which were jarred by periodic shouting from the depths of the windowless expat bar on the corner. The clientele's swagger proclaimed that it still laid claim to the turf.

The neighborhood converged on a strip shopping mall whose crown jewel was a Bradlees discount department store, fronted by a glass-littered parking lot so open and desolate that it seemed somehow safe to venture through.

Shea struck up an acquaintance with Ozzie next door, a fortyish car wash attendant from Mississippi with a pleasing schoolteacher wife and two dark skinned, sloe-eyed teenage daughters who were maddeningly unaware of their emerging powers. Shea kept his distance. Instead, he managed to connect briefly with a series of young women whose jobs as Fields Corner bank tellers or Bradlees cashiers made the dance of initial contact less awkward. Inside the yard he kept a nervous distance from Patty.

On the far side of Ozzie's house lay a simple block structure from which rousing gospel music reached out every Sunday. Shea walked past the church every day on his way to the MTA and noticed a line of Hebrew letters carved in the stone lintel over the door. Underneath, a translation in the stone observed "How Goodly Are Thy Tents, O Jacob". The first time he considered the scripture and then the bar across the street, he laughed.

*****

Walking by the church a few days later, a glint at the corner of the building caught Shea's attention. Between waist-high bricks, a rolled-up piece of paper stuck out from a gouged crevice of weather-beaten mortar. A silvery chain peeked out from the paper.

Shea edged closer and pulled them out. Written letters on the paper looked similar to the Hebrew carved into the building. He had no idea what they said. The chain held a round metal medallion with two marks in what seemed to be the same script.

He looked at his watch and calculated, then started over to Levinson Realty instead of heading for the train.

Lou looked up from the files on his desk. "Problem with the house?"

Shea shook his head and held out the pendant and paper. "Any idea what this is? Thought you might know."

Lou unfolded the note and read it for a long moment.

"It says *Ikh vel keynmol fargesn meyn klein sheyn shul.* I'll never forget my beautiful little synagogue. It's Yiddish, which is written in Hebrew letters. Our people have a habit of leaving notes in places we don't live anymore."

Shea nodded. "And the necklace? Like a St. Christopher's medal?"

"Not quite," Lou said. "It says '*chai*' in Hebrew. It means 'life'. Hebrew letters also have a meaning as numbers. The two that spell *chai* mean eighteen."

Shea said, "I knew a lot of eighteen year olds got dead in Nam. And a kid from my old neighborhood named Sean Malley was eighteen when he got killed by the cops in East Cambridge. You know that story from the papers?"

Lou said, "White kid several years back? I do remember hearing about that."

Shea took back the necklace. "You think it's okay if I wear this thing? Good memory for him, like he's still kickin' somewhere. He's one big reason I see the world like I do. Puts a lotta the pieces together." He looped the chain over his head.

"Sure," said Lou. "Think of it as part of a cycle of good thoughts."

32

The morning heat spread over the river and sucked up dew from the piles of steel plate rimming the shipyard. Shea was already at his table in Ziyad's. He had a view to the bar and, if he turned his head just a bit, through the cafe windows and across the street to the guardhouse and main gate. For over an hour he had been in the yellow vinyl chair, rocking slowly above the *Patriot Ledger* spread out before him, his palms flat on the table, nibbling his moustache. He'd gotten up only once, to grab another cup of coffee at the counter.

When he came in about quarter to six, a few old timers had looked up from their seats, bleary but noticing the new guy from nights. They staked out their tables, staring at crumbs by their lunch pails. Shea saw plainly that in the gray corners of the early mornings, the old timers ruled.

Around the room, small groups of men at tables tucked rolls of denim and protective canvas outerwear under their arms while they spoke in low voices and swished coffee and donuts and cow flaps between their teeth. A squad of white Nam vets passed by Shea's table and nodded at his fatigue jacket.

By six-thirty the crowd had swelled until it was younger and raucous and, finally, crushing. From a liquor-lined shelf behind the bar a radio informed the room that the white student population in Boston's public schools had declined sixty per cent since the court busing mandate came down a few years ago. Little Z turned from the cash register and switched the station to disco. The Bee Gees took over. Ziyad grimaced but kept his eyes on the grill.

Livezey the drunk, more commonly known for bingeing than analysis, stood up from his table and announced, "Anyone with half a mind woulda pulled their kid. And the ones that's left there got rocks in their head."

Shea looked up from his paper.

A small group of young guys hunched near the counter. They all wore brown welders' hard hats and green South Boston Marshal's windbreakers. One of them called out, "Damn right, Livezey!" before turning to the bar, "Hey Z! Give that man a donut on me." Harsh laughs complimented his wit.

Two of the Southie kids tore past the rail in front of the bar. A third one, who had hung back, tossed a crumpled lunch bag at them overhand, like a football.

The bag sailed along the bar. The two receivers jumped for it and banged hard. Their elbows dug in for a vicious moment before one of them came out on top and then lost the pass in the bare light bulb glare of the ceiling. The bag popped off his fingers, skittering behind the bar and hitting the floor at Little Z's feet.

The welder jackknifed across the bar rail and swung down onto the kid he had elbowed out of the play. He brushed off his Marshal's jacket and cuffed the other kid on the arm. "Watch the fuckin' merchandise," he said amiably.

Ziyad broke off from pre-frying a batch of lunch-rush burgers, and without moving from the grill stabbed the air with his spatula. "Hey, hey! Cut it out, Donny!"

Little Z looked up from the cash register and frowned at his father while the old-timers offered a round of grunts from the gallery.

"Fuckin' welders," one of them muttered.

Little Z leaned over and flipped the bag back to the welder, who stuffed it inside a pouch above the waist band of his Marshal's jacket, then grabbed a warm sausage roll from the bar, peeled back the wrapper and took a bite. He searched for change in the front pocket of his jeans and counted it out into Little Z's palm.

The clock edged toward seven o'clock. The old timers in Ziyad's Grill heaved and began to trickle onto the street. They picked up their hard hats, mostly brown but also mauve for sheet metal guys, green for riggers, orange for grinders and burners. They shuffled out the door. There was still plenty of time for them to make it to their workshops near the gate.

Clusters of men covered the sidewalks outside. Without the bar walls to bounce back the sound, their chatter faded to a soft buzz that rippled up and down the street.

Here and there a woman's hair peeked out from under a hard hat. A close bunch of them sat circled on the grassy knoll to one side of Ziyad's, each wearing a brown helmet or wrapping one under an arm.

Welderettes, Goldy the old Jew in the Stiff Mill called them, and usually the girls laughed along, their eyes unknowingly seductive against the drab male backdrop of the yard. At the end of the shift their nails still sparkled crimson with polish they shared in the bathroom.

The ten-of whistle blew. Gulls that had perched over the security shack at the gate fluttered, cawed and then settled defiantly before the end of the blast.

The whistle transformed the doorway at Ziyad's into a tangle of bodies. The younger guys were suddenly all business, churning out the door to eat up the quarter-mile of asphalt between the gate and the boats before the last whistle blew and the whitehats pulled out their warning slips.

The white Southie kids squeezed through the doorway out of Ziyad's. Their green Marshals jackets brushed against three mid-thirtyish black welders heading in with their gym totes. The backs of the jackets were embroidered with their neighborhood's no-busing slogan: *South Boston Marshals— You Know Where We Stand.*

The black guys were too seasoned to take offense. They moved into the bar with an aloof yet studied air of reserve. Each picked up a coffee and with one of Ziyad's tissue-thin napkins selected a sticky, last-minute cow flap that they stuffed into their totes to wolf down at break time. They settled over a pinball machine while the rest of the hardhats began to get up and flow across the street toward the gate.

Through the windows by the door, the Goliath crane rose from the ground, glinting ferociously from a thousand yards. Bad sun today, thought Shea. He took the last bite of his egg and cheese sandwich, threw down his coffee and got up.

At the bar, Little Z had set out a couple dozen freshly poured, plastic-lidded styrofoam cups of coffee between the cash register and a stack of sandwiches that were leaking spots of oil through waxed paper wrappers. Shea grabbed another cup. He ripped a hole in the lid with his teeth as he walked. Coffee slopped onto his jeans and hit the floor, where it disappeared among unvarnished boards. "Shit," he said quietly.

The mess would dry out soon in the heat. At least it wasn't winter when spilt coffee iced up the instant the door out of Ziyad's cracked open and the wind charged in from the waterfront.

33

"Looks like you're it," Lonny summed up. Shea and Cotty nodded.

Shea smiled broadly. "That's great. Thank you. But we're not finished. I can't run alone. We need a full ticket, just like the other side." He pointed to Cotty and Lonny. "I need you two with your bright faces shining to the shipyard. We want to show them what we mean by unity, not what Rashford and his crew think it means."

Shea expected them both to object, but Cotty nodded and said, "You got it Shea. I'll do it. You gonna win."

Shea looked at Lonny. "If you don't run I don't."

Her face crinkled up and she took a big breath. "I'll do it," she said, "Just to piss Farrell off."

*****

From the outset of his election campaign, Shea pushed himself to roam into unfamiliar territory at lunch time. First shift was a tumult of mostly unfamiliar faces, as alien to him as his first evening out of the school. Even the first shift welders themselves were different. The average one was more senior and much whiter and more likely to be enmeshed in the web of favors doled out by the union's old guard. And unlike night shift, where almost all of the welders were jammed onto one or two hulls in the basins, day shift employed many more crews on ships spread over

153

three of the yard's six drydocks. Hundreds more brownhats squirreled away in the boiler shop, the Stiff Mill, the Turret Shop and the sheet metal and pipe shops, their bodies and concerns a mile away from a boat-bound welder like Shea.

As he probed, Shea found unexpected support in the shops. Even a few of Rashford's guys in the soft welding department jobs understood that the old shipyard deal was changing. And he tugged at a soft spot when he reminded them about McKinnon's needless death.

Goldy from the Stiff told Shea that he was pulling for his candidacy in the mill. "It's time for the old guys to go. Get in some new blood," Goldy confided. He tugged hard at the lapel of Shea's denim jacket. He looked around the assembly area suspiciously, pressing close to Shea's face with slightly bitter old man's breath. "Lansky's talkin' it up for you over in the Turret Shop, too. We got all the Jews in on this one." Shea laughed uncertainly and Goldy put on an offended expression. "Hey, there's at least a dozen old Jewish welders around this place. And the Italian guys listen to us, too, even if the Irish don't."

Goldy suddenly reached out toward Shea's chest and touched his necklace. "What's this?" he asked hopefully.

Shea said, "It's just to remember someone who died."

*****

On his way out of the Stiff Shea hustled down a short flight of stairs for a pit stop in the dugout, the lunch area below the shop's work floor. He passed a couple of indoor picnic tables and proceeded to the back of the concrete shelter, where he luxuriated in front of a real ceramic urinal. Quitewhite's trademark commentary stared down at him from the wall: *Niggers Swallow White Man's Cum* and below that, at an angle, *Lonergan Sucks Black Dick.*

154

Shea walked back topside and hailed Goldy down. "What do the guys in here think should be done about the graffiti in the shithouse?"

Goldy said, "Don't know. No one really talks about it."

"What if it said, 'Kikes suck'? Would that be okay?"

"No, you're right. I know that can't make Elroy and Hicks feel too good." Goldy touched Shea's arm. "I remember when the union was getting organized. At the vote the company hired a bunch of guys to yell at the gates. *'You'll pay your dues to a pack of Jews! Pay your dues to a pack of Jews!'* Big Jim O'Donnell went over and ripped them a new one and they shut up real quick. That's when the union was really something."

Shea said, "Yeah, I heard about him at the school."

"Big Jim thought it would be easy for the company to tear guys apart by playing the groups against each other, and he wasn't gonna let that happen. He thought the same thing about whites and blacks."

"Yeah? Back then?"

"Yeah. There weren't really any blacks in the yard before the war—or after, really—cause of layoffs. And not that many during, either. Anyways, Big Jim thought that if there was more blacks then the company would stir up the race thing between union guys, so he was always against gettin' them back in. In the end the yard stayed pretty much white and we didn't have an issue."

Shea said, "I guess that's one way of looking at it. Not sure it worked out so good for the blacks."

"Well, now the government's forced them back in with the affirmative action thing," Goldy said. "But that's talk for another day. Just win the election first."

*****

Cotty and Byron weighed in from second shift with reports of solid support on nights for the campaign. "That won't hold on its own, though," Cotty warned. "Make them believe you remember them on nights, that you still got those roots on the shift. Me bein' an alternate on the ticket ain't enough by itself."

So three or four times a week Shea drove home after work, showered and returned to the shipyard for the seven-thirty dinner whistle, waiting at the gates to meet the brownhats streaming out for a bite or a nip. He never once ran into Charney or his election team.

34

"*Forward Motion: Vote for a Stronger Union.* That's the slogan," Lonny said.

By the next week, the yard was awash in yellow stickers sized to slap on the side of a helmet. Anyone boarding a boat could see dozens of them on clusters of brown hardhats. Cotty told Shea that on nights the stickers gleamed in the yard's harsh klieg lights and it seemed that every welder had one. Even a smattering of fitters and burners stuck them on in a show of support.

Hauner the guard passed the word down to Shea. "They're goin' crazy on the stickers up front. They don't know whether to ignore them or confiscate the helmets. Either way they're fucked."

In the end Industrial Relations ordered welders to remove the stickers from their hard hats, which were company issued.

"They sure know how to juice our support," Shea told Lonny. "Piss people off."

The Forward Motion ticket paid for a round of buttons to replace the stickers with the same slate name and slogan. They were snapped up by welders and pinned on their coats or their leathers.

A few days later flyers called for a Forward Motion protest outside the main gate at lunchtime. Shea addressed the crowd, demanding the right of expression, safe working conditions and respect for every welder on the job. Hundreds of welders turned out.

When money for printing flyers and buttons ran low, Lonny hit on the idea of a fundraiser. She enlisted the help of a welder who did disc jockey gigs on the side. Shea volunteered to host at his house. Notices for the party appeared in every shithouse and by the Saturday night before the vote, Shea and Lonny agreed that the turnout would be a referendum on the campaign.

That night, several hundred slicked-up welders breezed through Shea's heavy front door and threw a dollar bill each into the bucket inside. Shea realized with horror that almost none of them had brought women. The scarce shipyard females flew from room to room in a sociable frenzy. Lonny boogied by in a long dress and makeup, accompanied by an absurdly attentive male entourage.

"What I won't do for the cause," she chirped to Shea as she danced by. A step behind, her newest girlfriend smiled as tolerantly as she could.

The party rolled on in waves. A second rush of young white kids flooded in. Then a dozen small groups of young blacks came by. Then more whites—no little thing in Fields Corner. The sloe-eyed teenaged daughters from next door flounced in and were swept into an eager swarm of studiously polite black welders.

Around three in the morning, after everyone else was gone, a tide of West Indians rolled through the door, and then still more African-Americans returning from *The Sunrise*, a private after-hours club in Roxbury. Shea was dog-tired, flushed with drink and success when, in the midst of that last wave Pretty Boy walked in with Patty Withers.

She was stunning in a slinky black sheath and strappy heels. Her regular chocolate features glowed in the soft party light as she shook to the music. Her plush mouth voiced the lyrics.

She worked in the Turret Shop, a long way from Shea's job in the basin. Since coming onto first shift he had seen her before work and around Ziyad's at lunch, but she'd shown little interest.

He pulled Pretty Boy aside. "Truth. You guys together or no?"

"My dick pantin' for her like a dog, but she don't want none of it. Can you imagine?" He laughed then realized that Shea was asking with a motive. "Go ahead. That girl sure open up my nose. But her tongue way too sharp for me."

Patty was dancing with Elroy when Shea approached and asked for a turn. Elroy said, "You the man of the hour, right?" He smiled and moved away.

"Hello," Shea danced close without touching. "So you and Pretty Boy aren't connected."

"Took you some time to figure that out. But it's nice that you asked him."

The pause between them lasted too long. He struggled to get something out.

"Nice seeing you, though," he finally said, "Hope you have a good time."

*****

On Monday he rose from his table in Ziyad's when he saw Patty working her way along the bar counter with her breakfast. "I got two things to ask you," he started. She turned from the line in front of the register, offering a wide, friendly smile. He said, "Do you want to help pass out the flyers tomorrow?"

Her eyes passed closely over him. "I'll think on it. I told you I'd help when I got back in town."

"And would you maybe want to work the polls at the hall for the election?"

Patty looked him full in the face and laughed a loud laugh that accentuated her full mouth and smile. "You are one funny white man. You gonna win, don't need me for no election." Her smile disappeared. "If you want to ask me out, just say so."

She looked him over. "You do appeal to me, though Michael. Yes, you do." She laid her money on the counter and walked toward a table of importuning black welders in the rear. Shea watched the sway of her jeans.

35

On election day, Rashford's official board was out in force promoting Charney. Farrell and the other markers made their way around the yard warning of dire results if the welding leadership didn't remain all white. Shea packed the steps in front of the union hall with volunteers handing out poll cards. Another two dozen welders stood at the gates to usher the brownhats to the vote.

There was a rush of welders to the hall in the morning before work, then speeding carloads at lunch and another outpouring after the three-thirty whistle. Like he was reading a jury coming in with a verdict, Shea could tell exactly how well he was doing by the eyes of the voters rushing past. It seemed he and Charney were running pretty close.

Second shift—voting before work and again at the half-hour dinner break—made the difference. Black American and West Indian welders deluged the union hall chanting Shea's name. The Cape Verdeans from Griswold's crew piled out of an auto caravan in bunches, pulling along newer arrivals from the homeland who had hired on since Shea had moved to days. The newer Cape Verdeans had been primed by the original group with the history of Shea's efforts with Rosa on their behalf and then given careful instructions on how to vote. They talked excitedly among themselves as they trotted up the steps of the union hall and showed off their marked-up sample ballots to Shea. He was impressed by the loyalty they gave for the little he'd done for them.

For most of the night, there were many more dark skins than white in the hall. Rashford's election committee was stunned. "Attack of the fuckin' Zulus," Salvucci grumbled. By eight o'clock, after the end of the second shift dinner, Charney had lost. Shea was the new welding steward.

*****

After the votes were counted, Shea drove home by Wollaston beach without stopping at the Beachcomber or at the Greek's for clams.

He stayed home as the evening deepened, sitting alone in his rocker on the deck off his kitchen. An exotic clash of music fought for attention from a dozen windows. Tin cans clattered along Dakota Street between teams of skirmishing youngsters. Shea threw down cashews and beer, sucked on a joint and listened to the sounds of his neighborhood piercing the twilight. Next door, Ozzie's daughters squealed and licked tangy, late season barbeque from their fingers.

He told himself that he would never get so comfortable with the steward job that he couldn't let it go. Kevin Charney had become addicted to the recognition and the perks, the time off and the tit jobs, the warm corner chair in the whitehat shack. He had forgotten what it was all about.

*****

The next day Shea stuck out his hand and suggested to Charney that they should try to work together. Charney still wore his Official Board badge. He said, "Go fuck yourself, mister. You and your commie friends think you got all the answers. You don't need anything from me. Stay outta my way."

"Look, Kevin," Shea said. "At least get me your old grievance records and seniority lists. I'm kinda lost without them."

A welder passed and said, "Hi, Kevin." Charney hung his arm protectively over the young hardhat's shoulder. They walked down the runway together.

36

Shea looked at the union pass that his day foreman Kearney held out to him. "They want you in the front office, at labor relations." He gestured toward Shea's gear. "Pack up your toolbox before you go, drop it all off at the Stiff Mill before you head up to labor relations. After lunch you report to Timmy Bronson in the mill."

"How come?"

"Hershfeld said they want you in pissing distance of his office when they need you."

Shea's name was written under the notation *Union Business Pass*. Next to *Employee* the pass read *Brian Gimple*. In the space after *Reason for Pass*, Kearney had written *Suspension pending termination—sleeping on the job*.

When he got to the Stiff Mill, Shea rummaged through his toolbox for the spiral notebook and pen he had brought in for his first day. He headed toward the administration building by the main gate. He got off the elevator at the fourth floor and followed a sign through double doors. An arrow indicated the employee benefits office straight ahead and labor relations to the left through a wooden archway marred by routed cut-outs where hinges had once held a door. Beyond the arch the front edge of a desk jutted into his line of sight from the hall. The desk was unoccupied, but on the floor behind something moved.

He peeked over the desktop. Cramped behind the secretary's chair, uplifted toward him, was a well-cushioned plaid-covered buttocks. A woman was perched below on all fours in front of a low file cabinet. She craned her head at the folders in the back, then tabbed through them and pulled one out.

Shea cleared his throat. "I'm Mike Shea, the new welding steward. I was told to come up on a grievance."

The woman swung around and sat up on her knees. "I remember you," she said. The recollection was clearly unpleasant.

Shea was taken aback. "I don't think we've met."

The woman shook her head. "No, of course not. I mean I remember your file. You were suspended for violation of rules and regulations several months back. An attempted job action on the boat."

"That's very good memory. And it was a very smoky tank."

The woman clambered to her feet. "Next time they'll fire you and it'll stick. You've built up a bad record for Mr. Hershfeld to use against you in an arbitration."

Shea cocked his head. "And you are?"

"Lynne. His assistant." She pointed to a door halfway down the hall. "The grievant is in there with Stan Rashford. They've been waiting for you."

Shea started down the hallway. The woman's sharp voice pulled him back.

"Your pass," she demanded. "I've got to sign you in. Since the strike." He handed it over and she scribbled her initials, then turned away and kneeled again at her files. "Door on the left," she called over her shoulder.

Shea walked down the hall and knocked.

"Come in." He recognized Rashford's baritone.

Metal chairs surrounded a metal table in the small conference room. Nothing on the walls. At the table's midpoint, Rashford leaned back in the only chair with armrests. Across the table from him, a sturdy young welder in aviator glasses fiddled gloomily with a piece of paper. Rashford studied the welder without a hint of expression.

Kevin Charney sat at the end of the table closest to the door. He stiffened when Shea stuck his head in.

There was barely enough space to edge past the men, so Shea stood where he had entered, shifting from leg to leg. Hardboard partitions rose to the ceiling around the furniture. On the far side of one, an unseen man barked angrily about someone's habitual tardiness and fondness for liquor. It was a one-sided discussion over a phone.

Charney spoke first. "Time to show us what you can do, hot stuff."

Shea avoided Charney's glare. He had no idea what he was expected to do. He looked at Rashford without eliciting any guidance and then tried the welder. "I guess you're Gimple? What's the problem?"

"They call me Junior." The welder lapsed into silence.

Rashford motioned Shea into a chair. "Siddown, I think we got this one licked. Gimple here had a tough night. Had a few winks."

Shea squeezed toward a seat. "Any witnesses to the alleged sleeping besides the boss?"

"Don't need witnesses," Rashford said. "Company doesn't require them and so won't an arbitrator. Besides, this guy can't go without a job for a year just to have a day in court, whether anything happened or not." He turned to Gimple. "Which it did, right?"

Gimple shrugged, "What's the difference?"

Rashford nodded. "Exactly."

"So?" Shea asked.

"So as president of this union, I've been working on it. Hershfeld offered to bring him back to work after a suspension if he signs the hangman's letter. Otherwise, he's gone."

Shea said, "What's a hangman's letter?"

Rashford gestured at the typewritten sheet. "Give it to him, Junior." The welder slid the sheet across the table.

Shea picked up the paper and scanned it. "Well, gets him back on the job." He held up a finger while he read down the page. "This makes it sound like we agree they can fire him if he's nailed for anything at all down the road. Can't even file a grievance. That right?"

Rashford nodded. "That's why it's called a hangman's letter. I already explained the whole thing to Junior here. We got a handful of memos like this one floating in the yard right now."

"What if some whitehat gets a hard-on for the guy?"

"That's why it's called a hangman's letter, kid. Look, nobody's gonna come after Junior. The shipyard don't work like that."

Shea said, "I'll remember you said so."

Rashford turned to Charney. "Hey Kevin. Take Gimple out to the hall and give us a minute, okay?"

Rashford pulled out his wallet and picked through it. He placed a laminated card on the table facing Shea. Under the plastic, the card was crinkly and smudged but easily recognizable.

"'Get Out of Jail Free'?" said Shea, "What's that supposed to mean?"

"It means 'This is how things work'. How many of these cards you got?"

"Me?" Shea sounded unsure, "Why would I have one?"

Rashford leaned back in his chair. "Right you are. You wouldn't. Me, I got hundreds. Thousands. In my head. Don't ever show 'em. I just tell Hershfeld 'I need this one' and the guy gets outta jail free. His problem goes away."

Shea said, "So you're tellin' me that a guy can get clear any time?"

"Nope," Rashford said. "Only when I tell Hershfeld or Pennock I need it. Like here. I been knowin' Gimple's old man for thirty years. Over time he's had things he needs. Maybe an insurance problem, or a chit taken away, or some OT. Right now he needs his son's job. That's a big one. A hangman's letter solves it for Hershfeld, least it does with my card. Which believe me, he'll remember to call in. So I do Gimple's family the favor and they understand when I ask back. Like a vote. All three of 'em and their cousins. Understand?"

"I guess."

"These hangman letters ain't nothin' new. We just don't make a big deal of them. You know, keep them in a drawer so's we don't embarrass the guy involved." He lifted his eyebrows until they were shadowed under his drooping silver forelock. "For example, your badass buddy Townsend had one in his file."

Shea couldn't hide his surprise.

"Didn't know that, did you?" Rashford continued. "How do you think I got him back to work when he threatened that boss before his election, sleeping then pretending to look for a line? Just a big joke to that clown."

Shea said, "So why did Townsend qualify? He was never one of your guys."

"He was gonna be the steward. If he went down and I didn't finesse things for him, the coloreds woulda wailed like I nailed him up on the cross." Rashford chose his words carefully. "They ain't all exactly in my camp."

"So other than Townsend bein' a steward and all, the black guys don't rate with you."

Rashford pursed his lips and motioned to the door. "Let's bring Gimple and Charney back in."

*****

Rashford leaned toward Shea and tamped on the memo with an index finger. "Just one detail you need to know. I already gone over this with Gimple here. The only one that can sign off on a hangman's letter is the department steward 'cause you're the only one that can file a grievance. I gotta have your name on this to get the kid back to work."

Shea's eyes fell on another clause in the agreement. "What's this 'not to be used as precedent in any third-party grievance'?"

Charney pounded once, hard, on the conference table. "Look, mister. We got about five minutes before they pull this offer. President Rashford spent the whole goddam morning gettin' this guy's job back in the picture. You don't sign and he's out on the street for good. Why don't you just look at your welder here and tell him why you're not gonna let him go back to work?"

Rashford put a hand on Charney's arm. He looked at Shea. "It means what it says. If we sign, we can't use this as a precedent in any future grievance. And the letter stays with the guy for as long as he's in the yard. They don't want the fact that they're willing to go easy on this guy to interfere with firing him or anyone else the next time around."

Shea turned anxiously to Gimple. "You want to sign this?"

Gimple said, "I already did."

"You think I should, too?"

Gimple looked at the table. "I need my job."

"So what really happened? You got a side to the story?"

Rashford threw up his hands.

"Hey hotshot, which is it? Sign and put this kid back to work, or leave him on the street?"

Shea stared at the paper for a long, uncomfortable moment.

"Where's your name go?" he asked Rashford.

"I'm not the steward. I sign the contract, nothing else. You don't wanna sign this letter, just tell Gimple here that he's out of a job."

Shea looked at Junior. The welder's eyes were full of tears.

Shea scrawled his name on the paper. "I hope this doesn't come back to bite him or the next guy they go after."

"Join the crowd," Rashford said. He picked up the memo from the table and motioned to Charney. "Kevin, you stay here with Junior. Call his old man and tell him I fixed things for his kid."

Rashford walked with Shea down the hall toward a closed door at the end of the hall. At the entry a plaque announced the Director of Industrial Relations. As they passed Lynne's desk, she shifted to dig deeper into the file cabinet. Rashford winked and whispered to Shea, "Wouldn't mind a bite of that, hunh?"

*****

By the end of his first month as a steward, Shea had been seen walking up to the administration building dozens of times, where he disappeared for stretches of hours into Industrial Relations or the grievance room. Watching him, the welders were suddenly uncertain.

"Guzzling coffee from the company percolator with the rest of the bums," they concluded. "Whattya think he's doing up there? Eatin' donuts and havin' a snooze?" But not one of

170

them uttered a word of their letdown to Shea. Hey, fuck him, they grumbled, never counted on anything different.

Shea heard in their silence that by getting elected he had somehow moved beyond them, in their eyes and his own. Got-a-problem-ask-Shea was no longer so simple. Too much of his time was dealing behind closed doors with the company or the union's apparatus. The steward who was supposed to be different now aroused their suspicions. By his second month as steward, Shea understood that learning the ropes while he waited to act was to lose.

37

"I need to get over to the South Yard today," Shea told a circle of welders at Ziyad's. "Can I tell my whitehat you need to see me on union business?" The challenge flushed out brash welders in every basin and shop. "Sure, why not?" they responded, "I got a pair." Crew by crew, the new steward cobbled together a network that tipped him off to the smokiest tanks, to the diciest staging, to the whitehats who needed a nudge to go easy.

He tapped Roach and Billy for a call every week, but when he asked Patty to sign on she said, "Always somethin' you want for the cause. Don't you got nuthin' else to say to me by now?"

"I guess I want to ask you out." Shea struggled to look her in the eye.

"Okay, I'll think on it. Meantime, you think how hard this would be for *me*. Every white man in this yard gonna assume a white boyfriend means I'm spreadin' my legs for all them, too."

"Guess I shoulda thought about all that already."

She flounced her shoulders in mock exasperation. "I *like* you, Michael. I really do. But this ain't gonna be easy for neither one of us." She smiled and moved closer. "Just think on that for awhile."

He felt the heat of her body next to his. "I will. And we'll talk."

*****

Shea was waiting at his table every morning when the earliest welders came in the door. "Can ya fix this lost time chit?" they asked. "Will they pay my time for my grandfather's funeral?" "Damn whitehat's after my job." And the one he heard most every day, "So much smoke in that tank we're chokin' to death." Shea gave them his attention, nodding as he listened to their problems. He jotted notes with a clip-on pen in a spiral pad that lay on his table. He told them he'd look into it and see them back on the job. They learned to trust that he would. They touched him on the arm and said, "Hey, thanks, man," then got up to leave.

When the last of them were gone, Shea got up to head in the gate. He spotted Elroy and two other black welders at the pinball machine and sidled over, coffee in one hand, paper tucked under his arm.

"Hey, Elroy... Sonny... Hicks." All three of them hunched over forearms laid flat on the glass. With easy wrist flicks Elroy and Hicks lifted their coffee cups at him.

Not Sonny. "Hey, Shea," he demanded, "when do I get my money from that grievance you filed?"

"I don't know, man. I don't got a wand."

Sonny looked down at his drained cup of coffee and spit, then flipped the cup into the trash can by the door. He turned his face up to Shea. "Goddam union."

Elroy said, "C'mon man. Ain't his fault. He's the one filed the damn grievance for you in the first place." He turned to Shea. "Don't pay him no mind."

Sonny worked his mouth and spit again. "Shee-it. Could've done better myself, man. Could've talked it straight out with Charley Johnson." He showed his teeth. "No goddam good at all." He ran his tongue along his upper gum.

"Thought you was gonna change all this shit, Shea. Make this a real union."

Shea rubbed away an itch on his forehead with a chambray sleeve. The tape over the front of the brown hard hat said *Shea—Local 8 Welding Steward*. He said, "Look, you won the case, Sonny. When this company loses, it stalls as long as it can. Whaddya want me to tell you?"

Sonny looked away and picked at a tooth. Shea turned and walked out.

*****

Each morning in the Stiff Mill Shea handed his new foreman Timmy a list of a dozen welders he wanted to see.

"Sure, I'll set these right up," Timmy told him. He looked Shea in the eye. "The guy up front don't see what you're doin' yet. Stupid shits don't realize they made me your secretary, tying up half my morning on the phone setting up meetings for you all over the yard." He picked up the phone and dialed. "Fuck Hershfeld, fuckin' guy. Bright idea this was."

Shea stuffed his notebook and a manual of government safety regs into a satchel. He trotted around the shipyard with the bag tucked under an arm. It was clenched in his teeth when he climbed ladders or crawled through the boats' most unlikely cramped spaces. In time, the welders expected him to pop up anywhere and soon, wary foremen did as well. Within an hour of Timmy's job assignment at the morning muster, he was off in the yard.

Rashford's lieutenants trailed behind him, muttering darkly to welders after he left. "Fuckin' kid's all show. He can't get nuthin' done," they insisted, and the hardhats could see that much was true. "But he listens and always gets back," welders of all stripes acknowledged. "Can't ask for more than that around here." Shea marveled at how little it took to lock in their loyalty. It was, he told himself, a little pathetic.

When the hardhats considered the difference in Shea, it was simple. He wasn't hiding in the shacks. He took up their side. He walked up to the whitehats, handed over his pass and headed straight for the welder who needed him, never asking the whitehat "What's the problem?" before getting his guy's side of it. Shea acted like the welder's story was more than equal to the company's and he took furious, scrupulous notes to capture it all. The hardhats were the ones he most wanted to hear from. All they demanded was that someone pay attention.

Whenever the new steward passed, the hardhats stopped for a moment to watch. And not only welders. Men in every trade tugged down the brims of their helmets or cupped their hands against the glare of the sun. Their torches and sledgehammers hung limply while they tracked Shea's progress along the open ways and through the basins.

They rubbed their moist July jaws thoughtfully. The guy's alright, said the trades, even some in the shops, and the welders nodded.

Yeah, some of them noted, but they say he's a red.

*****

Hot Slag was renamed as the department's official *829 News* and saturated the yard in now-weekly editions. On publication days Shea and Lonny dumped stacks of newsletters in front of the shithouse stalls. The size of their delivery squad grew. Cotty and Byron helped out on nights. Richie Millis and a small network of others pitched in for the midnight shift.

When they tried handing out the *News* at the gates again, the welders gobbled them up and dropped dollar bills into collection boxes. The other trades picked up discards of each edition to read in the stalls or squirreled away copies in their shirts to mull over later in the gloom of the tanks. The flyers grew bolder and more angry, but never once did they exhaust the hardhats' hunger for accounts of the work that shaped their lives. Shea felt their support, that the work had begun to pay off.

38

"Drop your jeans and hop up on the table."

Keefer shook her head at the doctor. "I get examined by my obstetrician. I don't need you."

He took a step toward her and held up an index finger. "I'm the company medical expert. You want me to say that you're disabled due to a pregnancy? I have to examine you."

"You're not gonna touch me."

"Then it looks to me like you can weld. Nothing about a normal pregnancy could affect that. Welding's a light duty job." The doctor took out a pen and made check marks on a sheet of paper lying on a rollaway tray.

"Okay," he said, "Get back to work."

"You fuckin' jerk!" Keefer exploded. "You're not even gonna look at my doctor's report? He says that pulling cable is not okay for me or the baby, and that the smoke is even worse."

The doctor looked up briefly. "I'm the doctor here. You can weld. Back to work."

He pointed his pen toward the door.

Keefer walked back to the Stiff Mill with her cheeks stinging.

*****

By the time Keefer finished her story Shea could hardly contain himself. "That butcher wants you to weld until you have the *baby*? How are you gonna drag that welding line? And the smoke is gonna kill the kid."

Keefer took off her gloves. "So what do we do?"

Shea shook his head. "I don't know. This has never happened here before, least not since the second war. Lotta women here then. But that was thirty-five, forty years ago." They each considered that for a moment.

"Look," Shea said finally, "what are you looking for? Are you gonna weld if they tell you to?"

Keefer squinched her eyebrows. "No," she said at last. "How can I keep welding? This is my baby! All I want is to go on disability like anyone else who can't work. Contract says twelve weeks with comp and six months total for a non-work disability, right?"

"You got anyone to help you? Baby got a father around?"

Keefer frowned. "I don't think that's any of your business, Mike."

"Whoa! I'm just tryin' to think of a way to get into this. Somebody else to help, win you some sympathy outside the yard. It's not just some routine grievance, you know? We're gonna need a different approach."

Keefer nodded. "I've talked about it with the women. In the bathroom. And on Fridays we go over to the Blue Dragon after work. You know, away from Ziyad's and all, just us. They want to help."

"You mean Lonny and Patty?"

"And Magdalena. All the women, Mike. If they can help me, I really don't care what kind of problem anybody has with them. They're good people. And I know you like Lonny."

"I can work on the grievance end," Shea said. "What could the rest of you do to push them to settle?"

"None of us knows what to do yet. I mean, who gives a damn about the women in the yard, anyhow?"

There was another silence between them.

"Look," Keefer suggested. "If you want to help, why don't you meet us there on Friday? Just to talk it over."

*****

Two dozen women welders butted a couple of long tables at the rear of the bar in the near-empty Chinese restaurant. All but Lonny were under twenty-five. Between sips of Mai Tais, their talk fluttered around the shipyard and their outside lives. As they talked, they played brightly colored paper parasols through their fingers and drew water doodles on the tabletops.

Shea poked his head through the glass foyer doors to search the shadows inside.

"C'mon over here, Michael!" Lonny called across the low-ceilinged room. "Don't be afraid of the girls!" The chorus of women laughed as Shea stepped in with a trapped look on his face. The women's chatter stumbled to an uncertain halt.

Lonny shoved over and Shea squeezed into a chair next to hers. He kept his mouth shut, inspecting the faces at the two tables until the conversation warmed up again. He nodded at Patty, then tried not to stifle the urge to keep looking.

The women spoke with increasing ardor. Even Magdalena, the normally quiet Haitian welder, spoke up in her difficult accent. "They want to kill the *babies*?" she demanded. One of the married women volunteered that she had been thinking of kids, but after consulting her checkbook, determined that she couldn't afford risking the job. The others nodded knowingly.

Magdalena asked Shea, "What do the union do?"

Shea said, "I'll file for disability time and pay. And if Keefer refuses to weld and gets fired, that's another one in the system. But I can't guarantee if the Grievance Committee is gonna pursue the case or let it die. I just don't know." His voice trailed off doubtfully.

The women watched water dribble down the rims of their Mai Tai glasses. Lonny stabbed a cocktail cherry with a toothpick and sucked at it.

Shea tried to explain. "Don't seem to me that Charney or Rashford have anything against women in the yard. Bringing in women wasn't their favorite idea, but they've sort of got used to it, same as when the first few blacks were hired in the early Seventies."

"Long as there weren't too many and they stayed welders," Lonny threw in. She gestured to the bartender for another round. "They're not so thrilled about it now."

"Look," Shea said. "The union just wouldn't do anything extra for the blacks, and won't for you, neither. Nothing that might piss off their hard core, anyway." He looked directly at Lonny. "And to tell the truth, it would be a lot easier if some of you learned to hold back on your opinions a little bit."

"Just like you do, right? You mean if we're good girls they might help us."

Shea grunted. Leaned back in his chair. When the new round of Mai Tais appeared, he asked for one. The women gurgled on their straws and moved on to the fresh drinks.

Lonny was certain that hardhats all over the yard would back them. "Even if they don't like women inside the gates, the average guy in the yard knows what's right and fair," she insisted. "Besides, they're gonna think of their wives. A lot of them work somewhere, even if they're not welders."

Shea said, "That's your Mai Tai talking."

Keefer was troubled. "I can't have a baby and no job. How long before I hear from a grievance if I'm fired?"

Shea said, "A year, maybe two. Hershfeld can string it out that long if he wants."

Keefer blew out her cheeks. "And I don't guess I'm gonna get unemployment comp either—not that it's worth much."

"Unemployment's easier to win than arbitration. I'd say your chances for that are better than even."

Lonny rapped her knuckles on the table. "This has got to be settled fast. We need a little guerrilla action."

"Fuckin' Che Guevara here," Shea muttered. "Let's get real."

"Michael!" Lonny said sharply. Shea gave her a small, apologetic wave.

Keefer relaxed the room with a mischievous smile. "Mike, you told me exactly the same thing, that this has never happened before. So, we gotta do something different."

*****

By the end of the afternoon the women were in equal parts boozy and eager to get started. File a grievance. Publicize the issue, inside the shipyard and out. The group figured there were another dozen or so women they could count on to talk it up through the yard.

As the conversation died down, Lonny cast around the table for anyone who hadn't pitched in much. "What about you Patty, what do you think?"

"This all is good. I'm glad to help with whatever." Patty turned and spoke directly to Shea. "But what I don't hear is much enthusiasm from our new steward here. He listen to ideas but never says 'Yes, I'm down with that'."

Lonny said, "That's true, Mike."

Patty said, "Maybe he wants to be in charge. Maybe he don't like it when womens take over. Seems to me when an invitation from a woman is straight and clear there should be some direct response. If he wants that woman by his side, that is." Her lips twitched up.

181

The table was quiet. Shea managed to croak, "Okay. I understand."

Patty's eyes were on him, dancing. "So that mean you comin' aboard, Mr. Shea?"

The other women exchanged glances. Lonny said, "This is about Keefer and her baby, right?"

Patty looked directly at Shea. "Most certainly."

*****

When Keefer was assigned a job the next day, she took out a paper and read it to Timmy. "I respectfully refuse to weld due to my pregnancy, my health and that of my baby."

"Don't make me do this," he told her. "You know I'll need to send it up front."

"It's not your fault, Timmy." She put her hand on his arm. "We know you're one of the good guys." She was walked out on suspension and terminated by telegram five days later.

39

Within days of Keefer's termination, the women circulated a petition. Shea was surprised when they gathered eight hundred names the first day, more than a hundred of them on a single list that Goldy hustled through the Stiff Mill and Boiler Shop.

When the *829 News* took up the issue, Shea was first at the gates, holding up the headline in front of his steward's badge: *Justice for Pregnant Welders*.

Salvucci shook his head as he brushed by, refusing a copy. "You've lost it, Shea," he said gruffly.

Lonny called the *Patriot Ledger* and set up interviews. When Keefer posed for the newspaper photo she made her protruding belly as obvious as possible. In the background of the published picture, another yard woman placed her toddler in a carriage. The headline asked: *Discrimination at General Shipworks?*

After that, all three Boston TV stations called Keefer for interviews. At another session at the Blue Dragon, the women agreed that Keefer should appear on camera, but with some of the less photogenic women, or the married ones and their kids. "Something for everyone to identify with," counseled Lonny.

The company press office in Omaha refused comment.

The *Patriot Ledger* article was followed by a sharp editorial. A female press flack for the shipyard flew in from Omaha to read a statement denying bad intent, adding that

183

"the pregnancy issue is a matter best left to representatives of the bargaining unit and the company's labor relations office." The phones at the union hall started ringing with calls from the media. Rashford issued instructions not to respond.

*****

A week later three dozen women welders showed up at the gates with picket signs calling for support from the men. Another barrage of coverage followed in the *Patriot Ledger* and this time, the *Boston Globe*.

When the women made a push to turn out the welders to a union meeting, Shea noted ruefully that they were much better at it than he. Keefer laughed and tossed her hair. She patted her belly until Shea looked more closely than he had intended. Her blue eyes gleamed as if that settled that. "Hey," she reminded him, "it's a shipyard full of guys."

The Grievance Committee threatened to drop Keefer's case. Salvucci booted Shea out of the grievance room and yelled down the corridor. "Go weld for a while and then see how you feel about it!"

*****

After a month of the ruckus, and over vigorous protests from Salvucci and Charney, Rashford called Hershfeld to see if they couldn't discover an out. They resigned themselves and brought in Shea. Within a day, the three men signed off on Keefer's grievance. She was notified by telegram that her termination was withdrawn and disability payments would be issued retroactively. Shea pulled the grievance and the women in the *Patriot Ledger* photo agreed to write a letter to the editor attesting to the General's recently enlightened outlook. From her Omaha office, the press flak refused comment on the resolution of a matter which she insisted was of concern only to the Shipworks family.

After it was done, Rashford summoned Shea.

"You know, Mike, I'm a little tired of you grandstanding at my expense."

Shea said, "That's not what this was about."

"So you say. But you're not as bright as I thought if you think this is how these matters end." Rashford threw a piece of General Shipworks letterhead across the table. It was an internal memo from the corporate board in Omaha to Pennock, the general manager. He had been given the go ahead to resolve Keefer's grievance, but was also instructed to make the pregnancy issue a prime target in the next round of union contract talks. "The substance isn't the issue," the memo noted. "However, you cannot let them think they can win in our shipyard. The board can't afford that. Neither can you."

"Always remember to have a negotiating chip you don't mind throwing away," Rashford said to Shea. He reached across his desk and plucked the memo from Shea's fingers.

"You're planning to sell them out," Shea said, "You pimp."

Rashford's face was impassive. "Get out of here, Michael. I'm done with you. For good."

40

"You don't want to put your thing in a black woman, is all." Patty pulled away from Shea. She took a big breath before bolting upright and punching him in the ribs.

"That's not it. I'm just having some trouble relaxing."

They were still for a long minute, panting on the rug in front of his fireplace. The dying flames thickened the glaze on their eyes and set off the curve of her hips.

She drew down close to his face and said, "Me for me, remember? I am right here with you."

She reached out tentatively and touched him. He hardened. With sudden assurance she fondled him and smiled.

She breathed in his ear, "Now don't that feel good as any white girl?"

Shea rolled on top. Their eyes fixed on each other. He said, "It feels like you. That's what I want."

*****

They began to spend long hours together. Shea marveled at her trove of North Carolina stories, mostly centered on the extensive clan she had left behind in Lenoir County. Sunday after church lunches each week, big family fish frys, a reunion each year that brought back relatives from the north. The experience of any family like that was completely foreign to him.

186

"Why did you leave?"

"Nothing back in Lenoir County for me 'cept family, and that's important, but not enough. Down there black folks don't make half what whites do. And I won't spend my time working with people all arrogant at me like that. My parents passed last year, just two months apart. My sister Alice was ready to leave even though she had a good job dancing at a place near to the Air Force base in Goldsboro. So when her boyfriend's great uncle left him his little hardware store up here, Alice was ready to go up north and I just now followed."

Shea told her about his mom and how she'd died.

"I can see that you're different, Michael," she said, "though I don't yet know why."

He said, "I dunno," then went quiet. "The black and Latin guys in my platoon in Nam had my back when I needed it, just as much as the whites. And not just in the field. Back at base, too. Their horror stories actually relieved me, like I wasn't alone.

"But the real change was back home. Some white and black kids pulled together to protest when this guy from my project was murdered by cops. I had a black friend who helped me see how important that was. My guys, the white ones, rushed back to the race war the next day. But to me, seeing those kids work together felt right and it stuck.

"Then a year or so before I started at the yard I went to Carson Beach in Southie on a Sunday. Hundreds of people swimming, just having a day off. Then five or six black guys showed up on the beach. Turns out they were bible salesmen from out of town. Didn't know better, but that didn't make no difference. Those hundreds of Southies tore them apart, chased them off the beach, put two of them in the hospital, fucked up their car. Cops came and got them out before they got lynched. And these guys were bible salesmen, for chrissakes! I had a hard time sittin' with that."

Patty said, "Uh-hum. That's good. But we gonna talk sometime about what you mean by those salesmen 'didn't know better' than to go to the beach."

Shea took her hand. "Guess I'm still learning."

*****

They decided that it would be best for them both if they didn't broadcast their relationship around the shipyard. "You ain't gonna win no votes with the whites," Patty said, "and I ain't gonna win no friends on the dark side. So for now let's keep us for us."

"I'm worried either way," Shea conceded. "The hiding makes it seem like I'm ashamed when I'm not. But I'd be lyin' if I said I wasn't worried about risking what we're trying to do in the yard. Makes me question myself."

"You on the right track bein' honest about that, Michael. Makes me feel closer."

*****

It took Patty a week to invite Shea back to the apartment she shared with her sister. "This is Alice," she said when they met in her kitchen. "She dances up by your way."

Alice was taller, with lighter skin than her sister, though she had the same even, wide eyes and riveting features. She looked at Shea shyly from her seat. "I'm at the Starlight by Four Corners. You ever catch my show?" Her drawl was like Patty's, but her voice was so soft Shea had to strain to hear her.

"Pleased to meet you." The Starlight was a club not far from his house, past Codman Square, with a sign hung out front that promised exotic dancing through the evening. "Never had the opportunity."

Alice smiled shyly again. "You should come by sometime with Patty. We can play cards at our place after last call."

"Alice is very good," Patty assured him. "At cards *and* at dancing."

On weekend afternoons, Patty took Shea fishing at a creek outside the city where they caught baskets of sunnies. He'd never fished before. They'd go back to her place, throw the little fish on the skillet and share them with Alice and her boyfriend Franklin at dinner. They ate half a dozen sunnies apiece and washed them down with beer. Patty, Alice and Franklin laughingly called the numbers at each other and eventually, more carefully, at Shea. They played cards for hours, betting with matchsticks. As they played, Alice ran a soft sportscaster's patter: "Franklin throw down a six of spades and she waits, sees him and raises, then she throw down a love ace and sets back to see. Now Michael look to raise, but wait, he show a six of spades and he calls. And yes, Patty lays 'em down and beats him again!"

41

Shea gestured at the shithouse walls scrawled with racial slurs and crude sex graphics of women welders. He read out loud, "'Lonny sucks nigger dick'. Would you show this crap to your wives?"

None of the two dozen white welders clumped by the heating pipes spoke up. Shea said, "All I'm asking you to do is tell your foremen you want the place cleaned up and the graffiti removed. And ask again every day until it happens."

Billy the Kid leaned on a pipe at the far end of the room and said, "It's not just this shithouse. It's all of them. You gonna file a grievance?"

Shea said, "Nothin' in the contract that touches this. I'm going to go up to industrial relations with some of the black guys to lodge a complaint." Soon as I manage to recruit them, he thought. "Maybe threaten to get some attention from outside." He looked around the room. "Anyone willing to join us?" Silence. Shea sighed. "Okay. How about talking to your whitehats and crews?" A few hands went up. "Good enough," Shea said.

Shea drifted back to floor of the Stiff Mill and asked Elroy Washington to lead a group up to Hershfeld's office to protest the graffiti. "I'll try to follow it up with some white guys if I can," Shea promised the machine operator.

Elroy thought it over before getting back to him the next day. "Okay, I got some of the brothers to go up after work."

Elroy looked hard at Shea. "You gonna have our backs up there, right?"

*****

At the whistle, seventeen black welders congregated at the ground floor entrance to the main office building. They rode the elevator up in three loads. When Shea arrived with the last bunch, the others were still waiting for them in the hallway. They started down the corridor together, watching the way their color and numbers were reflected in the startled faces of passing executives.

Elroy looked around at the group. "I guess we some bad stuff, hunh?" The rest cackled and bolstered each other with wild forecasts of the scene that lay just ahead. With a hint of a strut they paced briskly through double doors and up to Irv Hershfeld's office.

The door was partly open. Elroy knocked on the jamb. The others crowded behind him. Hershfeld jumped up from his desk and circled around it. He swung the door toward the group, leaving a narrow slot open to the welders. His head peeked anxiously around the jamb. "What is it you want?" he asked in a low, urgent voice. After a few exchanges with Elroy, Hershfeld swung back the door and allowed the welders to shuffle past. They flowed around the corners of his office, then assumed standing positions on either side of his desk and behind the two empty chairs in front of it. After a brief hesitation, two of the welders plopped into the seats.

Hershfeld assessed them from the door. He waited until their eyes turned toward him and then walked slowly to his desk. He straightened his tie with a self-conscious twist and sunk into his high-backed chair.

The welders told him they wanted the shithouse and warming shacks cleaned and painted. "Don't care 'bout no contract," said Elroy. "You got a barrel of hate down there and you're giving it space and a voice. There been stories about Klan papers circulatin' through the shipyard for years, too. Nobody up here ever tracked those down. Now you let this Quitewhite shit pollute the whole place, and that ain't no rumor. Don't sit right with us and I don't think it's gonna set real well in the community."

Shea added, "We still got the numbers of those reporters from the pregnancy issue." He didn't mention his call to the *Globe* business reporter who'd cut him off just that morning saying, "We can't cover every sneeze in that shipyard."

The welders turned toward a scraping at the door. One of Hershfeld's assistants stuck his head past the jamb and looked the question at his boss from the hall.

Hershfeld shooed him away. "It's okay, I can handle it. These guys have only come to talk." He turned to the watching group of black welders. "Am I right?" Too late he heard the insult in his own words.

Elroy stood up and motioned the others. "Thanks for your time," he said to Hershfeld, "We'll see where we stand and decide if we need another talk or maybe something else. Maybe you gonna hear from us tomorrow."

*****

One of Hershfeld's labor reps called Shea the next morning. Together they toured the dugout underneath the Stiff Mill and the main bathroom closer to the boats, paying special attention to Quitewhite's artwork. That afternoon a small army of gray-helmeted cleaners spread over the yard with orders from Hershfeld to blast the graffiti, clean up and paint.

To Shea's surprise, Elroy put out a request to see him and held out his hand when he arrived. "My man, maybe it ain't so much. But it's the first crack I seen in this damn company in all my time here."

Shea took his hand. "You're wrong if you're saying that I'm the one that got this done. Congratulations to you and the guys."

The word spread among blacks and whites alike that the Stiff Mill bathroom and the shithouse close to the basins now boasted the cleanest break areas in the shipyard—and that the rest were on the cleaners' schedule. "Okay, we get it," Roach allowed. "You went in for a black issue and everybody made out. The shithouse is clean. You got lucky."

That evening, Patty waved at Shea with the fork she was using to scale a mess of sunnies. "Now look, Michael, far as I know this is the first time black people in this shipyard ever asked a white steward to join with them for anything." She fanned her hand against the greasy air in his kitchen. "Elroy didn't go to check it out with Charley Johnson first, neither. I give you a special little pat on the back for that later. For now, you give yourself one."

*****

From the bottom of the open circular cargo hold Shea heard a single clank above him and jerked his head up, scanning the top of the hold, ten stories up.

A foot-long shipfitter's wedge, looking from the distance like a ten pound tomahawk, arced end over end across the hold. The wedge bounced against an angled sidewall and changed direction, its graceful somersaults mesmerizing Shea—until he realized it had no predictable trajectory. The wedge accelerated as it flew down, clanking against the ever-changing angles of curved steel plate along its descent.

The wedge careened down the walls of the hold, rocketing madly from one sidewall to the next, faster with each clanging bounce, carving its own crazy path, impossible to duck, banging the sidewalls again and again, racing wildly toward the bottom. Shea searched frantically for cover. There was none. He dropped to the steel floor, squeezing his knees to his chest, fighting to stop the tremors that coursed through him. At last he looked up. The silence in the basin was its own terror.

From the far away out-of-sight deck, a voice called down, "Heads up, nigger lover!"

42

There was no sign on the door when Patty and Shea climbed the stairs to the Sunrise Club in Roxbury, but the smoky second floor was awash in black people wearing finer clothes than Shea had ever owned. Jewelry hung from the men and women alike. The men wore suits in an array of colors, most with widely spread collars. Shea knew he was underdressed and wished that Patty had warned him.

The floor was stuffed with draped card tables and cushion-seat folding chairs. Patty maneuvered toward the center of the room, Shea tagging close behind. He spotted a dozen or more shipyard workers among the hundreds of people at the club, though he had to look hard to recognize some of them through the camouflage of pressed suits and pomades.

The disguised hardhats nodded to him. Several extended a hand and said, "Hey, Shea, what's happenin'?" Elroy, Hicks and Sonny waved at him. Still, Shea had to fight an urge to whip around after he and Patty walked by. He was certain that unfriendly black faces would be staring at the two of them.

He said, "You sure you want to be seen here with me?"

"Hey, somebody don't like it, they can just leave. Simple as that." Patty watched him through slitted eyes. "Or maybe you don't want to be seen with me."

"Just checking," said Shea, more airily than he felt. "Let's go."

He started to move further into the room, then faced her. "This is a mistake." She stopped in her tracks, then reached her arms around his neck and pressed her forehead to his. As she spoke, she grazed her lips on his cheek.

"You know, this ain't like you a black man on the beach in South Boston, Michael," she said softly. "Black folks won't trash up their own club just to go after a white man."

Shea squirmed under the heat of her affection. "Why are you doing this?"

She backed off with an irritated pout. "I told you. I do what I want. Besides, what do you care? If there's heat here, I'm the one who's gonna take it. Just don't make me sorry."

Shea nodded.

Patty spotted Alice and Franklin. Alice's cocktail dress was cut low and scooped on the sides, revealing the curve of her breasts. Shea looked away.

He ordered a round for the table. When it came, they toasted and Patty smiled quietly as she tipped her glass to his, then to Alice and Franklin. She made a joke and laughed, tucking her head and placing long fingers over her mouth.

Shea looked past Patty to take in the room. And froze. Over her shoulder, sitting at a table with two women, Charley Johnson stared directly at him.

Shea excused himself and took a lonely, conspicuous walk across the floor to the superintendent's table. He stuck out his hand. Johnson took it stiffly.

"Didn't know you did clubs," Shea said.

Johnson smiled tightly. "This is my territory, not yours." He didn't introduce the women. "I see you brought company from the black side of the yard. Course I knew about that already, but I thought you'd be more discrete. I been tryin' to figure out how to deal with you, but you make it easy. This is gonna be all over the yard by Monday. There's a hundred

196

people in this room itchin' to say it out loud. And she's not gonna win you many white votes, either."

"Well," Shea said uncomfortably, "have a nice evening." He was pretty sure Johnson hadn't really known about Patty—why would he have kept it quiet until now? But he hadn't considered what Johnson might do with a secret that he and Patty had kept from the white yard.

Johnson said, "You make some interesting choices. But not smart ones."

Shea said, "I'll keep that in mind."

Patty watched Shea return to their table. "You don't need to mix it up with him in here."

"No, I don't." He was trembling and so dry that his throat hurt. He picked up his drink and drained it.

"Now you're talkin'." Patty put her hand in the air for the waiter. "Nother one on the way." She turned full-on to Shea. "You need to understand. Nobody likes Charley Johnson for what he does in that shipyard, but sometimes he's the only one can pull out a favor that any white guy can get in dozens of places. Now, Charley is always out for Charley and we all know that. But he belongs here, too, in a different way."

Shea said, "Okay, I get it. I guess. Tell me why we came if you thought he might be here."

"Don't worry, Michael. If he makes trouble on the outside with anything he sees in here he won't get back in again. He understands that."

"He much as told me he's gonna spread this around. Us. You're saying he won't make trouble for you just to get at me?"

Patty shook her head. "That's not how it works this end of town. He's tryin' to scare you, put you in your place."

Their drinks arrived. Shea was more than a little woozy when a few minutes later a heavy hand gripped his shoulder from behind.

His anxieties about the club flooded back. Without moving his head, he darted his eyes around the big room, searching for an exit. He steeled himself and turned.

With relief he saw it was Cotty. The old man was cologned up and wearing a sports jacket over an open lavender shirt. His stubby fingers tightened on Shea's shoulder.

"Glad you here, boy," Cotty said, looking around the table. "Scuse me, nice to see you, Miss Patricia. Miss Alice."

Cotty guided Shea a few feet from the table. "Shea, what you doin' about Pretty Boy?"

"I don't know what you're talking about."

"He been fired. That motherfucker Pody walked him out last night. Same one what got me before on suspension. They say Pretty Boy was sleepin', Shea! He sleep all day long, you know that. Not on the job!"

Shea tried to focus through the liquor. "He have a bad night?" He knew immediately it was the wrong thing to say.

Cotty drew himself up rigidly and gripped Shea's elbow. His fingers dug in painfully. "I ain't asked him. He told me he wasn't asleep and that's good enough. And what if he was? White guys get away with that shit all the time. Man, when I was on third shift, Pody actually invite his white boys up to his office for a nap."

Cotty relaxed his grip. "If Pretty Boy lose this job, he gone to the gutter. This job is the only shot he's ever gonna have."

Patty tugged at Shea's elbow.

"Cotty, you leave my man alone, now. I brought him to party, you just let him be. I'll see that he calls you tomorrow."

Cotty looked at them both balefully. "We been behind you, Shea, and we been trusting you. You know Pretty Boy's like my own son. Don't you let me down."

43

Pretty Boy hugged a double shot of ginger brandy, straight up. Shea told him that he looked as though he had aged two years in two days.

Pretty Boy said, "My momma's been cryin' all weekend. I can't get her to stop."

His story was plain. Eight months ago he was transferred from the boats into the Turret Shop, where the crews were gearing up to assemble smaller units and load them onto number 42 boat. At first Pretty Boy was glad for the break from the tanks—out of the stale air, out of the rain. But he soon realized that the wide-open floor was a whitehat's paradise. His new foreman, Ned, leaned on the balcony perch in front of the second floor office, easily picking out slackers with no need to move his own butt. It was a different sort of game with fewer places to hide. Pretty Boy no longer thought of it as a break. In a way, he wished for the end of the push so he could get back to the boats, but no luck. Even after 42 boat had floated under the Goliath, the last stop before leaving the shipyard, they didn't let him out of the shop.

"Now ain't that a bitch?" he asked Shea. "Who would've thought the boats would ever look good?"

Towards midnight on Tuesday, Ned asked Pretty Boy about working over an extra half shift. Pretty Boy wanted the money but he had to decline; there was no way for him to get home at four in the morning. He thought he might be able to hook up a ride for the following evening if Ned kept the offer open. Ned moaned that all his welders knew how to do was to fuck him. Pretty Boy saw through his act and waited him out. In the end, Ned agreed.

On Friday night, third shift trickled in a few minutes before eleven to begin its first hour of welding while second shift was still winding down. That last hour overlap between the two night shifts was always clumsy, with second still working and third pretty much hanging around until the whistle. There was always an opportunity for the shifts to exchange scuttlebutt. Tonight, Pretty Boy learned before his shift started that Pody, the graveyard boss, needed a man in the chain locker.

Pody had a reputation among black welders, so Pretty Boy knew right then he was in for a bad night. He considered tracking down Ned and begging off, then realized it was pretty late to cancel out on the guy. And Ned was fair as whitehats went, so why fuck him up?

Pretty Boy looked across the shop floor at the chain locker—a long low alley sealed off at the far end, not even knee-high, almost too tight for an air sucker and a welder to fit. Built to reel in and store the ship's anchor chain. Shit job if there ever was one.

Pretty Boy knew some whitehats would put their lowest seniority man in there. A few of the better ones, like Ned or Timmy Bronsan, might even try to figure out which guys had their fill of bad jobs for the month. On the other hand, it was crystal clear to Pretty Boy—like he told Cotty—that a cracker whitehat like Pody would solve it by sticking a black man in the hole.

Pretty Boy had watched the unit sit in the shop for three, maybe four months, just taking up space. He had never once seen a wisp of smoke anywhere near it or watched a welding line snake into the unit.

The chain locker had languished patiently in the corner of the shop waiting for some planner to notice it. Marty Farrell had painted bright yellow numbers on its side that clearly marked it as a wayward piece of 42 hull, long after the boat itself had floated under the Goliath. The chain locker would just sit in the shop until the time was ripe. Or later.

Pretty Boy had even joked about the unit with the guys. "One day they'll remember it's here. Damn boat be hoistin' up anchor and some whitehat gonna say, 'Shit, no place to haul this anchor into! Some motherfucker forgot the chain locker!' Then some poor ass welder gets pushed inside with no sucker, no air. Maybe me."

And sure enough, Friday night the unit was suddenly hot. The planners had barged into the Turret Shop during second shift and sniffed around, then took off without a word. They returned before midnight with their clipboards waving and Pete Rosa trailing after them. It was Pretty Boy's bad luck that they found it just before the only third shift that he had decided to work over all year, the only black guy welding for Pody that night.

"He comes up to me, Pody does, and he says 'Get in there, that job's too nasty for any white man'." Pretty Boy drew back at Shea's startled expression. "Don't look at me funny, Shea. I swear to God, that's what he said. Everybody knows Pody's like that. You don't recall hearin' Cotty talk about how Pody walked him out just for sassin' his ass?"

"Yeah, he just reminded me about that," Shea said. Cotty had first complained about Pody back when Shea was on nights. Pody had been a cherry whitehat back then.

Cotty had been stashing his street clothes in his toolbox just before the whistle along with his copies of *Muhammed Speaks* and the *Bay State Banner*. Even after spotting the papers, Pody had only given him the evil eye. But before the night was out he issued the old man a warning slip for low production and then, when Cotty disputed it, Pody walked him out.

When he returned from suspension, Cotty went straight to the War Room, hopeful that the yard's only black superintendent would jump on the problem.

Charley Johnson said he sympathized. It was too bad things had got so far out of hand. He settled the problem by moving Cotty to another crew.

Cotty never forgave him. "That man just put there by white trash to front for more white trash." And whenever Pody's name arose in any context, Cotty savaged him, too. Over the years, he systematically collected tidbits of Pody's racial slurs and bad treatment. "Sooner or later," Cotty would say, "gonna sweep out the garbage."

Pretty Boy knew all that about Pody, but it wasn't in his nature to rise to a fight he could avoid. So he pulled his welding gun and gas line over to the chain locker. He dragged the big spool of wire from the unit he had worked during second shift.

He peered into the long low alley of his new job assignment. No portholes, no vents. The electricians hadn't even considered crawling inside to string up a line of bulbs. Just wasn't no room. And as he predicted, there was no sucker. He yelled out to Pody.

The whitehat yelled back across the shop floor. "Sure, sometime tonight. Now get moving."

Pretty Boy groped through the deep gray interior of the unit by the beam of his flashlight. Once he positioned himself at the job, he jerked his head to bring the shield down over his face. The hiss from the gas line was steady and the wire flow smooth. Pretty Boy's outstretched arms ached. He arched to extend the flow of his puddle until muscle fatigue won out. He was almost done with the worst.

"That was it," he told Shea.

"Whattya mean, 'That was it'?"

"I mean the next thing I know, Pody's flashlight is shinin' in on me, and it's the only light in the locker so maybe I was between arcs. 'Hey welder', Pody says real loud, 'You asleep!' And then he says, 'Caught that nigger in the woodpile.' Somethin' like that."

"You didn't deny it?"

"Look, I'll say what I gotta say to get back my job. Truth is, I don't know what happened. I felt okay goin' in. Pody surprised me. I jumped when he yelled in that unit. I don't remember nothing before that flashlight hit my eyes. Maybe I *was* asleep."

Shea said, "Don't say that again." He dug into his bag and came up with a copy of Pody's report. The whitehat claimed to have come upon Pretty Boy around one AM, almost two hours after the welder had crawled into the chain locker. His eyes had been closed.

"He says your shield was off. Said he could see your eyes."

"No way. Last I remember I was welding. How could my shield be off?"

"Luther, if you were welding, how could he have looked past the arc?"

Pretty Boy considered his brandy. "So maybe I wasn't welding when the flashlight caught me. But my shield was on. It was hot as hell in there, too much trouble to get that thing on and off."

"This isn't good."

"Man's a racist. What about what he said to me?"

"I'll work with that, too. But we gotta find something to go with. Maybe a witness sayin' Pody was after you. Just calling him names won't help you right now."

"Fuck the witness. You think Pody's stupid? And I know what he said." Pretty Boy threw back the gold-colored brandy and slapped his glass on the table. "I can't tell you what happened in there. But I don't sleep on the job."

Shea said, "I know you don't."

*****

In the grievance room, Salvucci let Shea have it. "You got nothin'. Take this shit outta the system or I will."

Shea chewed unhappily on his mustache.

"You know what?" Salvucci said. "You got a sleeper guilty as hell and instead of suckin' a little dick to get him back all you can do is claim it's racial. If you can't fix it in the yard, then leave it in the grievance process and I'll make sure it dies."

"Just bring in Hershfeld," Shea demanded. "Maybe you should duke it out with the fuckin' company for once, not me."

*****

Shea started as soon as Hershfeld sat down. "You got a foreman out to nail black people. You let that graffiti poison this place for years before you got convinced to do something about it. Somebody like Pody feeds on that."

"We manage the shipyard and we do it within the contract and the law."

"What about Gimple? You brought him back."

"We have a hangman's letter on Gimple. You're the one that signed it. You can't raise that case here."

After the meeting, Rashford pulled Shea aside. "They're right, you got nothin'."

"That's just what I'd expect from you."

"You listen to me, you little fuck. So Pody don't like colored guys, what else is new? Stop whining. Strike a deal or your welder is gone. Otherwise you'll wait two years and still lose, even if we take it as far as arbitration."

Shea hung his head. "Hershfeld won't deal, not even a hangman's letter. And Pretty Boy can't wait for arbitration to pay his mom's rent." Shea heard himself making the same argument that Rashford had used to justify Gimple's hangman's letter.

Rashford repeated, "Just put it in the system and move on."

"This whitehat's bad news."

"You haven't shown it. If you want to waste time on this, make your case."

Shea said, "I will."

44

Shea found Elroy Washington at his job in the Stiff Mill, watching a row of synchronized torches track the gap between long L-fitted plates and fuse them.

"You heard Pretty Boy got fired the other night."

Elroy nodded. "I heard. Pody done it." He pulled a hand towel from a bar on the machine and patted down his face. The automatic welder's multiple arcs jogged along overhead tracks, hissing above the rumble of its casing.

"There's some thought that he isn't so crazy about black welders. I need to round up the stories."

"That's Cotty's department. He been out for Pody for some time."

"I also thought it might help if we could pull together a bunch of the guys for another visit to the front office."

Elroy frowned. "Look, man, this is about some kid probably been out to party, then fall asleep. Goin' up front on that graffiti was righteous. This ain't that. This 'bout some kid take a nap and get caught by the wrong guy." He wrapped the towel around his hands. "You want me to put my job on the line again, you show me a reason."

"This is a black kid who got nailed by a whitehat looking for a reason. Plus, Pody made some comments."

"If I worry about all the *comments* around here, as you call 'em, I got no time to work. You tryin' to make this into my fight and you ain't havin' no luck, Shea. Sorry."

"Listen to yourself—this is a good kid! I've known him since I walked into this shipyard. You talk to Cotty when he comes by this afternoon. He knows Pretty Boy. And he told me Pody lets the white guys on his crew get away with shit all the time."

Elroy knitted his brows like Shea was a crazy man.

"I don't doubt that, Shea. But if that's the issue you don't need no damn kid and his sleeping case to get started. And don't you go lecturing me!" He tossed his towel onto a toolbox and slowly made his way back around the automatic welder, his eyes on the torches once again. Suddenly he wheeled and gestured at the hissing machine.

"This thing cost more than a million dollars, man. They put me to handle it. *Me*. In this shop. Clean. No damn tanks. I get fifty cent an hour bonus and I earn it, too, do 'em a fine job. Charley Johnson the one got me in here. And you want me to go after his whitehats? Shee-it." Elroy swung his head emphatically from side to side. "Unh-uh."

*****

The story made Patty wince when Shea told her. "Those chuckleheads want to see a smokin' gun. Makes their asses feel safer if they can tell themselves there ain't no real problem."

"I didn't think he'd be so worried about calling out discrimination, even if he thinks the case isn't perfect."

"On the outside is one thing. In here it's their jobs." Patty considered for a moment. "You talk to Charley Johnson?"

"Not yet. I guess I need to."

"He got a real hold over some of these fellas. Leastways might help educate you to it."

*****

Johnson ushered Shea into his office with a big wave. He sobered quickly when Pody's name came up. "I take it personally when you tell me I tolerate a racist foreman in my department."

"I thought you might. That's why I'm bringing it to your attention."

Johnson worked up a game face. "Not a single black welder has complained about Pody in three years. Last one was Cottaway, and I took care of his problem."

"You mean you transferred him. Seems like that didn't take care of anything."

"No one's been back to me about Pody since. Not the union. And no black welders. I call that solved."

"You know there isn't a black welder in the yard would've gone to Charney or Rashford on this. And you're management. Why would they come to you?"

Johnson leaned back and clasped his hands in front of his stomach. His scowl gave way to a genuine smile.

"If you don't understand that, I got less to worry about with you than I thought."

"How's that?"

"When a black guy in this department is in trouble, who do you think he's gonna look for, you or me?"

"Black welders supported me, voted me in."

Johnson smiled. "Sure they did. You say all the right things. You might even mean some of them. But when those guys really want something done, they come to this office, and they'll keep on doing it as long as I'm in this chair. They don't tell you that, right? I look out for them and they know it."

Shea started to protest, but Johnson cut in. "Don't get me wrong. You want to make an issue of Pody, stir things up for Hershfeld, more power to you. Elroy's been here about

Pody and Pretty Boy, and I already told him to do what he wants."

Shea reddened at the news.

Johnson said, "Didn't know he beat you in, did you?"

"So why don't you care if Elroy makes a stink about Pody?"

"Cause then Hershfeld comes running and asks me to please get the black guys back in line." Johnson thumbed his own chest. "He comes to *me*." He put on his whitehat and rose. "That's all I got time for."

*****

On Rashford's orders, Salvucci and Charney charged around the yard accusing Shea of playing politics with the race issue.

Roach came back from the shithouse with worried, sour reports. "They're sayin' you only care about the blacks, that it's a payoff for the election."

"That's just Rashford's best line."

"I didn't hear it from him, it's the guys. Not sayin' they're right."

Roach had vaguely heard about Pody, too, though he hadn't given it much thought. "Guy's a redneck, whaddya expect? Anyways, you're not winnin' many friends."

"I'm not here to win friends," Shea said, though he felt like he could have used some. Pretty Boy was still on the street, and Shea was no closer to getting him back on the job.

45

Cotty pushed his way down the bus aisle and tore past the others, his scalp hot and furious as he made his way through the yard. He'd preached the old saw many times; whatever a black man won in life he owed to those who had come before him. Today it felt like those guys were weighing him down.

He huffed as he ran toward the Stiff Mill, searching for Shea.

Shea spotted Cotty from inside the mill. The old man was jogging over from the time clocks, waving a piece of paper and stamping his feet on the platen.

"Get over here, you lying motherfucker! What you call this?" Cotty held out the paper to Shea, shaking with anger.

Shea took the sheet and his heart sank. It was a copy of Gimple's hangman's letter.

"That your signature down the bottom?" Cotty demanded.

"Where did you get this?" Shea asked.

"Why you pretending 'bout Pretty Boy? You already killed his case, signed away on this white boy."

"This happened on my first day, Cotty. Rashford cornered me into it."

"That so? You think I'm stupid? I don't see no Rashford on this damn paper!"

"He made it sound like..." Shea dropped off. There was no convincing way to describe the pressure he had felt in the front office cubicle on that first day as steward. "I'm sorry it happened. I've been killing myself trying to get Pretty Boy's job back, but I can't use this at an arbitration—says so right in the letter."

"Now you listen to me," Cotty shot back. "This Gimple got caught sleeping, like they say Pretty Boy done. He gets brought back. Pretty Boy gets fired and can't get back in. And now I find out some other white kid got caught nappin' in the same damn unit as Pretty Boy, and *he* come back to work, too! And you can't do nothing to help my boy? Shit!"

The news was rushing by too quickly for Shea. "Whoa, Cotty. Another guy was caught in the same unit as Pretty Boy?"

Spittle agitated at the corners of the old man's mouth. "How can you not know that? A couple years ago, on number 41 hull. Before you start as the steward. Right in the chain locker before it move to the basin, exactly like now. You supposed to be on this stuff, boy!"

Shea reached out for Cotty's biceps to calm him. The old man wrenched away.

Shea said, "Look, Gimple's case was already settled when I got up front. The letter was all written. Rashford worked out the deal and I was just told to sign this." He pointed to the memo in Cotty's hand.

"Agh!" Cotty snapped his hand in the air. "Now you do what they tell you? And what about this other guy? Sleeping in the same unit they nailed Pretty Boy!"

"I swear, Cotty, I know nuthin' about it." Shea knew the record would have been in the grievance files that Charney had never turned over. "You got this welder's name?"

Cotty pulled a scrap of paper from his pocket. "Vince Cardinale. Italian fella. Some surprise he got his job back, hunh?"

"How do you know about this?"

Cotty said, "I know. That's all."

"Who gave you this stuff?"

Cotty's eyes flashed. "Maybe I heard about it on the boats when it happen and I just now remember. Question is, what kind of half-ass looking you been doin' that you don't know about it?"

"Cotty, nobody told me about this guy or anybody else that was caught in the chain locker. There was no way I could follow up."

Cotty stepped back, heaving. Shea saw tears in his eyes. The old man squeezed the balled-up piece of paper in his hand, drew back and threw it. It hit Shea's hard hat just above the brim and dropped at his feet. "My boy dyin' on the street, fella. *Dying*! Either you tellin' me you turned on him or you stupid. You pick which. Ain't no never-mind to him or to me!"

Cotty looked down at his watch. His wrist trembled. He drew the watch up to his face to read it. He wiped his eyes and when he looked at Shea again, they were dark with pain.

Shea wondered how everyone else knew so much more about this case. So many back channels from so many sides—how could he ever compete?

Cotty broke into his thoughts. "I gotta get to the boats, where the honest men work. They fire old niggers like me, we be late."

Shea watched his friend jog slowly, almost painfully, all the way to the superstructure. Cotty's lookin' old, he thought sadly. He can't take the boats much longer.

46

Shea stood behind the deckhouse on 42 hull and stared at the chain locker. The cut-out entrance that Pretty Boy had crawled into was still unsealed. He jotted down the dimensions of the locker and the access hole. He kneeled and looked down the alley inside. No light and bad air. He put his satchel on top of the unit and crawled in, working his way to the end of the tunnel. He tried to turn around but the chain locker walls were too tight. He inched his way out backward. Splinters of slag cut at his knees.

He crossed the yard to the Turret Shop and stopped at the double doors. The steel-on-steel clatter of a pneumatic air chisel deafened the work floor. Shea let a transporter crawl by with a unit, then looked around the shop. He reached into his pocket for a pair of yellow foam plugs and crushed them into his ears. They barely muffled the noise.

He spotted a whitehat on the work floor and ambled over to check in. The whitehat looked at his pass and pulled Shea close against the jackhammer bursts from the chisel, then pointed to a far corner. His mouth pressed at Shea's ear. "On the deckhouse unit!" he screamed.

Shea climbed onto the deckhouse and felt his way over a dozen loose planks. Although it hardly seemed possible, the air chisel's fearsome rattle intensified.

He watched a welder strike an arc and hunkered down next to him, looking away from the glare. He waited until the guy released the trigger of his gun and lifted his shield to inspect his work.

"Vince Cardinale?" Shea tapped the welder's shoulder and yelled the name when he turned.

The welder pulled off his shield and nodded emphatically. He held up a gloved hand, then ducked inside the unit. The racket ceased and the welder reappeared a moment later. Shea realized that he had gone to tell the chipper to take a break.

"Yep," Cardinale picked up the conversation. "That's me. And what an honor. Our steward."

Shea said, "How's it goin'?"

Cardinale adjusted his glasses. "No new trouble."

"Look, I got a sleeping case. Story's similar to yours."

The welder nodded. "Yeah, I heard. Sounds tough. You got that guy Gimple back to work, didn't you?" He paused. "Not much I can do to help."

"Why's that?"

"The letter. Charney told me I couldn't ever testify on what happened if I signed it."

Shea suddenly deflated. "Charney set you up with a hangman's letter?"

Cardinale nodded. "That's what he called it. I was out thirty days on suspension for sleepin' on the job." He sighed at the memory. "Worst day of my life, gettin' sent out of the mill to the boat and that chain locker."

"Yeah, it's a different world."

"Especially draggin' that goddamn auto welding gun around."

Shea frowned. "I thought this happened almost two years ago."

"Yeah."

"You had a gun on the boats back then?"

Cardinale nodded. "I was good with it in the shop and they were beginning to test it on the boats. That's why they sent me out to the basin in the first place. You know, before they gave it out to everybody. Didn't even have the gas manifolds set up. On top of the spool I had to pull the fuckin' cylinder with me everywhere I went."

An idea stirred in Shea's head. "You were using the gun that day?"

Vince nodded. "Sure. Every day." He reflected. "Y'know, I could never understand it, fallin' asleep and all. I was feelin' pretty good at the time."

"Maybe there's another way you can help me, Vince. The day you got walked out—did you have an air sucker in the chain locker?"

Vince gestured to the job in front of him. "Nah. Like here. I don't like to wait around for that shit. Besides, get a sucker too close on the gun and it fucks up the weld. You know, messes with the gas shield the gun throws around it."

Shea's heart skipped. "You're certain? When you fell asleep there wasn't a sucker on the job?"

"No. Definitely not."

"Let me ask you something. Your job's safe now. If I ask you to testify to what you just told me and help get the guy back, would you do it?"

Cardindale said, "I'd like to, but I gotta think about it. They could come for me again, with the letter and all. Just make somethin' up."

Shea nodded. "Well, think it over. It would mean a lot. I'll come by again in a couple days."

*****

As soon as he got back to the mill, Shea used Timmy's phone to dial Pretty Boy. When his mom answered, Shea

215

identified himself and was immediately sorry. The woman wouldn't let him go. She assured Shea a dozen times that Luther was a good boy, a hard working boy. Shea had no answers for her questions, and still fewer when her voice began to quaver and weep through the phone. Finally, she composed herself and begged his pardon, then continued in a clear, firm voice. Her boy Luther was out on the street. He never, never hung out on the street before this all happened. She would have him call Shea the instant he got home.

When Pretty Boy did call, Shea couldn't tell if he was drunk or just high. He decided to keep it short.

"Did you come out of the chain locker at all once you were in?"

Pretty Boy's tone was close to a growl. "I told you. It was a motherfucker in there. I just stayed and burned wire to get it done."

"With no sucker. And the gun."

"Already told you that, too."

"Did you know that some guy on days fell asleep in the chain locker on Number 41, maybe a couple of years ago?"

There was a silence. "He get back?" Pretty Boy asked.

"Yeah," Shea said. "We can't use that. But he gave us something else."

*****

He spent the next evening buried in the library at Copley Square, reading up on metal inert gases. At the end of the night he gave up on finding a way to convincingly present his theory to Hershfeld on his own. He called Lonny, who leafed through her address book and came up with a cousin who was taking a chemistry course at UMass Dorchester. Lonny thought that she might be willing to do some research.

216

A few days later, Lonny brought Shea a sheaf of paper. Her cousin knew a teaching assistant who was eager to get in her pants. She had convinced him to review the research and print an analysis on UMass letterhead.

"I think I got it," Shea told Pretty Boy that afternoon. "The guns are shielded with gas that gives off monoxide at the weld. In a closed area like the chain locker, the gas eats enough air to put somebody to sleep pretty quick." He handed Pretty Boy some photocopies. "I think we got something here that's gonna get you back, Luther. With pay!"

Pretty Boy scanned the pages. "I guess maybe you are. Too late for that poor guy Cardinale with the letter, though. Gimple, too. Signed away their money. You can let Charney explain that."

"Maybe I would have found out about this earlier if Charney had bothered to tell me about Cardinale."

*****

Shea walked the UMass report over to Hershfeld and left a note asking for an oxygen test in the chain locker. An hour later, Timmy called him over to the phone in the Stiff. Hershfeld was on the line.

"The chain locker unit's already aboard ship and completed," he told Shea. "Too late."

"I was just out there," Shea protested. "There's plenty of welding left inside to seal up. Enough to monitor for oxygen. I wouldn't refuse to test it if I were you, Irv. We got proof it could happen and you're not gonna even check it out?"

There was a silence. "I'll run the test," Hershfeld said finally. "Just don't count on it meaning anything."

Shea pressed the next day. "What about the test?"

"There's some question about the results."

217

"Bullshit," said Shea. "You're just making the end of this worse for yourself."

Lonny put together an *829 News* calling for a welding department rally across from the gate. The welders gathered at dinner in front of the grassy knoll opposite Ziyad's. Shea stood on the rise with Luther, Cotty, Lonny and a visibly nervous Vince Cardinale. A *Patriot Ledger* photographer snapped the picture of the five of them for the next morning's paper.

Shea picked up a bullhorn and faced the crowd of about seventy-five, mostly black welders.

"Here's what's wrong in this yard. Two white welders get fired and blackmailed into silence for their jobs. A third one, black, with an unblemished record, is fired for the same supposed offense and the company refuses to budge."

"Ain't right!" someone called.

"But not one of the three welders should have lost a minute of pay, much less their jobs. And why? Because you *can't breathe carbon monoxide*! They are all victims of this company's core value: Production over safety! And now that we know the truth, the guys with the hangman's letters still won't get their lost pay—because of a lazy solution pushed on them by some of our own union leaders!"

To shouts of support Shea continued, "I'm proud that we're gonna win it for Pretty Boy with the help of Vince Cardinale, one of the victims of this whole mess!" He reached over to Vince and held up his arm.

Cotty had come in early for the rally. "Look at us! This is the unity we need!" The crowd clapped and whistled.

On the far side of the street, surrounded by a clump of markers and pipe welders, Farrell grimaced. "Guess he's not gonna try to get any money for the white guys. See if they offer anymore of those letters to save somebody's job."

Next to him in his orange burner's hat, Frank Salvucci scribbled notes on a pad. "Public attack on the union."

*****

"Alright," Hershfeld said. "We'll give the employee the benefit of the doubt and bring him back."

"What about his money?"

"Don't push it."

"You'll pay ten times as much to your lawyers and still pay Luther in the end. Why stall the inevitable?"

"We win more arbitrations than we lose."

"Really? When we have a paper from a major university that says you're wrong?"

Hershfeld took a breath. He said, "Alright, I'll pay. If you agree that I don't see it again in that damn newsletter of yours."

"You're doing the right thing, Irv. Doesn't it feel good?"

*****

Cotty's reviews were grudging. "Sure, I'm happy my boy's gettin' back. The way I see it, though, you near cost Pretty Boy his job to save a white man who done the same thing. That's not what you supposed to be about."

"No, Cotty, it's not. But this turns out to be about gas, not Pody. And I think at least some of the guys got the message."

"Yeah, I heard what you said yesterday. But every time you turn around in this place, some Pody gonna be out there messin' with people. Ain't no accident that Pretty Boy was the one put in there in the first place, any more than he be the only one they didn't offer that hangman letter. No different than keepin' us off of the pipe crews, giving us the shittiest jobs every night, keepin' us outta the shop trades."

Even Charley Johnson seemed satisfied to sign off on the grievance and get Pretty Boy back to work. "The man needed a sucker and went in without it, no skin off my nose." Then he looked hard at Shea. "Don't ever try and make me look bad in front of my black welders or I'll go after you with everything I got."

It finally occurred to Shea that Rashford wasn't the only one who could have leaked Gimple's hangman's letter or the file on Cardinale's case to Cotty.

*****

Shea leaned over Patty and pulled their chaise close to the grill for warmth. Though the evenings were brisk, he insisted on stretching the barbecue season out on his postage stamp deck. Ozzie and his family next door had long since disappeared inside for the winter.

They traded a joint back and forth, toking while he recounted his conversations with Cotty and Charley Johnson.

Patty sucked on the joint and exhaled. "You really won something and I'm telling you right now it don't make no difference. They done already forgot."

"You're a real picker-upper."

"Look," Patty said gently. "Sometime somethin' else gonna come up on Pody. When it does, they gonna blame you for not finding it sooner. 'Til then, they gonna go back to Charley Johnson. So just be prepared." She toked again.

"Hey, don't eat the damn thing!" Shea feinted at her playfully and grabbed for the joint. She pulled it away and sucked greedily, choking on her own laughter.

"You listen to me, will you? That's just the way poor folks are."

47

"Hey, black girl, you scared of us? Come on in and have a drink. We can be real friendly when we want."

Patty crossed the street to avoid the clump of drunk white guys in front of the bar just opposite Dakota Street.

"Don't get rude with me, you black bitch!" The guy threw a bottle that crashed at Patty's feet. Her back stiffened with fury. Fear quickened her pace. The drunk staggered into the street but was too far gone to follow.

She burst into Shea's house. "I'm driving to the Bradlees next time I got something to buy. No more walking 'til this place gets cleaned up!"

Shea said, "I'm gonna go talk with them right now." Patty blew out an exasperated breath. "You lookin' to get really hurt? You the white guy gonna run out and defend my honor? I don't want you dead."

It wasn't just Patty. During the previous month, the visceral bitterness emanating from the bar across Geneva Avenue from Shea's house had intensified. Weekend nights and not a few weekdays had become a nightmare of screams, drunken fights and sidewalk provocations, many of them directed against the largely Puerto Rican residents of the apartment buildings around the corner on Josephine Street. There were a number of clashes and more than one neighborhood kid was hurt. A thirteen-year-old boy was slashed up after jumping to the defense of his older sister. From his backyard Shea could hear the angry meetings at the neighborhood's storefront Pentecostal church. "We need to take action ourselves! The cops don't do shit!"

After weeks of increasing tension, Shea woke up with a start in the middle of the night. The air smelled darkly of smoke. He got up and ran through rooms until he was satisfied the source was outside. He threw on a pair of jeans and walked the half block to Geneva Ave. The bar was in flames. Smoke from the ashes choked the spring air.

Shea stood in the swirling red fire engine lights and watched chunks of ash glow in the rubble. The apartment buildings on Josephine Street had emptied onto the curb, where their residents conversed festively in Spanish. Entire families seemed to be out on the street, some watching while others danced in couples or with children. Around the fringes of the crowd, strings of firecrackers celebrated the death of the bar. *"Ha estado ardiendo durante una hora,"* someone sang tunelessly.

Shea supposed if there had to be one more vacant lot in the neighborhood, this was the right place to make the room.

In front of the smoldering wood frame, Shea surveyed the neighborhood. It was not improving as he had hoped. Here and there a business started and failed, apartments were fixed and then left to deteriorate. There were plenty of attempts, but it was a neighborhood with too few paying customers.

There was a bulky movement toward him. A familiar face stood before Shea with his arms folded in front of his chest.

"Hey," the man said in heavily accented English. "Been a while since I see you."

Shea recognized Ramos, the big Puerto Rican welder who'd calmed Lonny and Townsend at the union hall. Though he and Shea waved when they passed in the yard,

Ramos had never called him on a grievance and they'd never spoken at length.

"Yeah," Shea said. "Nice to see you."

Ramos held out his hand. "So now you the union guy. Congratulations."

"Thanks. You live around here?"

"Yeah. Long time now."

"Funny I haven't seen you around." Shea pointed toward the ruins. "This was quite a fire. Fast. Almost like they set it for the insurance money."

Ramos' face was studiously blank.

"You know," said Shea. "Insurance. Or a kitchen fire? Maybe one of their fights inside got outta hand?"

Ramos tilted his head. "They say in the shipyard you a smart man. The trash in that bar no burn their own place. *Claro*? You make a joke, right?"

"So what then?"

Ramos shook his head. "Man, you live around here. The guys in that bar only want us to know that they still own this area. For a long time we ignore them, no matter how much problems they make. That's the extra cost to live here with some peace. Now the cost to live with them is too high."

Shea said, "I guess."

"We want quiet and this trash gets in the way. Where else can we go? We ignore their smaller trouble, but no one can accept the way they act now. Cost is too high, kids hurt, not worth staying quiet. So somebody send this message. Now we will see. I think maybe this message is pretty clear, no?"

"Agreed. Pretty clear. You didn't call the cops to sort it out?"

Ramos snorted. "You mean the same cops what grew up with this trash? That ignore their *asaltos* every day? Really?

Like I say, only these guys in the bar have the power to give us some peace.

"The shipyard is the same, no? The company gives us money. We trade our work for nasty boss, everyday stuff we ignore because this is the only place with a job and pay like this. But sometimes people there have enough and also send messages. Like that girl willing to work with smoke but not to hurt her baby. Or the black guys that ignore that they get the shit jobs, but not that they got to piss with that Quitewhite in their face. You went with them. I heard."

Shea said, "You got a lot goin' on in that head of yours, you know that?"

"Sometimes the message is confused by white guys," Ramos went on. "Maybe one is more qualified but Charley Johnson gives a pipe job to another with a connection to some big union man. Then the more qualified guy tells himself that his real problem is not this connection thing but the big Puerto Rican, or the blacks or the *comunistas*. That's bad for him and for us. Of course, the white guy he don't see that."

Shea said, "You know a welder named Elijah Cottaway on nights? Old black guy? He talks about stuff the same way as you, calls it a color tax."

Ramos shook his head. "I read these ideas in *Claridad*, the Spanish newspaper. *Claridad* calls this monopoly rent, like the game."

Ramos brightened. "Maybe you come to my *futbol* club sometime, yes?" He waved at a storefront down the street with a sign hanging over the door that said Club Sport. "We try to build here in spite of this trash. Now it will be more easy."

Shea smiled apologetically. "I'm not much of a football player."

Ramos hit Shea playfully on the arm, jarring him slightly off balance, "Not football like you know. Soccer *futbol*... That's okay. We watch, have some beers. It is my club."

Ramos walked off toward the crowd of onlookers. Two small dark-haired children broke away from a woman on the curb and ran into his arms. Ramos swept them up in a single motion and kissed each of them on the cheek.

"Don't forget!" he called back to Shea, "The Club Sport."

48

"How 'bout a little company?" a male voice asked.

Magdalena turned her face up to the stranger. One of the white kids from the other side of the patio stood over her with a drink in his hand. She lowered her eyes and shook her head.

"No thank you," she murmured. She pointedly placed her ringed left hand on her root beer.

The kid sat down.

"So, you wanna go someplace?" His chair scraped against the cement patio until it almost touched hers. From her seat Magdalena could smell the alcohol on his breath.

She shook her head. "I read now, you see, then go to work."

The kid glared at her, then got up and stalked back to a table full of his friends.

Magdalena had only recently volunteered for third shift. She thought it was the best decision she had made in years.

When she'd been on first shift she had been persistently late to work and in trouble. But there was no possible way to deliver her kids to day care and then get to work by seven every day. At the three-thirty whistle she ran for the clock and beat a quick path to the parking lot ahead of the rush, then sped to the day care center. The welders she jostled on her way out marked her as the squat, curt, black one. An unfriendly image that her taciturn modesty and clipped Creole accent only reinforced to strangers.

Once she got home she settled the kids, poked over their day, exclaimed at their art work, made dinner, washed their dishes and then washed them, and finally got them both to bed after reading two story books aloud, one in halting English, one French. She concocted and packed the next day's lunch and set out the kids' clothes, put in the necessary loads of laundry. She felt herself weaken as the steam gushed from the iron.

By ten she could drop into bed. She set the alarm for midnight, giving herself a half hour to prepare before Pierre arrived home from second shift, muscle stiff and grumping about Fat Sal and unreasonable demands from the welders. For a vent man that no one really bothered, it seemed to Magdalena that Pierre complained an awful lot.

She stayed with him in the kitchen each night, leaning heavily on the worn formica counter, serving him food and beers in the cramped dinette while he talked at her. Afterward, there was maybe sex, maybe not, she could never tell in the first hour or two how tired he would be. And always the insults afterward. She could usually count on being back to sleep by two, cherishing the solid three hours until her day shift cycle started again.

Now that she had started working third shift, she put the kids to bed and then left for work before ten. Her aunt from upstairs checked on the kids and stayed until Pierre showed up. When Magdalena arrived home in the morning she took over from Pierre, who was just sleeping anyway. Then after the children awoke, she played with them before driving to the day care and then going to sleep herself.

Later, when Pierre returned from second shift, Magdalena was already gone and the kids tucked in bed— truly a change for the better.

Magdalena quickly realized that she could stretch her night shift premium pay to cover a babysitter one or two early evenings a week. On those nights, she tucked in the kids and drove toward Quincy a few hours early. Her aunt stopped in just as the sitter was cleaning up her traces. The aunt stayed until Pierre came home and he never knew the difference.

The first night she had driven in early, Magdalena pulled into one of the bay side parking slots at Wollaston Beach and turned her face to the cool nighttime breeze. The tables outside the patio bar on the boulevard reminded her of home, the pastel cafes on the ocean that had given her the feeling of being far from the desolation of Port au Prince when she was young. The illusion made her smile.

That first time at the Beachcomber, Magdalena scanned the patio facing the water and selected the table most distant from the others. The plastic top was tacky with the residue of sugary drinks and the chairs wobbled unevenly on the concrete.

She delved with slow concentration into a Harlequin romance while crowds of young white kids of both sexes drank seven and sevens and sized each other up. The young boys showed off pale white chests beneath shiny disco shirts and the girls tottered on bright leather mules, their painted toes edging the fronts of the soles. Magdalena sighed at their foolishness and returned to her book. She felt totally and peacefully alone.

The beach was addictive. She parked by the bay and sat at her Beachcomber table. She ordered root beers to odd looks from the pony-tailed waitress. A few hours later, she gathered her things and entered the shipyard gates to spend the night welding.

Her evenings at the Beachcomber relaxed her so wonderfully that even Pody's insulting attitude didn't bother her much. She could just ignore him until the night ended and she went home to her babies, shutting out Pody and the yard and Pierre.

*****

She tugged a light sweater around her shoulders and smiled at the nearby kids, then pulled out her paperback, the bookmark an inch into the book. She let it fall to her lap. She was pleased with her progress, no need to hurry. She closed her eyes and listened to the surf.

"Y'know," the kid was back, towering over her. "Reading's not what you're here for." He reached out unsteadily and cupped her breast.

Magdalena shot to her feet, upsetting her root beer. It soaked her leg and washed over the edge of the table, slopping onto the kid's disco shirt tail and pants.

A taunt floated over from someone in a kelly green jacket at one of the far tables. "Wet your pants over some black pussy?"

The kid snarled, "Shut up, Donny," and turned on Magdalena, "You some kind of whacko?" His friends chortled and egged him on with obscene gestures.

He darkened and pointed at her. "This beach ain't for niggers. Just pack it up." He shoved her harshly. She skittered backwards and fell. Her head snapped back and bounced off the concrete. The patio whirled about her, an ellipse of pain and confusion. Her book lay face down in a root beer puddle.

"I said get the fuck out!" The kid nudged her hard with his foot. He stood over her with his fists clenched.

Magdalena looked up and sobbed. She scratched for her purse and held up a bill.

"I am sorry to you," she choked between sobs. "My babies at home. Please do not hurt me." She looked around wildly and appealed to a face she seemed to recognize from the shipyard, a tall, stringy welder with a crooked nose and a green South Boston Marshall's jacket.

"Please," she begged him, "Please."

*****

In the two years since the strike, the pain had eased for Slidell. Some of the hardhats still gave him the silent treatment. So what? He had survived the worst of it when other strikebreakers had been driven out. Now he was a graded welder mechanic. Some of the guys he worked with these days didn't even know he had been a scab.

And not all the fallout was bad. The company was still concerned about retaliation, still kept the scabs pretty much out of sight, so Slidell rarely found himself assigned to a job in the tanks. And like the others, he had avoided the night shift no problem. That was a godsend. He could still count on evenings at home with his little girls. He had no regrets.

For the first time in months he had pulled some serious O.T. and wouldn't be reading his girls to sleep. He knew it was a little thing, and unavoidable; they needed the money. Still, it bothered him.

He was thinking about the twins when he leaned into the long curve of the beach boulevard by the sea wall.

He pulled in at the Greek place for fries and a coke. He slowed for the left hand turn into the lot, then noticed a crowd milling in front of the Beachcomber next door. He looked closer and saw a black woman on the ground. He recognized her without knowing her name. The Haitian girl. He watched a kid kick her and she cried out.

Weakness shot through Slidell's arms. He clutched at his steering wheel, pressing his head into the back of his hands, trying to think. He threw the car into reverse and readied to gun it back to the road.

He willed himself to stop and released the wheel. He beat his palms a single time against his head, then did it again and again. He shoved the stick into neutral, jammed down on the parking brake and turned off the car. He opened the door and reached under his seat for a short hardwood club he had stowed there since the strike.

The crowd saw him coming and opened. Magdalena threw up her hands and crossed them in front of her chest as if to ward him off.

"Go away!" she cried out. "They kill you!"

Her attacker turned around to face Slidell. "Awright!" he grinned. "A real nigger! Wicked mean lookin', too." The kid turned to the crowd and shook his head as if at a joke. "Shit, this is the last time I take a dare from you, Donny."

Then Slidell was on him. Donny stepped out of the crowd and motioned the others to give him some room, then whirled and kicked Slidell in the kidneys. Slidell fell to the concrete. The others waded in.

*****

Magdalena was more than two hours late to work. It had taken almost half that time for the ambulance to arrive and strap Slidell to the stretcher. She followed the screaming van to the hospital, then called the number Slidell had painfully drawn with the EMT's pen on her soggy romance novel. His wife answered the phone and after a tearful rush of questions, hung up to call for a cab. Magdalena paced the emergency room in the hospital until Slidell's wife arrived with the twins.

Slidell had been badly bruised up, nothing worse. The ER attendant looked at Magdalena with an air of skepticism.

231

"What were you doing there? Making a point of some kind?" She fled the hospital, and only later became aware of how her head still ached where it had smacked the concrete.

*****

As she entered the door to the Turret Shop, Pody called from across the floor. "Hey Magdalena, get your butt over here!" She started to explain that something terrible had happened at the Beachcomber, but her stammering, accented distress angered Pody and he cut her off.

"You work slow as they come, anyways," he sniffed. "Now you even cheatin' me on eight hours of that." He raised his voice for the benefit of some white welders nearby. "Goin' to pick up some white boy at the beach, what you expect? They tell me you island girls got some hot blood, though I don't see the attraction myself." He clicked his gums at the other welders with mock regret. "'Course, I gotta do the right thing and tell that fucknut husband of yours when I see him tomorrow."

Magdalena blinked. Her head throbbed over the piteous wail of Slidell's pretty wife and little girls as they hung on the rails of his hospital bed. Her words came out a low growl.

"You a bad man, Pody, you hear me? You tell me respect or I cut out your tongue."

Pody chuckled and stepped closer. "You stupid bitch," he said quietly. He raised his voice for the others. "Hey boys, you hear what she said? Threaten ole Pody like that?" He curled a finger at Magdalena. "You come with me while I call for the guards. You just lost yourself a job, lady."

49

"You can't just forget it and move on like that," Lonny said.

Shea plopped a dumpling into a bowl of tamari sauce, burped and excused himself. He gestured with his chopsticks between bites. "We did what we could. We got Pretty Boy back. We should pat ourselves on the back, not worry too much about what we lost at the edges."

"Hiram Pody can't be lost at the edge! He's a racist who needs going after. I know it and the black welders do, too."

"I suppose you have some inside line on what the black welders are thinking."

Lonny shot back. "Sleeping with Patty doesn't give you one either."

They glared at each other.

Shea's face softened. "Look, I'd like to get Pody. Magdalena's case is in the system. If we play up Pody's attitude at the arbitration I think she'll win."

"If the Grievance Committee takes it that far."

"I haven't found anything I can use to force Hershfeld to take her back short of an arbitrator's decision."

Lonny spread her hands. "Then let me look for it. I feel like I've been sitting on my hands since you became steward."

"Look into it how?"

"I worked graveyard before I met you. I know a few guys on Pody's crew."

"White guys, I hope?" Shea said.

233

"Pody pretty much makes sure anyone not white works for another whitehat. Magdalena was an exception 'cause he wanted to push a black woman around. Besides, why is anything the white guys say more valuable?"

Shea stiffened. "Don't start that stuff with me. You know why."

Lonny closed her eyes in frustration. "Okay, yes. I know white guys on Pody's crew."

Shea squished a dumpling with his chopsticks and it oozed grease. He swirled it in a red puddle of chili oil and tucked it in his mouth.

"Good luck," he said. "Keep in touch."

As Lonny got up to leave she asked, "Is Patty still looking for a place to live? Or are you two moving in?"

He shook his head. "No to moving in. We're not ready for that and we don't think the shipyard is, either. She's decided to stay on with her sister for now. How come?"

"I've been thinking about getting a couple of roommates. My place feels kind of big these days."

He thought of his house in Fields Corner. "I know what you mean."

He stayed on at the restaurant after Lonny left, easing into a Mai Tai fog. His neck and shoulders loosened. He felt too sapped to stand up. That was the trouble with rum after a day at the yard. Once your shoulders relaxed it was all over.

Keefer came in with her latest boyfriend and went straight for the bar without noticing him. She had been hugely pregnant the last time Shea saw her. Now her belly was flat. How old would her baby be now—couple of months?

Shea called to her and she swung around. He looked at the pull of her sweater, her falling blonde hair and then, as she faced him fully in the bar's blue overhead spotlights, he saw the flash of her lipstick and eyes. She waved, and she did it with more encouragement than she had offered to Billy the Kid so long ago in the welding school. He tried to recall if she had ever given him any hint of a come-on aside from her usual teaser stuff, decided she hadn't.

He wished he was feeling less groggy.

He brought his bill to the bar and leaned on it next to her. They said hello again and she introduced him to Butchy Something, who looked Shea over suspiciously.

"How's motherhood?" Shea asked.

"Lotta fun, lotta work. What I expected. My mom's driving me crazy. Nothing I do with the baby is right."

"When are you coming back to work?"

Keefer tapped her fingers over her lips like it was the first time she had thought about it. "A few months, I guess. When I can't afford to stay out anymore. Or I can't take any more of my mom."

"You know, you just missed Lonny. She's looking for someone to move in with her. I bet she'd let you slide on rent for a while."

"Really? Jeez, I passed her on the way out. I'll give her a call."

"Okay, then. I'll see you." He threw some folding money on the bar and turned to the door.

Outside, icy flecks of wind cut at his face. A harsh gust almost pinned him to his car, and then, just as abruptly released him. All at once he was very awake.

He drove home by the beach. As he cruised by the patio in front of the Beachcomber, he braked to a crawl and stared, trying to reconstruct the assault on Magdalena and Slidell.

He felt guilty that Pody had still been around to go after Magdalena. And pissed off. He was doing everything he could, and that was all they ever asked for. That was what Cotty had told him early on. It was all they had asked of Townsend.

But with every new issue he sensed watchful distance, not trust and support. As if Pretty Boy's job and getting rid of the graffiti hadn't been anything at all. What the hell did they want?

He asked Patty the same question later. He'd had this conversation with her before, though when he talked about it she mostly sat looking at the burning logs in his parlor fireplace and murmuring "Un-huh, un-huh." Once he had called her out for not paying attention.

"Oh, I'm payin' attention, Michael," she said. "You want to know what we want? *Honesty. Justice.* It ain't right that Pretty Boy spent months on the street. Ain't right that Pody put him on that job in the first place. Ain't right that black guys get shit thrown at them at every turn. Not right that Magdalena got fired and those Southie kids what beat her get off scott free."

"I know all that," Shea said. "It's not fair."

"Fair's got nuthin' to do with it! Not never! Ain't never gonna be *fair* for black folk in this shipyard. Ain't never gonna be *fair* for women. But we want a demand for justice, for honesty about what's goin' on and for payback that means somethin'. We want to see you fight for all that, not be feelin' sorry for yourself."

She sat up straight on the couch. "You want everybody to see your white horse, Michael, and pet it. Okay, I see you." She whinnied playfully, then laughed again, deep in her throat.

"Goddam it! You think I'm in this for myself? My life would be a lot easier if I'd never run for steward."

"I'm sorry this is all so hard for you. But you not the victim in the story. Yes, you in it for the good stuff you do. But I'm also pretty sure you don't mind the attention that come with that."

"Fuck that!" Shea stalked upstairs and lay in bed, open-eyed and waiting in the dark. When Patty crawled under the covers, he pulled her close.

"That was very nice," she whispered in his ear when they finished. "You good for me, Michael, I ain't lyin'. But that don't change what I said."

He jumped to his feet and, snatching his pillow, stomped to the bedroom at the far end of the hall. He expected her to come after him. Instead, she rolled over and, with a small groan, went to sleep.

*****

Lonny napped after work and left for the yard at nine-thirty to catch the third shift coming in. She made sure that her Alternate Steward pin was visible to anyone walking in the main gate.

"Hey, Vince!" she called when Cardinale approached the gate, "how's third shift treating you?"

"Hey, Lonny. It's okay. Still getting used to the change. But mostly I like it."

"And how's Pody for a whitehat?"

Cardinale made a face. "Not so great. He's not real thrilled I helped get the second shift black guy's job back. Lets me know a couple times a week he's not a fan."

"Has he harassed you? Done anything to make you worry?"

"No. He's just letting me know. For now. He's really not a nice guy."

Lonny had approached a handful of other welders coming in, but after a brief exchange about Magdalena, none of them wanted to talk about the incident. A couple alluded to Pody's vindictive bent. Vince Cardinale might be her last hope tonight.

"Were you around when Magdalena got fired, Vince?"

"Didn't see it, no."

"Well, what about Pody? Did he say anything to the crew about it after? Did he have it in for her?"

Vince shook his head. "Not that I heard. But look—and I'm only sayin' this 'cause it struck me wrong, and this time it ain't comin' from me. He did give us something you might want to see." He pulled a paper out of his lunchbox and gave it to her.

*****

Lonny reached into a drawer and pulled out the three-color tabloid. The masthead read *Blitzjezt*.

Shea scanned the front page. "This is Nazi stuff."

"Look inside," Lonny prompted.

Shea opened the paper. Coarse baboon-like caricatures jumped from page three. Opposite was a mock certificate with the heading *Nigger Hunting License: Good for Unlimited Bucks*.

He looked at Lonny. "This is Pody's?"

"He showed it to his crew. He made copies of that license and passed it around."

Shea stared at the pages until Lonny grew defensive at his silence. "I thought this was a great find. Makes sense of all those stories about Klan propaganda in the yard."

"Yeah, it really is." He tried to be excited for her sake. "I'm just tired. Can I keep it?"

She forced a smile. "Use it well. And soon." She put her hand on his shoulder and gave it a squeeze. "This is the smoking damn gun."

50

Charley Johnson scanned the racist cartoons and the hunting license with steady hands. "Think you can make me look bad?" he asked, tossing the copy of *Blitzjezt* on his desk in front of Shea. "I'm covered on the whole Pody thing. You lose."

Shea smacked his fists on the desk. "That's all you care about? You're the only black manager in the shipyard who can do something about him!"

Johnson got up from his chair and leaned tensely across his desk. "I made recommendations on Hiram Pody to the front office months ago. It's Hershfeld's problem now. And Pennock's." Johnson pointed at the paper. "This isn't worth shit, but you put down on the record that I'm passing it up to the office."

The superintendent abruptly tightened his stance, arms wide like a tackle at the ready. "How dare you judge me? You connect my name with any of this and I'll come after you. At night."

Shea stared back, more shaken by Johnson's threat than he could ever admit.

*****

"Here's the Pody file you requested, Mr. Hershfeld," Lynne said, placing a thick folder on his desk pad.

239

He opened the folder and leafed through Pody's background checks, his promotions, production reviews and at the bottom of the stack, page after page of disciplinary actions taken against welders. Cotty. Luther Sims. The Haitian girl Magdalena. Then a long list of lower-level suspensions and warning slips, almost a hundred over the last two years. Hershfeld had to read it twice—even Elroy Washington had somehow gotten on Pody's wrong side. Black after black after black. And now the damn Hunting License.

Hershfeld sat back in his chair and closed his eyes. No one would believe the company didn't know. That he didn't know. He anticipated the calls that Shea would instigate from the EEOC, the inquiries from the press. But if he just fired Pody now, General Shipworks would look guilty, pressured into it by a wild steward and his rabble rouser friends. He himself would look like an idiot and, inevitably, he'd become the scapegoat.

Hershfeld shivered, anticipating Pennock's grim, haughty disapproval. He sighed and then straightened his shoulders. He just needed to tough it out until he developed a plan.

*****

When Shea appeared at the main gate for lunch, Cotty was waiting and waving a copy of the *Bay State Banner*. He danced his way toward Shea from Ziyad's. "Hey Shea, now *this* is somethin' fit to print!" He held up the tabloid. "They published the whole thing! Front page picture!"

Shea looked at the photo of Pody's Hunting License. "This is gonna help, for sure. Nice job pushing that to the *Banner*, Cotty. I'll bet Hershfeld's heard from the feds by now, too. And I got one more thing to do."

*****

As soon as Hershfeld entered the corner office, Pennock poured himself a scotch from the console behind his desk and cocked his head at the bottle. When Hershfeld declined, Pennock lifted his glass and peered through it. "I'm disappointed," he said.

Hershfeld reached for the second glass on Pennock's desk. The general manager shook his head and took a sip. "I mean I'm disappointed about the whitehat. Who the hell is this Pody? Never mind, I don't want details. You should have taken care of this whole situation sooner, one way or the other."

As he spoke, a dribble rolled from the corner of Pennock's mouth. He caught it with a finger and licked it. "Make this go away before the feds get riled and bring in their Contract Compliance office. However you do it, don't leave any doubt inside the shipyard that *we* manage this place and *we* make the decisions...All of them."

"Of course," Hershfeld said. "I'll take care of it."

*****

Shea waited a day before calling for a meeting with Hershfeld. When Rashford got wind of it he demanded to sit in.

Hershfeld opened. "This whole Nazi paper thing seems to be part of a frame up. Just a little too neat and clean. Anyone could have planted it. Come back when you really have something for me, will you?" But the furrow between his eyebrows deepened as Shea produced details that Lonny's painstaking conversations with welders who knew Pody had unearthed.

"We got signed statements from several of them," Shea finished.

Hershfeld tapped steepled fingers against his lips for a long, pensive moment. He stared at the pad of notes on his desk.

In the silence, Shea realized how grim the room felt. The only thing on the wall was Hershfeld's diploma. The entire admin building had the same feel—no visible connection to the six thousand hardhats outside. The few scattered hangings in the hallways were sterile, staged christenings of ships built since the General took over the yard. Not a single shot of workers building them, much less of groups of hardhats talking or laughing at lunch or hanging out before the whistle, as if the actual shipbuilders didn't exist except in manila folders.

Hershfeld broke into his thoughts. "Mike, would you mind stepping into the hall?"

Shea looked at Rashford and back at Hershfeld. "I would mind, yes."

Hershfeld's voice hardened. "It's not a request." When he opened the door, Rashford pointed to it.

Shea reddened. "You're taking *his* side? In front of the company?" He stomped out and slouched by the empty assistant's desk a few feet down the hall. Lynne walked up with a batch of files under her arm. "Still here?" she asked. "I thought they would have nailed you by now."

Hershfeld stood at the door and waved him back in. "What are you planning to do with this... thing?" He pointed at the *Blitzjezt*.

Shea said, "Maybe nothing. If you get rid of Pody and rehire Magdalena. With pay."

"That's not going to happen."

"Doesn't Pody's reading material turn your stomach just a little, Irv? Jewish guy like you?"

"I'm not going to answer that."

Rashford put a hand on Hershfeld's arm and asked Shea, "And if you don't get your price?"

Shea ticked off the possibilities. "There's the papers, of course. You've seen the *Banner*, but obviously there's *The Globe* and *Patriot Ledger*—if they don't pick it up on their own."

Hershfeld glared. Shea suppressed a grin.

"And of course I'll go to the affirmative action people. File to get General Shipworks disbarred from federal contracts. Maybe the whole corporation."

"You little shit," Rashford said quietly. "That's the end of the Navy work."

"That would never happen, Stan." Hershfeld tried to sound confident. "Not to *this* company." He swung to Shea. "And you know it would get you nowhere."

"Maybe not." Shea felt the grin break through. "Want to test out the theory?"

Hershfeld waited him out.

Shea said, "We can see what it costs you in legal fees, though I guess you don't care about that. But I'd like to sit in on the call you get from Omaha after we file downtown and the networks pick it up."

Rashford said, "My turn, Irv. Will you please excuse us?"

Hershfeld got up and gestured expansively at his desk. "Be my guest, guys." He started into the hall.

Rashford turned full face on Shea. "Trade the black girl for Pody. Forget about her case."

"*What?*"

"You heard me. That's the deal I gave him. She goes and he goes." Rashford hit the *Blitzjezt*. "Forget this shit. I don't need to tell you that girl doesn't have a chance in hell at arbitration. *If* we let it get that far. She threatened a boss." He went with the sweetener. "I'll get Hershfeld to guarantee that he gets rid of Pody within a week. From our side, it'll be without any publicity."

Shea said to Rashford, "You are one slimey bastard. But not dumb."

"Nice of you to notice, asshole."

Shea's fingers closed around the grips of his satchel. Before he could lift it, Rashford pinned the bag on the table with one hand. "I'm not finished. You turn down the deal, that's your business, I could give a shit. But if this shows up anywhere," he slapped the paper again. "Or if I hear anything else about filing downtown, you're dead meat. I'll have you in front of the Sanctions Committee so fast it'll make your head spin."

"For getting rid of a racist whitehat?"

"For killing any chance of new work the yard has left. Why do you think Hershfeld needs this deal? On our side, that's our men's jobs, and that's how I'll play it."

51

Pody kicked at a can of welding wire and watched the rods rattle across the steel. He looked around the Turret Shop floor, daring someone to notice. He stomped upstairs to his office and ripped open the door, revealing his lead man in a worn swivel chair with his feet propped on his desk. "Get the fuck outta here," Pody said. "Go do some work."

"Jesus, Hi, I'm your lead man, remember? I don't weld."

Pody spun the swivel chair. "I'm in no mood for smart talk from you. Go check on the guys or I'll make sure you have something to weld. Now get!"

"Jesus," said the lead man again, "okay." He stood in the doorway. "By the way, that 603 unit? It's loaded with piss, from before it got to the shop, I guess. I told the guys to hang tight 'til you move them."

A steady drum beat hard at the top of Pody's skull. The last thing he needed was a production problem for Charley Johnson to jump on. That black bastard would take it right to the Jew. On top of the bullshit about the damn license. The two of them were probably in this thing together.

"I don't care what the fuck it's full of," Pody burst out, "I want that unit tonight. Tell them to get on it."

The lead man pursed his lips. "I'm no whitehat, Hi. I tell 'em to weld over piss, they'll tell me to get fucked. You better go on out there and tell them yourself."

"You're useless as tits on a bull, you know that?" Pody slammed the door on him.

"Hope so," the lead man mumbled after he'd gone. "Hope Shea stays on your ass, too."

*****

Hershfeld and Johnson entered the Turret Shop twenty minutes before the end of third shift. Welders crouched in twos and threes on the platen, killing time before the whistle while first shift filtered in. They didn't see Johnson in the shop very often and didn't like it when they did. They puzzled over the front office guy, though. A suit in the shop before seven o'clock? These fuckin' guys never quit.

Johnson and Hershfeld split at the door. Hershfeld walked around the perimeter of the work floor while Johnson headed straight through the middle.

Johnson strutted his stuff, casting mean, heavy eyes around the shop. The welders scrambled in circles in search of make-work to fill the minutes before the end of their shift. Johnson surveyed their units, absorbing them with scowls of concern. He ignored the welders and lit on a telltale heap of welding rods that betrayed someone's lunch time game of pick-up sticks. The sight seemed to please him; he made a note on a three by five card that he slipped into his breast pocket: *6:46 AM: Destroyed company property found on unit. Pody absent from the floor to observe.* The welders hunched over their lines.

Another pair of welders skulked out of a storage area. Like Johnson, Hershfeld didn't bother with the welders themselves, just jotted an incident report on his note pad: *6:48 AM: Two welders idle and loafing. Pody absent from the floor to discipline.*

The two bosses met at the bottom of the stairs leading up to Pody's office. Johnson indicated the shack at top with his thumb and said, "He's gotta be in there."

They trotted up the steps, Hershfeld behind and huffing to keep up, Johnson in front, enjoying the other's discomfort. They stopped at the landing on top while Hershfeld put his hands on his knees and puffed a few times. Then, without bothering to knock, they barged into Pody's office. The door closed behind them. The lock clicked.

At first the welders heard nothing. Then shouting broke through to the floor. Pody stormed out. His lead man trailed after, bug-eyed, with Pody's white helmet swinging in his hand.

Johnson stepped out of the office and leaned across the rail at the landing. He called to the lead man. "Hey you, get back here!" Johnson pried the white helmet from the lead man's fingers and plunked it, off center, onto the man's head. Johnson tapped the brim so that the helmet sat firmly. "You're a foreman now."

Pody banged through the door at the far end of the shop. He sucked in the air when he saw the security jeep. Hauner reached across to the passenger door and opened it. "Grab a seat, Hiram. I just do what they tell me. Now try to go out in style."

*****

"It's got nothing to do with your charges," Hershfeld told Shea. "Pody was up for routine review. His crew's productivity was problematic. Charley Johnson documented two instances of Pody's malfeasance in a single on-site review. And we discovered that he had been distributing unauthorized written materials inside the shipyard. Just like we'd fire anyone who handed out your *829 News* inside the gates."

"Nothing, of course, to do with the content," Shea said.

Hershfeld took off his suit coat. He leaned forward on his desk and seethed through his teeth. "And just who the fuck is Louis Levinson?"

Shea said, "Lou? A realtor friend of mine. Why? You happen to run into him somewhere?"

Hershfeld purpled and stood up straight. "You know goddam well he lodged a complaint against me with the fucking rabbinical court of Boston. 'Violation of the commandment to recognize all people as made in the image of God.'" He searched for words but just managed to spit out, "Some guy in a black fedora brings a demand for appearance at a tribunal to my house and hands it to my wife! Are you out of your fucking *mind*?"

Shea said, "Sounds rough. What about Magadalena?"

Hershfeld took a breath and sat back down. He wiped his forehead and pretended to review a sheet of paper on his desk. "I've taken another look at her case. Without Pody, I admit I have a tougher nut to crack at arbitration. I'll bring her back to work if she signs away rights to her grievance and any civil rights complaints."

"Her money?"

"Not a chance. She threatened a foreman."

"Not just any foreman."

Hershfeld spoke as if to a stubborn child. "Talk to her. Tell her that she can be on the job tomorrow, if she chooses. You have that obligation. Let me know by three-thirty."

When Shea called Magdalena he could hear her kids running riot in the background.

Pierre had left home, for good she hoped. Hershfeld's lawyers had twice postponed her unemployment appeal. Every afternoon since the last delay, she'd rushed to the mailbox, looking for a notice with a new hearing date. "But not all bad," she told Shea. "My first month of food stamps arrive just yesterday."

Shea accepted the deal before lunch. He wanted to call Lonny and gush, but the job with no money felt like a hollow victory. The sell was a hard one out at Ziyad's, too. "Six months with *no pay*?" one welder exclaimed. "You said she would win the whole thing!" Another welder squinted at Shea. "All that work for a black girl that barely talks English? That's bullshit." He flicked the ash from his cigarette into an empty coffee mug. "Well, at least you got rid of Pody."

Shea told them Pierre had run off and asked for donations to help pay down Magdalena's bills. The hardhats shook their heads and wondered what the matter really was with those black guys, never had it together to stick out the tough parts. A few of them dug into their pockets.

52

The coffees were lined up, as usual. Ziyad hunched over the grill, also as usual, but he slid his spatula under the burgers so listlessly that they almost rolled onto their backs rather than flipped. When Shea said, "Morning, Ziyad," the guy never looked up.

"Fuckin' Arabs," the old timers groaned at their tables, though they didn't look at Ziyad when they said it. They focused instead on the front page of the morning paper. Still, the grill man cringed at his station without a word.

Little Z couldn't keep it to himself. "They're Iranians, not Arabs, you jerks! *We're* the Arabs!"

His father wheeled from the grill and smacked Little Z with an open hand. "Shut up!" he yelled.

Shea frowned at the old timers at the tables. One of them said to him, "The fuckin' ayatollah's done it now." He shoved an open *Patriot Ledger* toward Shea and spun it around so he could read the headline: *US Hostages in Teheran.* And in type just as large, a second headline: *LNG Tankers Jeopardized.*

Shea scanned the article. Under the Shah, Iran's reserves had been a sure source for the gas cargo trade. With a hostile regime in Teheran, the prospects for shipping LNG dropped dramatically.

Number 43, the next to last of the yard's firmly contracted LNG tankers, would float under the Goliath crane in a few months. The last guaranteed ship, number 44, was well on its way.

Repair and maintenance work on the small Navy frigate that had just docked in 6 Basin wouldn't last long. The keel for the third of four modest chemical barges would be laid before summer. Now it seemed that the five contingent LNG tankers the shipyard had counted on would fall victim to the revolution in Iran. Without a miracle or, at least, another bone from the Navy, the place would close in less than two years.

*****

Jimmy O'Donnell hailed Shea as he passed by the school. "I'm back on the tools next week unless I retire," Jimmy said. "No one left at the school. Now you're gonna find out how it is with no work." The slag-scarred whites of Jimmy's eyes gleamed with weary insight. "Course you're a steward now, last one to get laid off. You'll see it all, you poor bastard."

The initial round of layoffs hit in waves, fifty the first week, a hundred the next. The hardhats spent their days calculating mortgage payments that stretched forbiddingly into the future, subtracting them from the diminishing number of paychecks they could still project.

Some of their whitehats began to hedge bets. "Watch it," they cautioned their crews, "they're squeezin' our balls to come after you, too. You gotta know that we're in this together now."

The hardhat response was distracted. They were busy scouting for culprits.

*****

When the lunch whistle sounded, the hardhats raced out the gate and headed straight for Ziyad's. Lonny had heard about it like everyone else, but she hadn't quite believed that the crazies would follow through on the promise they'd made in their flyers at the gate that morning. No one could be that stupid. A flag-burning at the shipyard?

A dozen unfamiliar young men in street clothes stood on the pavement in front of Ziyad's. Lonny recognized three brown helmets among them: the white guy with the *Workers Unite!* pin; the small black woman who'd called Rashford a fascist at Townsend's special union meeting; and a welder who'd talked to her once about his photography hobby.

Icy clouds of breath puffed in front of the demonstrators' faces as they tried hard to sound militant. They chanted, "Support Iran's revolution!" as workers gathered on the other side of the street. A few of the demonstrators held placards on sticks or leaned them upright against the brick facade of the Grill. In the center of the cluster, the tallest of them, an outsider, clutched a loudspeaker in one hand, an American flag in the other. He tugged his Donegal cap down over one eye. An enameled red star flashed at its brim.

"We spit in the eye of the imperialist menace and this flag, its symbol of oppression! The Iranian people have thrown off the blood-soaked shah and his CIA backers! We salute their just struggle!"

From across the street a welder yelled, "Stick it up your ass!"

The roadway was filling with hardhats. They churned in small groups and shouted at the guy holding the bullhorn. His loudspeaker squawked on, each burst triggering fresh anger from hardhats who windmilled their arms to friends coming out of the gate.

Eddie Hauner stood by his counter in the security shack and leaned out the window toward the street. Through the iron spikes of the fence he saw the hardhats coiling into a mob. He shoved the flyer he'd collected that morning into a drawer, intending to forward it upstairs at the end of his shift. "Stupid fucking kids," he breathed. He walked out of the shack toward the yellow line in front of the gate. After surveying the agitated mass of hardhats, he grabbed the phone and dialed the cops.

"You commie fucks!" shouted Farrell at the line of demonstrators. He turned to the crowd. "These are the same assholes that beat up those kids in Southie during busing! Don't let them burn our flag!" His eyes found Salvucci, who nodded approval.

The guy with the bullhorn held up the flag.

A warning shot out from the mob, "Don't touch it!" The hardhats hushed and waited.

The bullhorn sounded again. "The working class understands that the Revolutionary People's Party is as good as its word!"

"How the fuck would you know what we understand?" Farrell yelled.

The demonstrator handed off his loudspeaker. He held a lighter aloft. The scratch of the flint was clearly heard, some of the hardhats swore later, down the length of the street. Before it was even lit someone yelled, "Flag's on fire!"

"Get the commies!" bellowed Salvucci. Farrell surged forward and the hardhats followed. Shea hustled around the corner of the guard shack, hearing the screams before seeing the action. He'd been flagged down by a welder with a chit and cursed himself for the delay. It had been in his mind to calm down the welders scattered among the mob.

He'd tried to recruit Billy to help, but the Kid just plunked down on his toolbox.

"Stay as far away as you can," he told Shea. And no matter how Shea urged him to come out and witness, Billy hadn't moved.

*****

The crowd pressed toward Ziyad's. It spilled over the street as it swelled. Screaming hardhats choked the road across to the gate. They spread over the small, grassy hill where in better times they had joshed each other and ogled brown-hatted women.

At the crowd's edge hardhats stood on their booted toes and strained for a view. For a few wobbly seconds some balanced on their helmets before slipping off. Shea saw there wasn't a single black welder in the crowd. "Smarter than me," he breathed to himself.

A piercing commotion broke from the doorway to Ziyad's, the rough thuds of punches and kicks. Screams ripped from both sides, hatred and agonies blended. The crowd rippled and swayed with surges of combat. The hardhats opened a path from the center of the brawl, allowing one of its own panting warriors to emerge and rest up, full of the lust of the hunt.

At the door to the Grill, Ziyad hopped in a lather, pointing and shouting, "Stay away from the windows!" Shea stood near the gate across the street from the crowd. His blue eyes were neutral, observing the carnage. His head shook in protest that no one could see.

Lonny sidled up to Shea. "Get out of here," she urged underneath the dull slapping sounds of the fighting. "Salvucci's gonna nail you to this if he sees you."

"And you. More you." Shea moved in for a better look.

A handful of commies squeezed free of the mob. They retreated at a run toward the parking lot, pursued by strung out knots of hardhats. A fitter threw a helmet and missed. The fiberglass brim of another sliced at the neck of a red, who crumpled to the sidewalk in mid-step. A platoon of fitters reached him first and lingered, taking turns throwing punches and kicks. The other protestors ran on broken-fielded with hardhats still in pursuit.

Out front of Ziyad's, kicked clear of the windows, four of the demonstrators twitched on the sidewalk. They shielded their heads with rigid clasped fingers.

Lonny saw the photo guy, Matt. Tall, nice curly hair, his head now bloody and streaming. He'd told her he'd set up a weekend business at markets, portraits and candids, enough to get by and away from this life. She'd asked, "From the shipyard or your comrades?" He hadn't answered.

The hardhats enveloped the four on the ground without mercy, kicking and slashing at unguarded organs. Matt was rocked by more kicks to the head. Gorged and exhausted, the inner circle of hardhats backed off. Second and third waves rolled up behind them and laid into the demonstrators with a relish all their own.

Shea floated forward, as if nothing could touch him. "Hey, that's enough, let them go already," he muttered again and again as he drifted.

Salvucci moved away from the feast of mauled flesh, coughing and heaving. Through sweaty eyes he saw Shea and heard his muttered plea. "Jesus Christ!" Salvucci thundered. "Shea's with them! That shit set it up, lost our jobs!"

"Fuckin'-A!" yelled Farrell. At the edge of the circle a ring of hardhats had been fruitlessly struggling for a turn at the commies. Now they switched course and followed Salvucci.

Lonny grabbed Shea and pedaled him toward the gate. "Get in there!" she barked. She shoved him toward Hauner. The guard craned to look up the street. Still no cops.

"You're a pussy, Shea!" Salvucci yelled from across the street. He pulled out his notepad and jotted it down.

Shea stood inside the shipyard by the guard shack. Lonny stood beside him, watching the ongoing assault on the now unresisting protesters. "This scares me, Michael. They just want someone to beat on."

Shea's fingers curled around the chain link fence. He stared out from the yard in despair at the waste they had made of their anger.

SUNSET

53

The charcoal November sky deepened before Shea arrived home from the yard. He drove up to his house and let his car idle in the street while he rolled away the trash can that reserved the parking spot where he had shoveled out a snowdrift.

When he hurried inside and stoked up the fire, the big house stayed drafty and cold no matter what incredible quantities of oil it sucked. The ancient octopus heater in the cellar rumbled with each thermostatic trigger, a backdrop to the rumbling unhappiness he felt in the house. He had thought the damn place was a castle when he bought it, but now the chilled, vacant space made him want to cry. Though Patty was supposed to have filled it for him she hadn't been able to.

Or maybe he hadn't let her.

"You pullin' away, Michael, I feel it," she'd said. "Please, talk to me." Her almond eyes glistened. "This makes my heart ache. You owe me that much."

"Sure," he replied, but never had the words or the will. Discontent shadowed his life but he didn't know why. It was her. It was him. It was everything beyond them both.

"You owe me more than that," she insisted. Her words drove him further away.

He promised himself time to think about what he was doing with his life. Started by sitting alone in his kitchen. Overhead, a naked bulb bobbed lazily in the gust from the air ducts. He popped open beers and munched on cashews and dried apricots from Lambert's Fruit and Vegetables. He gulped at the beers and licked salt from his fingers, shoveled more handfuls of nuts in his mouth. Soon he thought of the twentyish girls who worked the registers down at Lambert's. Of the suggestion he wanted to read in the sway of their bodies. He popped another beer and watched the dusk darken his unwashed kitchen. Through the window, his deck dissolved into night.

For a week, then a month, he sat in his kitchen from late afternoon through the evening, determined to solve the dilemma of being the person he had envisioned since leaving the projects. When Patty came by she pushed him to grapple with her questions. Her persistence and insight annoyed him. After a couple of beers the desire to talk rolled away like the retreat of distant thunder. His dreams of the girls down at Lambert's seemed to fill him so much more easily.

"They're just monkeys with torches," Hershfeld said to Charley Johnson, "so train them to dance."

Johnson had long ago learned enough not to dispute.

Another voice came from behind him. "I been in this game a long time." Pete Rosa slouched in a leather wing chair that cloaked his short wide frame.

Rosa had been a welder himself, easing his way into enough tanks to fill all the years since Pearl Harbor. He had welded chain lockers and bilges and the worst of the pin butts, the first Cape Verdean to work his way up.

To make it Rosa needed to study every day, sizing up dangers and men. Over the years, as a brownhat then whitehat and then general foreman, Rosa had watched thousands of them. He knew how to get them to work. What it took was the knack to push and to pull, to be pushed at times without anger. And like Charley Johnson always said, Rosa had it. He never needed to look at a blueprint, never studied a budget, but he could still find the one job on a nine-hundred-foot ship that would clear the way for the rest of his schedule. Once it was spotted, he spent time talking it through with the welder who worked it.

Now he peered at the big shots through basset hound eyes.

"This place ain't an assembly line. You can't expect the guys to work like it is. Every job is different. Has different issues, needs different men."

Pennock and Hershfeld exchanged a glance. Hershfeld did the talking. "It's our shipyard and we'll task them as we see fit."

Rosa smiled wanly. His voice notched down half a tone. "Sure you will, Irv. Hey, what do I know? I'm just an old welder."

Hershfeld's eyes lingered on Rosa before turning to Johnson.

"Charley, you'll see to it that your foremen understand the new direction?"

"Of course I will, Irv." He nodded at the desk. "Mr. Pennock." He stood and Rosa stood with him.

Together the two whitehats walked back to production. Not a word passed between them. They passed by the mill, the card shack, the South Yard. Johnson started to enter the door to the War Room. Rosa moved toward the basins. Johnson spoke to the smaller man's back. "Pete, please watch it."

Rosa said without turning, "Thanks, Charley."

*****

Shea gouged the uncoated end of a welding rod into brittle gray paint. He cupped his other hand to catch the falling flakes and then ground them between his fingers before displaying the residue to Rashford. Far above the heads of the two men, a bridge crane rattled along the superstructure. Shea said, "Lead paint."

"You think I'm a fucking idiot? I know what it is."

"My welders are hurting. Some of them have kidney pains. They feel tired all the time."

Rashford ran a hand over the metal plate. "This is just like the stuff that was on the Navy oiler repair we had back a couple years after the wildcat. Nobody got sick then."

"I heard that was all outdoor work. Or maybe it's just that nobody complained fast enough. It was a smaller job."

"C'mere." Rashford still had his pipefitter grip and locked it down on Shea's shoulder as they walked. "Number 43 is gone. We got one more tanker, those last barges and this little frigate job the Navy just rushed us just to help keep things goin'. After that we got nothin' in the hopper. And you're worried about some goddamn *paint?*" Rashford looked Shea over with distaste. "What you see here is all there is. We gotta win some real Navy work to stay alive. This frigate job is a test."

"You don't want me to make waves."

"I don't want to lose jobs! You make an issue here, maybe the company loses money and time. That don't look so good on other bids. Or maybe you run to OSHA or have a demonstration for the TV. Suddenly everybody's shaking their heads about big labor problems in the yard. Then you've fucked the new contracts."

"I'm trying to keep people from getting hurt."

Rashford said, "Don't trip us up, kid, or I'll be coming after you."

*****

Shea worked his way down to the frigate's engine room through a twisted maze of piping and ducts. The boilers were chugging and the smell of sweat combined with an irritating, acrid smoke drifting from the pipe welders scattered around the room.

He had reached deep to move on after the riot at the gates. "I'm just not sure we can make a real difference, anymore," he told Lonny. She rubbed the back of his neck like a sister and said, "It's not all in the winning, Mike. You make them feel like they're worth something."

A voice reached out to him from the engine room floor. "Well if it ain't my old night shift buddy made good. Griswold would be proud of you." It was Farrell with his little bucket of yellow paint, brush in hand and a rolled-up blueprint sticking out of his back pocket. "Surprised to see me out at that commie stomp at Ziyad's? I got tired of the back shift, so when Griswold went on days I came with him."

Farrell looked around the engine room theatrically. "And you know what? The pipe welders around here been talkin' about you. They're not too crazy about reds. Or about a certain steward more interested helping niggers than his own."

Shea said, "Why don't you just shut up, Farrell?"

The marker said, "You're a big man now. Ask 'em yourself."

Shea looked. Half a dozen pipe welders, all white, looked on with hostile expressions. One said, "I hear you dance around wedges pretty good, Shea."

Farrell took a step forward and pointed at Shea. "If you had moved any closer to those commies out there we would've had your balls for lunch instead of Portagee fish salad."

Shea looked at the pipe welders. They were still watching. "I'm no more with them than I am with a scumbag like you, Farrell." Not the right time for this, he decided, then turned back to the ladder and climbed out, struggling to focus on the hundred other guys on the boat breathing lead.

✱✱✱✱✱

"This is Navy work," Shea said over Mai Tais at the Blue Dragon. "We've got to get it right or we'll be crucified. Maybe your cousin can help us with some research again?"

263

Lonny nodded. "She's living with me now in the smaller bedroom, so I don't think she'll turn us down."

She got back to Shea with a manila folder full of paper in just a few days.

"Here's the main thing," she told Shea. "The lead fumes can make them lose their hard-ons. And if they put their work clothes in the laundry at home they can wind up with retarded kids. You keep talking to these guys about giving themselves brain damage or losing kidney function and they'll laugh at you. Tell 'em their pricks are gonna fall off or their kids are gonna get hurt and you got yourself a winner." Lonny cleared her throat. "This is gonna make a stink."

Shea knew. "Yeah. Rashford won't be happy."

*****

The 829 News went out the next morning.

Grind Out the Lead Poison!
We're More than Monkeys With Torches!

Most of the shipyard picked it up at the gates and read it cover to cover by nine o'clock. Hardhats congregated on the runways at break time and argued over its claims.

Early that afternoon, Shea was summoned to the frigate. He found the same crew of pipe welders huddled underneath the ship, shivering by a ladder that poked through an access patch into the hull.

Griswold came out of nowhere. "Tell these guys to get back to work or they're fired."

A pipe welder took a threatening step toward the whitehat. Shea put out an arm and brought him up short, then motioned the rest of the crew for quiet. "What's going on?"

"We got assigned to the tank this morning," the welder said. "Griswold tells us it's hot. But that paint's still on every joint and your flyer says it's supposed to be blasted off before we weld it."

The welder pulled a creased copy of the *News* from his pocket. "Then at coffee, I go over the newsletter again and get scared. The damn tank's a smokestack, all heavy smelling like lead. I ask the guys, 'You feel sick?' We all do, like somebody's sitting on your chest. At lunch we talked it over. We won't go back in until they sandblast."

Shea said, "It could mean your jobs."

"Your newsletter says the paint is supposed to come off, goddammit, and we're goin' with it. So make sure you damn well do *your* job!"

Shea turned to Griswold. "They're not refusing to work. Just give them a place in the open to weld until you blast off the paint."

Griswold reached for the closed circuit phone that was anchored onto the basin wall. "Gimme Rosa," he rasped. "*Now.*"

55

Pete Rosa smiled grimly. He knew Griswold from nights, too much nervous energy. There was no point getting excited. He looked at Shea and then at the welding crew camped under the frigate. One of them raised a hand and said, "Hey, Pete, how are ya?" Rosa felt relieved.

He had always liked Shea. Distantly, of course. The kid was wild, but good-hearted. Now Rosa was glad that Shea hadn't gone overboard crazy, misread things and called for a ship-wide walkout. One day, he suspected, Shea would be escorted out for good. He didn't want to be the one to do it.

Rosa shuffled over to Griswold, who had been waiting impatiently for a signal to suspend the welders for refusing a job. "Can't you see they aren't going back in?" Rosa said evenly. "Get the sandblasters. Close off the tank while they go at it. And for chrissake, get the welders on other jobs. Whattya think, fuckin' Pennock's gonna weld up the ship himself?" Rosa turned and climbed back up the basin stairs, mumbling to himself all the way to the gangway.

Griswold called Charley Johnson, who sighed and put in a call to Pete Rosa back on the ship. Johnson waited a half hour with no response, then reported the story to Hershfeld. From there it went up to Pennock.

"I don't give a fuck what kind of paint's on the steel," Pennock confirmed to Hershfeld, "No one but me calls a halt to production."

Hershfeld phoned for security.

*****

After lunch, Rosa worked his way to the rear of the ship. The pipe crew was busy with outdoor assignments while the sandblasters worked inside using air lines. He tapped a pipe welder on the shoulder, motioning him to break his arc. Rosa leaned over the weld. His nose pressed close, examining its rounded underside. He turned to speak to the welder. Instead he faced Hauner. "Pete," Hauner said, "they want you up front."

Rosa's dark eyes were confused for a moment. Then his shoulders slumped and he threw up his hands. "Charley Johnson know about this?"

Hauner said, "What's the difference?"

Rosa looked around once. Noise from the welders stopped as he climbed the ship's ladder with the guard and vanished from the shipyard.

*****

Pennock's handwritten memo had been waiting on Tommy Kelly's desk when he came in before the start of third shift. A meeting up front first thing in the morning. Kelly was too busy shepherding the last of the deckhouse units into the basin to think much of it, even though the note said that the brass from Omaha would be there. Kelly knew that the heavyweights visited once a year or so, just to impress the locals. Waste of time.

With the LNG tanker program down the tubes, he guessed they were in for a pep talk. No skin off his nose. Kelly figured he was the only super in the place that could get whatever he needed from the graveyard shift in a pinch, though that thought came with a twinge since Johnno McKinnon's piggyback lift had gone wrong.

When his shift ended, Kelly broke away from his stuffy War Room office and inhaled the salt air. The cold clear scent exhilarated him. He opened the door of his pickup, decided to walk to the administration building instead. Matter of fact, when he got there, he would take the stairs four flights up to Pennock's corner office.

He arrived, scarcely puffing and proud of it. He gave Pennock's secretary a big smile. "Hey Tracey, how's my honey today?" The girl blushed and playfully threatened to tell her old man.

"That's okay," Kelly leered, "I bought him off. Promised him a whitehat the first time you and me do it." He patted her hair and took a step toward Pennock's office.

"Mr. Kelly," Tracey struggled for his attention, "I don't think he wants you in there yet."

Kelly frowned. "Whaddya talkin' about? Mort Pennock's got an open door policy with me, you know that."

Tracey shook her head in confusion. "Mr. Pennock told me no one goes in unannounced anymore." The secretary hesitated. "He didn't tell you?"

Kelly went hot at the temples and forced a big breath. "Sure, he did, Tracey. I forgot, is all."

The girl gave him a puzzled look. "Well, please have a seat. Mr. Pennock said he would be right with you." Kelly stood, motionless. She asked, "Is everything alright?"

Kelly reached for a chair and lowered himself into it. "A-OK, there, Trace, thanks very much." He murmured quietly, "Sonuvabitch."

Pennock buzzed and told Tracey to send Kelly into the corner office.

"It's nothing personal, Tom," Pennock told him, "we just need a change. The guards are bringing your items out now."

"You're nothin' but a fuckin' accountant," Kelly snarled.

"I'm the accountant who's still running things," Pennock answered. "We're staring at an opportunity to elevate this shipyard and you can't help me."

Kelly and Rosa weren't the only ones walked out. The shithouse wisdom had it that Charley Johnson only hung onto his job as welding super because he was black and kept his mouth shut, while friends like Rosa got the axe. With a touch of annoyance at his own sentimentality, Shea realized he felt badly for Pete Rosa. In the week before Shea had left second shift for days, the crusty general foreman had stopped him on the runway.

"You're makin' a name for yourself in this yard, so did I," Rosa told him. "To get where I am I needed a set of balls bigger than you'll ever see. These days it's different. I go to lay my wife and *phiffft*, it just comes out dust." Rosa had given Shea a tired smile before continuing down the runway. "Just don't expect it to last, kid," he said.

56

A stranger in a yellow helmet strolled onto the South Yard and unsnapped a black bag that hung from his shoulder. A camera slid out. He aimed it at a group of welders on break. The flash popped.

"What the fuck!" one welder bolted for a ladder. Others splashed out their coffees and jumped behind bulkheads.

The first one yelled across the plat. "Pecker checkers!"

Shea heard the call and ran toward the yellow hat, who had chased the welder to the ladder. The yellow hat's lens shutter clicked. He turned it on the others, clicked again. Shea grabbed him from behind and growled, "Who the fuck are you?" The yellow hat pulled away and showed him an ID stamped *Industrial Relations*. Ignoring Shea, he scanned the plat, finding welders who'd broken for a smoke. A shutter and flash. Across the South Yard, a platoon of cameras repeated the scene.

At the end of the shift, whitehats gathered their crews. They jerked their heads toward the blinds that stretched across Hershfeld's bank of windows on the front office building. They whispered that the blinds had been ruffling all day. Binoculars had jutted through slats. Or so they had heard.

"Don't know what's coming," the whitehats buried their words in their crew circles and licked dry, worried lips. "But it's all of our asses, for sure. Keep your heads down."

270

*****

In the weeks that followed, Pennock bunkered himself in his office, communicating to his army of whitehats with an avalanche of written directives and after-hours meetings that dragged on until early evening. The whitehats rushed their crews to work at the whistle and then fled to the War Room, sweating like schoolboys over endless report forms. Reams of tractor green spreadsheets cascaded into their mail slots, drowning them in the paperwork of jobs they had thought they knew inside out. The shelves by the coffee pots in their shacks sprouted more bottles of Maalox than mugs.

At the end of each morning, the whitehats returned to their crews. "Look," the most panicky among them begged. "I gotta get back on the tools. Can you get me a message to Rashford, on the QT? And can I pick up my old seniority level?"

The hardhats met them with noncommittal silence. The contract didn't allow it, and besides, they didn't care. They looked away, their eyes glittering as they recalled the whitehat parade a few years back through the struck and picketed gates.

*****

Shea felt later like he'd been sleepwalking through a nightmare. He was able to foresee it step by step, yet unable to alter the script. One of the Nam vets jokingly called it the Spring Offensive. Lonny adopted it as a lead line in the *829 News* and it stuck.

The first shots were fired in April. At the first morning whistle, the hardhats funneled into the gate and hustled around the Stiff Mill. They lined up at the punch clocks halfway to the basin, pushing their cards into slots. The time clocks dinged and spat the cards back. The lines moved more quickly than the previous springtime, or during the winter, or last week for that matter. There were just fewer cards to punch in.

At the start of second shift, a convoy of pick-up trucks rolled through the yard. A pair of warehousemen spilled out from each. They unfolded and studied diagrammed sheets, then tracked down and unplugged the vending machines plotted on their maps. They joggled the machines to their trucks and hefted them up to the beds. The trucks and their cargoes lurched through the yard. A dull silver jackpot of coins trailed a path to the gate. Less coffee, more work. "Damn," Cotty said, picking up coins, "they finally give me a bonus."

After lunch, the pink slips went out. In a week half the vent men were gone from the yard and with them the suckers they brought to the boats. Smoke lay dense in the tanks. Equipment repair crews were cut to the bone. Fat Sal's coffee business crumbled with the layoffs, though his betting game sales remained brisk.

Cleaning crews were laid off. Fermenting piles of garbage soon fouled the shipyard. Blast grit and trash piled up until welders trudged over mounds of debris that shifted under their weight. It all had a price.

One minute Roach was crawling down a ladder, slapping the rungs with his right hand while he held onto forty pounds of equipment. The next minute a cracked piece of two-by-twelve staging gave way. He flipped over nine rows of stiffeners before he hit bottom. If his fall hadn't been broken by some air suckers it would have been much worse than a broken shoulder, badly sprained back and a compound leg fracture.

Billy found him at break. The lift siren wailed and the crane hoisted up. Roach flew past the superstructure, surrounded by the crane's travel bell ring and the trolley screech of the rails. He pictured Johnno McKinnon, crushed to death in the basin, hauled out the next day in a basket like this. He sneaked a look down and seized up in panic.

The meat wagon shuttled non-stop to the clinic and back to the boats.

*****

Lonny sat with two crew mates on stacked spools of gun wire in the sun. They poured coffee, warming their palms on their mugs and speculating.

"How many guys are left, do you think?"

She said, "There's still a few hundred on the welding list until they get you. You'll be here for the contract."

"Think that we'll strike?"

"Keep the wet dreams at home. We're fucked and they know it."

She pointed toward the superstructure. At the back on the plat's tallest unit, Charley Johnson's stiff figure roosted against the sky. The welders screwed up their faces.

Johnson walked a slow, ramrod lap around the top of the unit, hands locked at his hips. All morning he picked at the air in front of his face, as if engaged in a fearsome debate with himself.

"Jesus!" Lonny said. "Don't the guy ever piss?"

Now and then Johnson beckoned a whitehat, who scrambled up the ladder to join him. Together they watched and appeared to be counting, Johnson pointing over here and now there. Swinging his arms, he gestured toward the basins: *Push those units, the assemblies, the crews.*

The whitehats nodded and nodded again until Johnson dismissed them.

At lunch time and break, even after the shift, the hardhats agitated with their foremen for information. The whitehats only scribbled initials on pads, shaking their heads. They refused to reveal their discussions with Johnson, or the view from the top of the unit.

The next day at lunch Lonny looked toward the basins, then tensed. There was Johnson once more, in the web of the superstructure that draped over the drydocks, two hundred yards off, half a football field up. Johnson gazed at the South Yard, then shifted and took in the basin beneath him.

She knew it was more than just one more ball busting scare.

57

Shea slid a token into the slot and pushed through the turnstile. He hadn't been in the station since he'd transferred to days, almost two years now. It almost felt like starting over.

He saw them by the bench near the tracks, just like Cotty had promised. "I got something to say, but you gotta be at the T for it. Two-thirty tomorrow."

"I haven't been on second shift in years, Cotty, remember? Two-thirty I'm in the yard."

"Tell 'em you got business up at the hall."

Shea had frowned. "Can't take time off for union stuff since the strike."

"You ain't got any lost time, Shea. Just tell 'em you're goin' home early, then. Eat the damn chit if you gotta."

*****

As Shea walked toward the bench, a rush of nostalgia coursed through him. Cotty, Pretty Boy, Byron, all there, their gear on the floor, paper bags in their hands. He was happy he'd come, relaxed by the memory for the first time in months.

"Looka here!" Cotty said loudly. "I told you this is new meat coming!" He tried to suppress a guffaw and couldn't. "Now pay up, you two!" He picked a fry from Byron and Pretty Boy's bags and chewed on them both. He waved Shea into the circle. "C'mere. Told ya once before, boy—I ain't gonna hurt you!"

Pretty Boy locked eyes with Shea for the first time that he could remember. "You listen to Cotty, Shea. He tell it straight." The words washed through Shea like it was yesterday.

The three welders smiled. Shea savored the words and the men and remembered.

Cotty said, "Don't know the exact day it was, but we makin' this your anniversary bus trip down memory lane, Shea. You goin' through hard times, seems like you feelin' alone. We know you tryin' like Townsend, don't nothing always work out. But we with you, man. You my boy much as Pretty Boy here. We just want you to know."

Shea asked, "Where's Rodney?"

Byron said, "Rodney dispatch back home a few weeks ago. Couldn't take this no more."

Cotty said, "Don't think 'bout that now. Today we tryin' to buck you back up."

Shea nodded and went to hug the old man just as the bus pulled up.

"None of that now," Cotty said. "Come ride with us for old times. Man's gonna bring you back to the station."

The bus door whooshed open. The driver leaned over and said, "Red carpet service as ordered." The steps to the fare box were covered in plush stick-on treads.

"For you from us, Shea," Byron said.

"Pull those up on your way out," the driver ordered.

Shea smiled and said, "Thanks, guys. I'll keep at it best as I can."

58

Even Joey Giacomo the union trustee was transferred to the South Yard as the shops emptied out. He called Rashford in a panic. "Make the call, Stan. Keep me outta the weather." Hershfeld found Joey a nice dry spot in the tool room.

"That's clout," Joey boasted to the board, "When they worry enough to take care of you like that."

The workload in the Stiff Mill lugged to a halt. Elroy's auto-welders shut down. The hissing torch heads went silent. In the cavernous quiet, the hardhats listened to their ghosts and their fears.

The last batch of stiffeners was readied to ship through the wide double doors to the plats. Crew by crew, the mill's hardhats were assigned to the South Yard and then, a couple weeks later, to the boats, where the only work remained. Like Elroy and Hicks, most had spent their time in the shop fusing plates that were spread flat before them, day after day, year after year, on the clean, titty welds. Overnight they were shunted to the boats, exposed to the cold and to junk-laden joints on jobs that required Houdinis to reach.

Goldy's arthritic fingers and knees had confined him to the shop for a decade. He was yanked from the mill and thrown onto nights, working with Griswold, who had missed his night bonus and was back on second shift. He was moaning before his feet touched the boat. Before leaving he put in a call for Shea, who had no Get out of Jail Free cards to stop Goldy's transfer. He gave the old man his phone number instead. "Call me at home if they give you any trouble."

Every night, Goldy limped to his job, leaning on Byron. Crawling twice a night through the tanks—in and out—was all that the old man could manage. After reaching his job, he collapsed on a plank while Byron fetched lines and welding wire for them both. "Brotherhood," Goldy observed, "is a wonderful thing."

He plastered himself to his job for the next eight and a half hours, certain that if he dared to go out, the return trip from lunch or the shithouse would do him in. He placed an empty coffee tin by his job, sealing in his piss with a plastic lid. Each night he weakened, ached more, welded less.

After a solid month of exasperation, Griswold took him aside. "You got pin butts tonight, like the rest of the crew." They both knew the job was a death sentence.

Goldy told him that he wasn't a kid, could no longer contort his body that way. Griswold ordered him to the shipside tool shack on the gangway, then went on ahead. On his way off the ship, Goldy tugged at Byron, who followed a few steps behind and waited outside the shack.

Griswold had the chit waiting. "I'm making this one for low production—a warning. Next time it's refusing a job. You'll be suspended." He held out the slip. Goldy trembled as he refused it. Griswold started to stuff the chit into Goldy's breast pocket.

Byron heard Goldy's wail and rushed in. He muscled between them and batted the paper.

"You set this man up!" he told Griswold.

Griswold shouted, "I can't carry cripples!" He stabbed at Goldy's shirt with the chit for a second time.

Byron grunted and pushed the whitehat away, then pushed him again. Griswold tripped backward, retreated and called the guards down.

*****

Shea found Byron at Ziyad's the next morning, cradling a blackberry brandy. Byron rose from the table. "I would rather weld in a car shop than suck dick with these boys. No justice, what they do to that man." He announced to the bar, "I would rather go home." He threw back his brandy, nodded to Shea and said, "Thanks for it all." Shea heard later from Cotty that Byron returned to Jamaica.

*****

As if he had spent all his years at a desk just preparing this entry, Pennock's awkward form came to life in the shipyard. He descended without notice on the boats, in the shops, to the basin. He watched his employees drink coffee on time that he paid them. He choked on his anger. He paced behind whitehats to jack up the heat that they put on their crews. His arms waved with fervor; his wire rimmed glasses tilted askew. He flew into rages, hurled light bulbs and spools at the bosses and bulkheads.

"Throws like a girl," smirked the hardhats, but their terror was barely concealed.

Pennock ordered parking lots padlocked, reducing the cost of the guards who'd secured them. Hardhats battled each other for space on the streets.

Demands on all sides escalated: more work, proper tools, decent staging, more firings, more layoffs, less work left to do.

The hardhats retaliated. Machines were stove in, rods bent and discarded, spools heavy with wire were thrown in the basins. Muttered threats of dropped wedges were rife through the shipyard, and actual drops were recorded. Steel plates were abandoned in faraway corners, then found very slowly or not at all.

From his post on the stool behind the door, Salvucci blamed the frightening turn of events on the commies. Rashford chased him out and screamed, "You ignorant fuck!" He pulled a bottle of Jameson's from his desk drawer and took a swallow. Fresh from the latest in a futile series of meetings with Pennock and Hershfeld, he sat at his desk with his head in his hands, boggled by his own impotence.

He tried to imagine what Shea would do in his place, then couldn't believe his own thinking. He clucked at the back of his mouth. "I still like that fuckin' kid, though. Godammit, he's got the piss." Rashford pulled another slug from the bottle. The taste of the whisky made him think of Big Jim O'Donnell, dead in the tanks these many years since. What would the old man think of him now? Rashford knew. Big Jim and Shea were two of a kind.

"You'd refuse to see how things are now, wouldn't you?" Rashford spoke aloud. "Just like fucking Shea." And then to them both, "You try sittin' here."

✳✳✳✳✳

In a slow, graceful bow to the gallery, the Goliath lowered its last aluminum sphere into 44 boat's fifth and final cargo hold. The ship readied for a week of sea trials, the puberty rites before launching and leaving the shipyard for good.

After 44 departed, the Goliath loomed over the empty basin beneath. The hardhats peered up at the god of power and motion they had built and then worshipped. They understood at last, with frightening clarity. It was an idol.

280

59

Shea and Lonny watched the filmy curtain on the kitchen window float with the wind. He could smell the leaves and the fall coming on.

"That's me," said Lonny, "lace curtain Irish." They allowed themselves a short laugh.

"I've been thinking of leaving," Shea told her.

Lonny straightened in her chair. "You think I haven't thought about it, too?"

"*You're* gonna leave?' he said. "For what? You got all the seniority you'll need for a while."

"Maybe I want a different life, same as you."

Shea said, "If I hand out one more flyer, I'm gonna go crazy. All we do is tell the guys what they already see. We're too weak or too chickenshit to do anything about it. They're killin' us in there." He put his hand on her arm as he talked, unsure if he was trying to comfort her or himself.

"You can't stop it, Michael, you know that. The newsletter just lets them know that what they feel isn't nuts. The company's a rabid dog, lunging out at anyone in its path."

Keefer paced in the next room. She cradled her baby to rock it to sleep. Shea snatched glimpses of her through the archway. He knew she'd moved in after Lonny's cousin had taken the smaller bedroom.

Drawn in by the talk, Keefer swayed back and forth at the archway. She cooed at the whimpering infant in her arms. "You don't mind if I listen?" she asked.

"It's fine," Lonny said, then turned back to Shea. "I've been reading about physical therapy, something like that." She looked at him curiously. "What about you?"

"Anything at first. Maybe a cab. I'll put in for the Post Office, the MTA. Something will happen." He said with transparent bitterness, "After all, I'm a vet."

"What about the guys?" she asked.

He didn't understand. Or pretended not to.

"In the yard, Michael. They'll miss you." She jostled him. "This really is important."

"I guess so," Shea said. "The place is just makin' me nuts." He pushed back from the table. "It won't hurt to think it through for a couple of days. I'm bushed. Gotta go home."

"Okay." Lonny tried to brighten as she walked him to the door. "Gonna turn in myself. We should talk about this real soon."

He walked to his car in the driveway. Pulled out his keys and rested his forehead on the roof of the car. When the kitchen screen scraped and he turned to the light, Keefer was framed in the doorway.

"Baby's down," she called to him, "want a drink?"

*****

When over the years any of the guys approached Shea and suggested getting together on the outside, he responded with an unconvincing excuse. It wasn't the particulars they noticed. It was the alacrity with which he said no, as if he had been assaulted by their offers of friendship.

Roach had long since become accustomed to his standoffish behavior. But it was a given that Shea would never hang out for a beer unless there was an issue to help wash it down. That was just the way he was. Roach felt sorry for him.

Once he and Billy drove from the South Shore to Shea's place in Fields Corner, hoping to pull him out to a bar somewhere nearby. Shea invited them in, then gently tolerated their visit in a way that made them realize their mistake. The few times other welders from Dorchester's checkerboard neighborhoods dropped by without warning, Shea remained politely resistant for as long as it took them to leave, too. They didn't try twice.

That's why he knew with perfect certainty it could only be Patty banging on his door. He had half expected her since he got home not long after daybreak. He considered letting her bang before he heard her hoarse judgement.

"I know that you're home, Michael. Don't you hide out on me!" Her pounding was fierce.

He slid back the bolt. She shoved the door a few inches before the chain jerked taut. "Open this door, Michael!"

"I can't undo the chain if you keep pressing on it."

She took her weight from the door without releasing the knob. He unlatched the chain. At the sound of the metallic rattle, she charged in, throwing Shea off balance. As if through a periscope, he watched her right hand whip at his face. He dimly anticipated the open-palm smack along the side of his jaw, yet was shocked when it jarred him. Even more when it hurt.

"Jesus Christ, Patty," he whined.

"You shamed me!" she shouted. "You damn well better ask him for help." She made a harsh, wounded sound. She lifted her hand to hit Shea again, then let it drop when he raised his arms to his face. "Shamed me in front of my friends. In front of my people," she wept in a whisper.

She had come by Shea's house the night before about ten, then left and returned after last call at Alice's club. Shea's house was still dark, his parking spot in front still vacant.

On an angry hunch that had long burned inside her, she wrenched her old Impala into gear and roared toward Lonny's place in Jamaica Plain. Her heart pounded with insult when she pulled up and saw Shea's car sitting in Lonny's driveway. It was all she could do to restrain herself from grabbing a whitewashed border stone from Lonny's perfectly groomed flower bed and smashing it through his windshield. Instead, Patty decided to go home and bide her time, maintain what was left of her dignity.

Unbridled accusations flew through her mind. Big talking white woman, all that sisterhood junk. Says she likes women then pulls shit like this. Patty flared her nostrils at the thought.

At the stroke of eight on Saturday morning, she lifted the phone and dialed Lonny's number. Her finger shook and caught in the dial. Twice she broke the connection and had to start over.

"He still there?"

"Who's that, Patty?" Lonny's voice was thick with apprehension.

"The man you been screwin'. Michael Shea, that's who."

"Patty, it wasn't me."

"I seen his car there at three in the morning. Don't you tell me he slept on your couch! He's there fucking *someone*!"

"Patty, please don't make me say anything else. I'm sorry it happened. You know it wasn't me."

"Who you hiding, then?" An awful certainty overtook her. "Keefer then? That little bitch?"

A silence, then Lonny said, "No, of course it's not Keefer. She's one of us in the yard for God sakes! You helped get her job back!" She breathed heavily for a moment. "It was my cousin. I'm sorry. I've already told her she needs to move out."

Patty dropped the receiver back on the hook.

*****

Shea hung his head when he knew that the slapping was over.

"I'm sorry," he said. "You know, we never really made any promises."

Patty flinched. "*No promises?* I love you, Michael, and 'no promises' is all you got to say? You just a cold white man. *Cold*!" She sniffed, bearing up. "You know what I put myself through to be with you? My own people say to me, 'Patty, you crazy'. All this time I been tellin' them folks to mind their own stuff. I been teachin' you, dammit! And you go and make me the fool." She slapped him again, suddenly and with force. This time she got a rise.

"Make you feel better? Do it again."

Her hand whipped out and raked him.

"No real promises? Well, all right, then." She gathered herself and strode out the door of his house. Like Billy and Roach, who had tried to befriend him, she never came through it again.

*****

Shea looked for Patty in the yard for a week before he checked his roster and realized that she had mustered out of the job. When he drove to her apartment past Codman Square Alice answered the door. She saw who it was and her eyes went cold. "She ain't here, Michael. And if she was I wouldn't be telling you."

"Ask her to call me when she gets back?"

"She ain't comin' back. She already gone home to Lenoir County. Now you go, and don't come here looking again."

Shea turned to go. Alice called after him.

"You broke her trust, Michael. And my sister is gone. You go sit with that."

60

Fat Sal shook his head. "I looked it over but I don't get it." He handed the paper to Shea. "From Hershfeld's desk. I sent a copy to Stan, heard nothin' back. Now I'm givin' it to you."

Shea read the memo aloud, slowly: "*Institute a three-strike progressive disciplinary policy already accepted by arbitration precedents. Discipline to be applied at the discretion of line foremen, but the three-step warning-suspension-termination progression becomes automatic.*"

He looked at Fat Sal. "Holy shit. How'd you get this?"

"I got cleaning people in the admin building, right?"

She blew out a breath. "It means they got a new policy to chit a guy twice over anything at all, then fire him the third time, even if the last chit is unrelated. Second chit is a suspension, third you're done. Frame anybody they want on dipshit stuff and look innocent when they fire him. Our hands are tied, they'll say, just policy. Go for the troublemakers. And old guys. Guys who can't work the ships or work too slow."

"Fuck," said Sal. "When?"

"Anytime they want."

*****

"Listen up!" Kearney told his crew, "I'm gonna read you a memo from up front. Every whitehat in the department is telling his crew the same thing."

287

"Does that mean you reduce the quota tonight?" Billy's sarcasm dripped.

"Just shut up and listen. 'Overtime is offered to every welder on every crew from this Saturday onward until further notice. When offered, overtime is mandatory.'"

"Okay," Billy allowed, "Time and a half. Good so far."

"Plus," Kearney added on his own, "A faster schedule means more flexibility for the company when it's bidding on new work, right?"

The crew nodded uncertainly.

Shea corralled as many welders as he could at lunch. "Faster production means quicker layoffs, so the OT's at the expense of everyone already outside the gates. Or if you're next up to get a slip." What Shea read in the memo—and that Hershfeld confirmed to him in a formal meeting—was that refusals would be subject to progressive discipline in combination with any other warnings. Three strikes and you're out.

What Shea *didn't* hear but certainly understood was Hershfeld's clincher when the plan had been presented to Pennock: "If they start to grumble that it's too much, only the union can organize effective resistance. Otherwise, any protest falls flat. If they do tell the men to refuse, the union would be liable for damages, our loss of production. Besides, Rashford knows that the men want the extra money."

Pennock considered. "But if they do refuse?"

"It will be the usual agitators at first, the ones just looking for an issue. With progressive discipline, applied consistently, we can remove them from the yard and win later at arbitration. In two or three weeks, the troublemakers will be gone."

When the whitehats read out the second week's edict from Hershfeld—forced first shift overtime Sundays as well as Saturdays for the foreseeable future—the response was mixed. Even Billy changed his tune. "Sure I want to bank some money for layoffs, but I got a wife and kids to spend time with, too."

Rashford and the board threw up their hands, insisting that a call for refusal was the same as a wildcat.

Shea rallied himself and his welders. "We can't let them bully us," he argued. "Besides, it seems like a bluff. What are they gonna do, fire the whole department before the work gets done?" He built the response through a simple whisper campaign. Just don't come in on the weekend.

On Wednesday, four hundred day shift welders were given mandatory overtime notices for the weekend, but on Saturday only half showed up. The other two hundred received written warning chits on Monday. Not one of them complained to Shea. By the middle of the week, though, he started to field calls from the welders with warning slips in their pockets. "What do we do next weekend?" they wanted to know. "Second time's a suspension." Shea told them to call Hershfeld's bluff.

The following Saturday another five hundred were told to work. Half of those were no-shows. On Monday there was a second round of chits. About a hundred of the disciplined welders had also been tapped to come in on the first round of forced overtime—this time the second-round offenders were suspended. Three days without pay and strike two on Hershfeld's three step ladder.

"So what now, Mike?" Billy felt disloyal but trapped.

That night Shea wondered how his mom would have coped with the three days lost wages that hung on each of his suspended welders. He felt the weight of a hundred families with breadwinners out on the street.

The hardhats were angry at Shea and the General, but Shea was the easier target. "What's the goddamn plan," they wanted to know. "How long does this go on?" The third week loomed, and with it, the threat of terminations. Shea had no answers. "You gotta tell them to come in next weekend." Lonny urged, "At least the guys with suspensions."

Shea caved. He told suspended welders to work the following weekend and no one got fired. Most of those with chits came in too, avoiding time off. He was saddled with the blame for a cause that the hardhats now saw as useless.

He felt a stab of pain for his mom who had died fighting for a little respect. In a way he'd never felt before, he was the target of his own guys' anger.

He felt he deserved it.

*****

Goldy's call came at night from the pay phone at Ziyad's. His voice was very small. "They fired me, Mike. Please help."

After his first warning from Griswold, the old welder had worked to the whistle every night without complaint to stay on his second shift whitehat's good side. It paid off. Griswold eased up, giving Goldy outside jobs when he could, avoiding the crawl through the tanks. There was only one further confrontation, the night that Goldy was simply unable to climb down a ladder to his assigned job. A couple younger welders had volunteered to switch with him, but Griswold had a stick up his ass that evening and refused. He wrote Goldy up, his second warning chit in the progression—a three-day suspension without pay.

At first, mandatory overtime had been a first shift-only concern. After two weeks it spread onto nights through a notice read out by Griswold after dinner break on Friday night. Goldy told the whitehat he had a hard enough time managing five days on the boat with bad knees. He couldn't do six. And his life and time were his own.

No one alerted Shea that the forced OT had spread to nights until Goldy called. The whispered counsel he'd been giving the welders to comply with the overtime demand had only reached first shift ears. But Goldy's knees wouldn't have let him say yes anyway.

It was his third violation. Three strikes and you're out. He was walked out the gate for good, his life reduced to an object lesson, the only welder fired for refusing overtime.

Befuddled by the turn in his life, Goldy wandered outside the gates every morning for weeks. He wore unwashed work clothes and clutched an old naval service book marked at the page with his picture. With a gnarled forefinger he poked at the image of a prouder youth for the benefit of passing hardhats. "See, I'm a veteran. They should never have done this to me."

Shea worried that the old man had come unhinged. He gripped Goldy's arm and guided him into a corner at Ziyad's to make sure that he really knew he was fired.

Goldy broke down. "It was all a hoax," he told Shea in tears. "My work clothes and all. My wife doesn't know."

That evening, Goldy began a ritual of nightly calls to Shea to conduct a minute-by-minute review of the day he was fired. Shea learned to soothe the old man but had no way to reassure him. Each night Goldy concluded his calls the same way. "Don't let them get you down, Mike. Bless you for trying to help." And every night after the line went dead, Shea understood that doing everything that he could just wasn't enough.

61

"Convene the damn Sanctions Committee and get rid of him!" Big Frank Salvucci demanded at the next Official Board meeting. But Rashford—and most of the Board— thought it was a mistake to give Shea a shot at martyrdom with yard wide elections only a year away.

"You're always a loser with a trial," Rashford told the Board. "But Big Frank's got a vendetta so I'm gonna let him move on this. The only thing we got going is that Shea fucked up with the forced overtime. Welders are pissed about their money and pissed that Goldy got fired." Big Frank had been too loyal for too long to say no.

*****

It was Saturday morning before Shea claimed the certified letter from the Sanctions Committee at the post office. As soon as he saw the Quincy return zip code on the slip, he knew what it was. He tore at the envelope, only mildly unsettled at the specter of a head-on joust with Rashford and the Board.

The official notice charged him with promoting an illegal walkout, endangering future work and fracturing the membership's unity. The Official Board had designated a few of its members as an ad hoc Sanctions Committee to oversee the trial. They would come to a verdict after a hearing. The decision would be confirmed by the full sixty member

Executive Board and then ratified by the membership at a special meeting.

Shea demanded a conference with Rashford. He arrived at the hall after lunch and was escorted to the dank basement boardroom. The union's top officers were already seated around a wood grain laminate table. Shea smelled cigars, though no one was smoking. Rashford sat in a padded government surplus desk chair while the other officers balanced on rickety folding jobs. One or two of them fiddled with memo pads.

Shea knew how meetings behind the Official Board's closed door were conducted. Rashford composed the agendas and chaired the sessions, rarely allowing his officers to take charge of anything more consequential than the sale of baseball caps emblazoned with the Local 8 logo or the post-meeting beer and cold-cut buffet.

The Official Board ringed the conference table and squinted at Shea. Salvucci opened by reading off the charges. "To top it off," he concluded, "We'll show that you managed to get a guy with thirty years seniority walked out the gate." He smiled. "Nice work, asshole. I'm thinkin' the Board's gonna find you guilty as charged in less than ten minutes."

"I've never used the *829 News* to attack other union officers," Shea said, "but I'll take this to the yard in a minute if you press it."

The Board circled the wagons in silence. Six faces looked apprehensively toward Rashford, who they knew didn't like this plan of attack in the first place. Salvucci held his breath.

Rashford's voice flowed like silk. "Do what you gotta do, Shea. You fucked up and we got you." He paused. "Y'know, this could have all ended differently. But you never wanted to listen."

"To what? The excuses you make before you give in every time to those bastards?"

"You still don't see how it works."

"Sure I do, that's the sad part. Anyone who wants to can see it."

Rashford sighed. "Not sure why I'm takin' up my time with this, 'cause no matter how this trial turns out, you'll never be elected again."

"They'll vote for me over you any day."

"Michael, don't you see? We'll never let that happen. No matter how many votes you get."

The Official Board nodded as one.

*****

Inside the shipyard, the graffiti on bulkheads announced *Reds Versus Retards: A Duel to the Death.* Below that a different hand had scrawled *How Can We Lose?*

Rashford encouraged Hershfeld to ease up in the yard until the trial was over. Hershfeld wasn't surprised when Pennock said no. The General's schedule was too tight to loosen the reins.

*****

Lonny and Shea spent hours outlining the terms of his defense before Shea concluded, "Who are we trying to convince, anyway? The trial's rigged."

Lonny looked at Shea with undisguised concern. "I need to tell you something." She drew a deep breath. "I will back you up as my steward for as long as I'm here. So will the others. Cotty will never desert you, of course. But what you did to Patty was wrong. There's not a woman or a black guy in this yard that'll really trust you like they once did. Including me."

"It was a mistake."

Lonny said, "No, it was a betrayal. And I'm not just talking about screwing someone else. Patty risked her place in her own world for you, and that just wasn't as important as your one-time depressed-as-all-hell fuck."

*****

The night of the hearing, a scant crowd of hardhats slouched in rows of folding chairs in the stuffy main hall. Four hours of wallbangers and stewing in front of Little Z's bar counter hadn't done much for their mood.

Reggie Leggiano, one of Rashford's trustees, opened the session by reading the formal charges. "Shea," he asked, "Do you have an opening statement?"

"Yes, I do." Shea rose.

"Siddown," Leggiano ordered, "You'll speak from your chair." Shea sat. There was an uneasy ripple from the floor and Leggiano banged the gavel to stem it.

Shea began. "The value of a union depends on its determination to extend equal protection to all its members—"

"You're out of order!" Leggiano bawled, bringing the gavel down again. "That's a speech, not a statement!"

"Let him speak!" At the rear of the room a weaving welder stood on his chair. His call was taken up by four or five others, not all drunk nor all welders. Shea spotted Roach on crutches, flanked by Billy the Kid and Ramos. A shock of red hair stood out in the crowd. Richie the rigger had driven back in after his shift to voice his support.

Leggiano relented, but his expression made it obvious that any reprieve was temporary. "Okay," he stared at Shea, "I'm warning you."

Shea said, "Forget it. Let's just move on to Lonny."

Leggiano said, "I recognize Alternate Steward Cheryl Lonergan to present Shea's defense."

Lonny was ruled out of order each time she tried to speak. Toward the end, her composure deserted her. She began to yell back at Leggiano. Shea walked over to her, took her elbow and shook his head. "The decision was made before we started," he said. "Save it for the vote." They sat without another word until the hearing was over.

The Sanctions Committee issued its report a week later to the officers of the full board assembled at the hall. Leggiano delivered the verdict: Guilty of obstructing the union's functions and endangering the membership. Then, to an approving hum from the floor, he recommended that Shea be suspended from his stewardship and barred from future elections.

As an Alternate Steward, Cotty demanded to speak. "What you doin' here is to kill the democracy rights of all welders, target the only white steward ever stood up for the black worker 'round here. You should be ashamed!" The Executive Board sat stone-faced. Without discussion, it accepted the verdict and the sentence. In addition to the three welding officers, only Fat Sal and Richie Millis voted to acquit.

The ratification vote by the full membership would take place the following week.

62

In the yard, anger over lost pay and forced overtime chits were largely forgotten. When Shea or Lonny tried to explain the Sanctions Committee charges, the technicalities were dismissed. "The bastards are after you, that's all," the hardhats insisted. "Don't make no difference what they say." As Shea walked through the boats, welders and even young workers from other trades bounded up to him.

"Who the fuck is the union to throw you out while the company is sitting on our necks?" the hardhats demanded. "*We* decide. We're the damn *membership*!" The insult drove their anger at whitehats who ushered them back to their jobs.

*****

Pared down by layoffs, the remnant of Shea's network circulated through the basins at lunch time, pleading for welders to attend the vote on the Sanctions Committee's verdict. Accompanied by Cotty and Pretty Boy, Shea visited the second shift gates during evening meal breaks to talk up the turnout. Afterward, he locked himself in his house and worked on his speech for the meeting, jotting an outline in the back of his black spiral log.

He knew that his notes were a jumble. How could he attack Pody's viciousness without mentioning the undeniable encouragement that the whitehat received from many of the

297

very welders that Shea now looked to for support? He had no way to condemn the General's onslaught in production, or Rashford's refusal to take it on, without acknowledging that Rashford, in his own way, was the bearer of a truth—a large segment of the hardhats would rather make peace with the terror than risk what little security they had.

Shea reviewed his notes, making changes and amendments, crafting phrases and ringing declarations. He worked feverishly, determined to make sense of the chaos that thrashed through the welders' world. He wanted to speak their repugnance. In the midnight stillness of his house, he refused to ask himself whether he wanted to win.

The second shift meeting was scheduled for two o'clock. Ratification of the Sanctions Committee decision was the only item on the agenda.

More than one hundred night shift welders showed up. Richie Millis had recruited a couple dozen guys from the other trades. Cotty hopped up and down excitedly in a corner, but Shea counted the room with dismay. He would need a much higher turnout at the first shift meeting to win.

Cotty's anger over Pretty Boy's firing and Magdalena's settlement was forgotten for now. "Don't you remember that meeting with Townsend? We couldn't get fifty guys here from second shift. And the shift was twice as big in those days!"

In the end, there were only three second shift votes to convict, over a hundred for acquittal. Cotty had held off his vote. "Savin' mine for the big show!" he crowed. "Wouldn't miss tonight for a million dollars!" Shea had gotten the margin he wanted and needed from nights, but the real numbers would make themselves felt at the day shift meeting.

*****

At three-forty, the union hall began to fill with first shift workers. Even Fat Sal's van full of Portagees prevailed on him to delay the return drive to Fall River. A line formed at the back door to the hall and snaked a quarter mile through the parking lot, down the driveway and around the corner onto East Howard Street. It was met by another column of hardhats coming by foot from the gates. Shea saw Cotty at the rear of the room, grinning at the size of the crowd.

Board members hurriedly arranged rows of folding seats in the basement and tuned on a second set of loudspeakers. Despite the layoffs that had hollowed out the yard, by four o'clock more than eight hundred workers packed into the hall. Shea was dizzied by the turnout.

Near the front, a contingent of Cape Verdeans shot him thumbs up. Saturday morning classes at the Y had notched up their English enough for Shea to finally understand them more as individuals than a collective—Pedro's striking friendliness; Tony's persistent concern about dental insurance for his kids; Joao waving his blue, white and red *Independencia para Cabo Verde!* cap to corral the others and talk through the news from the homeland. Shea returned their thumbs up with a pump of shoulder-high fists.

The crowd was already stomping and whistling when Rashford emerged from his back office. He looked over the room and blanched, then reluctantly moved to the podium between the Official Board tables up front. He leaned over and whispered angrily to Salvucci, who conducted a dour study of the hair on the back of his hands.

"Before I call this meeting to order, any second shift workers present must leave the premises now."

Cotty was on his feet. "Goddam if I'm gonna leave! I saved my vote this afternoon so I get the pleasure of watchin' you get whupped in front of this crowd tonight, Stan Rashford. You ain't denyin' my vote!"

"I will have the Sergeant-at-Arms take you out, Mr. Cottaway."

"Then you got a fight on your hands. That what you want? Throw out an old black man what's just tryin' to vote? With all these witnesses?"

"*Let him vote!*" The solitary voice was met with a cascading rumble of support from the crowd.

"Mr. President." Elroy Washington stood and spoke in a soft, clear voice.

Rashford seemed relieved. "Good to see you, Elroy. I hope I can count on you for some sense."

Elroy wheeled around slowly, showing himself to the crowd. "You all know me. I been here long as almost any of you, keep my mouth shut, do my work." Murmurs of assent rippled through the hall.

"Like Cotty, I'm here to vote. And I'm *gonna* vote. So is he. Everyone here, black and white gonna vote 'cause we all see that you, President Rashford, you afraid. You see us all here together, intent on callin' out these false charges—endangering the membership, favoring some over others, puttin' out a paper that tells us the truth, jeopardizing our contracts—all straw men what can't trick us about who Mike Shea is, or what we know about justice.

"So I say to you directly, President Rashford—too late for your fear! Too late for you tearin' us apart. Too late for your kind! Now, we gonna listen to each other, we gonna vote. And you, Mr. Rashford, this time you gonna abide by that count." Elroy sat down. The room was silent.

Rashford stood for a long moment, then hit the gavel. He coughed and cleared his throat before saying, "I call this meeting to order."

The hall quieted for the pledge of allegiance. Rashford started to read off the charges and verdict but thought better of it. He motioned Reggie Leggiano to approach the lectern.

"The chairman of the Sanctions Committee will report on its decision," Rashford announced and turned over the microphone.

Scattered catcalls from seated welders punctuated the lull. Leggiano fidgeted behind the lectern and began to read somewhat less forcefully than he had at the trial. He listed the charges in hesitant spurts as the catcalls notched up. "He's our steward not yours!" "Stop the railroading!" "Fight the damn company, not us!" Halfway through, Leggiano's words could barely be heard above the general clamor. He came to the end of his page, stopped and retreated from the lectern.

The noise in the room grew until Rashford filled the breech, repeatedly banging the gavel, this time with force. From the back of the hall welders led by a gang of vets chanted in unison at the Official Board. *"Mu-tha-fuck-as! Mu-tha-fuck-as! No-balls! Mu-tha-fuck-as!"* The angry pulse of it battered the Board at the front of the room.

Shea stood to speak from the floor. The noise in the hall snowballed toward a life of its own.

"Give him the mike! Put him up front!" a dozen hardhats yelled. Elroy rose from his seat. His gold necklace twinkled in the overhead lights. "We here for you, Shea!" he called out loudly.

Rashford clung to the podium with both hands. Richie Millis bulled into the aisle and took two alarming steps toward him. "We're here to vote, you lying bastard! Remember the lead paint! Remember the smoke! Remember Johnno McKinnon!" His eyes swept the room for approval. The hardhats cheered wildly.

Rashford moved away from the lectern and beckoned to Shea, who walked slowly to the front and waited for the crowd to quiet. He moved to the podium. After a hesitation Rashford gave way.

Shea held up a copy of the Sanctions Committee's printed verdict and threw it on the table. He understood that the hardhats had sacrificed a night watching hoops to channel their anger, not to save his position. Now he twisted that insight with a vengeance into Rashford.

"We have the right to refuse unsafe jobs!" he announced firmly. The crowd's anticipatory silence met his own. "We have the right to read the truth about our lives!" Approval rumbled from the floor.

"Respect for the guys who build ships—from the company and from the union—is as important as the ships that we build! That means every one of us, every color!" The hardhats stomped and shouted support.

Shea declared, "We are more than monkeys with torches! And we have the right to defend ourselves to anyone who says otherwise!" He swept an arm at the row of hapless union officials seated on either side of him.

The chant picked up: "*Vote! Vote! Vote!*"

Shea stood aside to let Rashford move back behind the podium. He banged the gavel. "I call for a voice vote," he said firmly. "All those in favor—"

"Voice vote's for cheats!" Lonny interrupted. "Divide the house!" The demand was taken up by the crowd.

"I said voice vote!" Rashford thundered. "Stay where you are!"

The membership ignored him. More than seven hundred hardhats walked over to Shea's side. Only the Board members and a handful of others stood across the room for conviction. Shea felt a stab of resentment when he saw the pipe welding crew huddled with the Sanctions Committee. "Fuck 'em," he thought. "Risked my job for those ungrateful bastards."

Rashford and the Official Board stood downcast and silent at their tables up front. Dusty nautical decorations vibrated on the walls and ceiling. Salvucci bent below the tumult to yell into Rashford's ear. Rashford shook his head violently and pushed him away.

The hardhats leaped over to Shea and piled on, pounding his back.

63

Rashford's Official Board hovered, glum and puckered, outside the cafe windows that fronted Ziyad's. They hung on each other, a circle of bean bags with badges. Rashford was nowhere to be seen.

The shithouse buzzed with speculation. Rashford had quit. Rashford had panicked. Rashford had been taken away. The profound hush on the sidewalk at Ziyad's fueled wild stories. At last, one of the rumors rang true.

At the postmortem board meeting the morning after the vote, Joey Giacomo brought out the coffees and donuts. He served Rashford first.

Rashford raged at his loss, then purpled. His breathing came short. Pain shot through his arms and he threw up his hands, clutched at his throat, fighting for air. Pastry mush spewed from his gullet. Big Frank Salvucci vaulted the table, pounding Rashford's back to dislodge what he thought was a donut. Rashford fell to the floor and convulsed while his heart crushed his chest.

Rashford motioned his men to come closer. His whispers constricted with pain. "Get the cops, not the medics. No sirens. Sean Macauley will know how to do it." He combed feebly at his forelock and bared his teeth in a gruesome attempt to reassure his boys.

Less than ten minutes later, an unmarked car pulled up to the hall. Captain Macauley climbed out with a young EMT who owed him his job and his silence. "Where is he?" was all that he said. They hefted Rashford onto a stretcher, laid him across the back seat of the car, then left as they had come.

Rashford lay in the hospital, weak as a puppy. Or so went the story.

The hardhats thought about Stan's forty years in the yard, a pipefitter made good, one of them. They shifted their feet, not at ease in their souls. Had the guy deserved all the shit that they gave him? The old timers recollected the days when the union was young, barely formed. Stan Rashford had stood next to Big Jim O'Donnell, the two best friends that a hardhat could have.

Young Jimmy O'Donnell, now over sixty, rubbed at the scars in his eyes. He spun his cinder-pocked cap in his hands. "Those were the days," he remembered. "Stan busted ass for the men in those days." At Shea's doubtful grimace, Jimmy held up a palm that foreclosed debate. "Yes, he did. And I don't forget."

While the rest of the Board mourned on the sidewalk, Big Frank and Charney made the circuit of shops. They strolled on the decks of the boats, calling men's names as they passed. A few of the hardhats even claimed to have seen them make rounds in the bilges. That one was hard to believe. What's more, when they asked what had happened to Rashford, Big Frank and Charney laughed like old times. You wait, they promised and winked. He'll be back.

✳✳✳✳✳

Fat Sal eased his bulk into the booth opposite Shea. He understood the question on Shea's face. "Game's changed," he said. "I'm still with Stan, but let's say you run against him next year—I think you win. Just a wild guess that you'll go for it. Am I right?"

305

Shea shook his head like Sal was a crazy man. "What's up?"

Sal hunched beefy shoulders forward. "Couple stewards thought they'd score points with Stan. Got him a small pot of flowers, and a bigger one, just the pot, no flowers. Put the little one in the big one, lined the space between them with a dozen Jameson's nips." Sal checked for privacy on both sides, then lowered his voice. "They took it to Quincy General to make him happy. Well, guess what? He's not there. So they called around to Mass General. Brigham and Women's. Shattuck. No Rashford anywhere. And he's not at the coroner's, neither. So, no heart attack?"

Shea couldn't puzzle it out. "So where is he?"

And Fat Sal, the beating heart of shipyard intel, said he just didn't know.

*****

At the gate a week later, the Board stumbled through a six AM fog. Shea had never seen them out and alert in the morning like this. In their left arms they balanced large stacks of leaflets and with piercing yelps slapped them into the palms of incoming hardhats.

"Hey buddy," the bunch of them called. "You gotta read this, it'll sure make your day."

Joey Giacomo patted asses as the hardhats shuffled by. "Easy, guy, take it easy," he urged. "Have a look at this flyer, willya?" And because they always did like Joey, because he was always good for a joke and, truth to tell, since they kind of felt badly for Rashford, they took one.

Beyond the line of officials, the hardhats stopped to stare at the headline. They looked to the Board, on the edge of real anger at the tease that they read on the page. The officials just laughed and mugged. "Hey, no bullshit, we got it!" Relief spread over the hardhat faces. Then they walked through the gates with a spring to their gait that they hadn't dared in a year, maybe more.

Shea stopped in front of Charney and put out his hand. Charney smirked and held out a flyer. Salvucci elbowed past him and thrust the paper at Shea.

"Read it and weep, cocksucker. You owe your job to the big guy."

Rashford Brings Jobs, claimed the flyer. *Announces New Ship Work with Pennock.*

*****

When Rashford showed up at Ziyad's he was mobbed. The guys wanted to know all about it. He recounted his flight over oceans and islands with Pennock. "We even did the little Jap bowing thing," he chortled. "I told 'em you guys, of all guys, are up to any job they got."

He surveyed the proud, happy faces at the bar. He relaxed and hinted of geishas, described the delights on the Ginza. He declined with a smile when Ziyad brought over a whisky on the house. "No thanks, guy," Rashford's eyes twinkled. "Your appreciation is all that I need." He made to play somber, then winked. "That is, and your vote," he guffawed. The hardhats guffawed and fought to be loudest.

Rashford cautioned the crowd, raised his voice for the ears at far tables. "It's an oil tanker. A repair and overhaul. She's hurt bad enough to keep us working at least a year while they find other work. We'll even have recalls, maybe restart the machines in the Stiff."

The hardhats yelled, "Alright!" and applauded. Some things you just can't take away from a guy like Stan Rashford.

*****

307

Engineers and draftsmen were called back from layoff and briefed. They were told that the tanker had been mauled in a storm, then a fire at sea. The tech men pored over shadowy photos that Rashford and Pennock had brought back. They tried to picture the damage. They looked to their budgets and cringed.

The ship was tugged up the river and drydocked. *Sea Shadow*, it said on the bow.

Timmy mustered his crew in the South Yard assembly area. "They're throwing us out to the basin." He lingered wistfully, scanning the long, empty rows of staging plats as if it were home he was leaving.

The crew hoisted toolboxes onto their shoulders and staggered toward the superstructure. Timmy stopped at the War Room to check on his orders while his welders stood outside in the sun. The *Sea Shadow* loomed over the crew, pervading the yard with secure, silent mass. Rain and salt water infected its wounds. What the grease didn't cover was mottled with deep, crackly rust that spread on the steel like a ravaging pus.

At the head of the basin, Timmy told the crew to stay put. He wandered off in search of the super. When he returned Shea was surprised to see Cotty with him.

They hugged.

"Goddam first shift," Cotty said. "Don't know what this is about, but they told me I'm here until further notice. First time in ten years."

Timmy said, "They told me all union officers 'cept Darby were moved to first shift."

"Want us all in a cage they can manage," Cotty ventured. "While second shift works on this killer ship with no union in sight."

The welders took in the length of the boat. The long, unbroken hull was painted sleek black. Waterline red peeked up from the basin. Like tourists in a cathedral, the crew drifted the breadth of the boat, hushing at vistas of damage. They gawked when the *Sea Shadow*'s port side came into view. Billy said, "Looks like my cousin. Downed out on ludes when he was a kid. Fell asleep cheek down on a steam pipe."

Heavy inches of black grease coated the hull, which was twisted and melted in places. Where the shell plates had ruptured, the welders could see into cross sectioned tanks whose bulkheads restrained swamps of dark, oily sludge.

Timmy came up behind the crew. "They tell me this tanker was struck by lightning. Blew apart in the water."

Shea said, "Blast off that grease or there's gonna be trouble."

"Hey," Timmy raised his eyebrows, "it's work."

The crew met in the shithouse at break time. "Weld on this stuff or be out on the street." They shook off their pricks and zipped up their jeans. "That's a choice?"

*****

Timmy scrabbled for jobs at the top of the ship, postponing the day that his crew would be forced to hunker down in the *Sea Shadow*'s tar pits. His welders mustered on the deck.

The ship's gnarled rib cage defied the stage builders, who fought back with planks that they tossed helter-skelter across twisted girders. Cranes strapped and slung injured hardhats in hammocks from tanks to the roadway, where the meat wagon never needed to wait for cargo.

Harried whitehats cornered nurses in the clinic and plied them with coffees. They pointed to hardhats whose injuries, they insisted, clearly called for the most urgent treatment. It was always a guy from their crew. "Patch him up, get him back," they pleaded.

When the deck work was finished the welders dropped to the tanks, where lightning-scorched grease hung from the sidewalls. Fitters scratched at the grease to make contact with steel. Welders inched over seams while fingers of flame shot up the sides of the plates that they welded.

Charley Johnson meandered over the ship, surveying the tanks. "Move along on those deadlines," he scolded his foremen, "Or move along some of those welders. We've got more on the list, there's more at the gates, they're beating the walls to get in."

Timmy gave the word as he signed the crew's cards at the whistle. "Put your noses in shit, guys, and like it."

Sweat itched at their backs. Grease dammed on their chests. Are we trash men or welders, they wanted to know. Their denims stiffened with sludge. Grease and sweat crabbed at their lashes like flies. At night they awoke, stinking like oil, sickened by smells that brought visions of men burst into fireballs, ignited by sparks from a weld.

The *Sea Shadow* seethed.

64

When the school shut down, Charley Johnson gave Manny Amado an option. "There's no more school, no instructors," Johnson told him. "Take the whitehat for the Cape Verdean crew or go back on the tools."

Manny had entered the shipyard a decade before, a kid with a family, fresh from Cape Verde. His parents begged Rosa to get him a job. The night that Manny took the whitehat, they toasted their son and Pete Rosa with mussels and vinho verde.

Johnson didn't like it when Manny asked for time to decide which hat he preferred. "I need you with them," Johnson said. "You're either their foreman or a welder. End of story."

Manny raised his dilemma to Fat Sal's riders at the turn of the shift. They debated his options all the way back to Fall River. Sal summed up the van-wide consensus to Manny. "You're fucked either way." Manny called up Pete Rosa, now retired in Scituate. Despite his own bitter end at the yard, Rosa counseled his protegé to accept the whitehat. And so, with misgivings, Manny took it.

Johnson assigned Manny's crew to the back of the ship and left them alone. Then Pennock's pecker checkers swarmed over the hull and conferred. They decided Amado was too thick with his welders.

Every day they scoured Manny's tanks, picking at him and his crew. Soon he felt more like a lap dog than boss. He

311

withdrew from the van pool and traveled alone. In his car he gloomily planned and replayed his days: the budgets, the crew charts, the insults, the threats. Soon he heard himself screaming at welders, saw himself writing out chits that he knew were a lie.

He told himself it was past time to quit. He just didn't know how to do it.

*****

The head of the basin was home to ramshackle sheds whose sheet metal walls shimmied and clanked along the gangway. A cramped whitehat office occupied the first of the shacks. Beyond it, a shipside tool shed with Dutch doors opened onto the gangway, commanding a view of hardhats and whitehats approaching the boat. Inside, the phones jingled with the latest from Fat Sal's central tool room—news via dozens of hardhats who dropped by for equipment or numbers each day.

Shea checked at the shed for an update from Fat Sal each time he returned from a pass. He was getting reports when a scream from the deck of the ship far above him cut through.

"Fire! Fire!"

The guy at the shed door jerked his eyes up past Shea. "Christ, it's the fucking grease." Shea wheeled around.

A speck of an orange-hatted burner leaned over the deck rail eighty feet up and halfway down the length of the ship. Behind him, flames licked over the port cargo sidewalls. They spun out the rim of the hold to the deck, then raced up and snaked through the grid of the superstructure. Above it they merged in a billow of flame and black smoke. No longer able to scream through the roar of the flames, the burner lunged and coughed his way to the stairs on the steel cage that cloaked the ship.

Shea raced up the stairway to help bring him down. Cascading shouts from below clashed with roars from the ship. By the time Shea reached the deck, the bow sizzled like butter in cast iron heat. The burner trembled against a water fountain bolted to the grid. Between slurps he choked out, "Welders . . . below."

A gust of pure heat sucked the breath from them both. Under Shea's hand, the metal grid warmed. The sting of charred paint filled the air. Shea tugged at the burner, who clutched at the rail and refused to let go. Broiling waves of air pressed at Shea's face. He tried to recall who worked in that hold. Anyone caught there was dead.

Manny Amado leaped up the stairway three steps at a time, his coveralls rank and heavy with sweat. "My guys!" he anguished and rushed past the landing, launching himself toward the flames.

"There's nothing to do!" Shea screamed.

Hardhats crammed on the stairway. The grid swayed with their weight. Flames smothered the crane, claws of fire forking above it. Encircling the flames, black smoke unfurled into clouds. Charcoal grease rained on the shipyard.

Manny emerged like a ghost from the boat. Ruptured blisters disfigured his arms. Not one of his crew had been where he'd left them. He wept with relief that he hadn't found bodies, and with fear for his guys.

He had a sudden vision and whitened. "They ran down below!" He threw aside hardhats who were blocking his way to an access hole at the bottom of the ship.

The hardhats clung to the grid like men possessed. Below, hundreds more clogged the gangway. The fire squad tried to push back the crowd. Their pleadings all fell on deaf ears. The holocaust roar commanded the yard.

A hardhat pointed. "Hey, look below!" Across the South Yard, the unwitting Cape Verdean crew emerged from the shithouse, laughing and joggling elbows at the door. They were jarred by the *Sea Shadow*'s heat, saw the flames rage at the top of the ship. To a man they launched into broken-field runs toward the hull, shouting for Manny. He emerged from his search in the bilges, shrieked and ran to them, hugging and kissing each of his boys with shameless relief. How could he have told all their families in Scituate? What would he have said to Pete Rosa? First Joao and then each of the others hugged him and kissed him in turn.

*****

Cotty and Lonny stood together on a landing, their arms entwined while the *Sea Shadow* burned. Through hours of flame, the hardhats around them endured the onslaught of heat, bolted to stairs and the gangway. They looked through the flames without seeing.

The fire died slowly. The embers left gifts—scalded odors of oil, the hot smell of fear. They remembered the feel of the grease, of the sludge, of the hot summer days, the welds spurting in flame.

Elroy and Hicks, new to the boat, had crawled high in their tank to hide from the flames. The greasy smoke found them. Now they lay in Quincy General like the dead. Tubes pumped their lungs. Twenty-three others lay alongside them, burnt and struggling for air. The hardhats remembered them, too.

*****

Shea smelled a bile rise from the hardhats. I know they can hate, he said to himself. But that's never enough. He braced against the grid and looked down at the crush of men hugging the cliff of the basin. They turned up their faces to him. Without any words they wanted to know, how do we cope with the madmen?

314

Shea spat at the *Sea Shadow*. "No one should live like this!" he proclaimed. He dreamed he would rouse them again.

They watched his familiar, faraway shout from the grid, a voice from above that exhorted them yet one more desperate time. In the flames of the *Sea Shadow*, they traced all their years. In their hearts they were glad it was burning. They thought of a few who should have burned with it.

They thought of the fears that they held for their world before the *Sea Shadow* floated up river, of the straw that it gave them to grasp. In their hearts they wanted the *Sea Shadow* back.

They thought of the hardhats still out on the street. Of the hope that the *Sea Shadow* brought them. They thought of laid off men crowding the gates, rattling the fences in chain-linked frenzy, begging reentry through fences and gates that defined all their meanings. That gave meaning to all of their terrible fears. They knew that the men at the gate would trample the gangway for the chance to break in. And they knew, as the ash choked the gangway itself, that they were the same.

They thought of their homes, fishing trips in New Hampshire, mythic fiberglass boats skimming over the water, the week, maybe two in a year that they prized as their own. They thought of their own little girls and their sons in their yards. All gone.

They knew they would go to their graves with a rage they could never concede. They stood by the basin and yearned for a bright, free beginning. For a start they knew they would never be given. They hoped that someone would save them from Shea.

He listened and learned that his moment was lost.

65

Shea made a left onto Dakota Street and pulled in by the tree that sagged across his front yard toward the curb. He spent a few minutes in the driver's seat inspecting cracked, drooping limbs which stretched past the sidewalk, almost as far as his outstretched fingertips. A fissure had appeared at the base of the main branch. It needed a lopping. His gut cried out for his eight-by-eight deck. A few beers, some cashews, a joint.

He walked up the steps to his oak paneled door and opened the screen. The door was solidly shut, but the lock was gouged at the keyhole. The lower right panel had been kicked in. Shea crouched at the hole and peered in. The splintered panel lay inside.

He ran to his car and snatched a bat from under the seat.

He slid his key into the lock. The door clicked and opened. He tiptoed into the foyer. Further on, the living room was thick with feathers that had been stuffed into his nan's velvet chair sixty years before. The chair lay on its side by the hearth. The velvet was slashed.

Her veneer hutch lay in splinters outside the kitchen. Shards from the glass cabinet doors glinted on the living room floorboards. The Chinese cabinet hung awkwardly, its lacquered panels wrenched from their hinges. Liquor bottles that Shea had stored inside made a trail to his second floor bedroom. Uncapped and half empty, they littered the stairs.

Liquor dripped down the risers and pooled on the hardwood at the bottom of the steps.

Shea crept up the stairway and tensed. Snuffles floated out from the bedroom. He tightened his grip on the bat, then nudged at the door.

A little black kid was curled up on the futon. Amber bottles were scattered like a halo around the room. Shea studied the kid with relief. Maybe nine, maybe ten.

The kid's eyes opened wide. "Hey, man, this your place?"

Shea sat on his futon, his head in his hands. Outside the window, he heard, almost tasted, the exquisite pork grill that Ozzie's daughters prepared in the yard next to his. They called at each other with hungry, expectant inflections that made him remember the night of his party, before his election, the night that he watched Patty dance.

Shea's shoulders heaved. "I really don't know anymore."

The little kid sighed. "Guess they made a mess of the place, hunh?" He slid across the mattress and he patted Shea's arm. "Don' be sad, man. Gonna be okay."

Shea looked into the small, earnest face. He offered a tired smile and put his arm around the kid's shoulders. He pulled him slowly to his feet.

"C'mon, little man," he said, "let's go find your folks."

66

Timmy took off his whitehat and cradled it under his arm. His shoulders slumped as he inched through the crowd. Once he'd been one of them, too.

The hardhats held back from their morning muster areas, massing instead on the gangway that led to the *Sea Shadow*. By the second whistle at seven, hundreds crowded the ramps, angry and fearful of boarding.

Timmy pulled himself up the stairway, stopped at a landing. He nodded at Shea, who stared dully back. Timmy rested his arms on the rail, his helmet between his hands. He spoke in a low, steady voice that carried along the metal grate stairs and over the heads of the men below. "Okay, guys, let's go back to work. Usual muster areas, starboard work only. They tell me it's safe."

At first just in dribbles, and then by the hundreds, hardhats shuffled to the ramps. Without a glance up at Shea, they walked through the holes that were cut in the side of the ship.

Lonny's arm was slung over Cotty, as if the two of them had frozen in place overnight. Beside them, a cluster of sullen white vets held out. And further down on the gangway, a few dozen young black welders stood together without a word.

Their silences broke in a unified storm. "Fuck Timmy Bronsan, fuckin' mouthpiece!" At the hundreds of hardhats walking in they called, "Fuck all you pussies, too!" They shoved at the men shuffling aboard who couldn't muster the strength to shove back. When the holdouts were finally the only ones left, they howled and cursed. Then they, too, plodded aboard ship.

Cotty and Lonny watched them go. They looked around, searching for Shea before they went in. He was the last to join the line.

Cotty said, "You did what you could."

Shea nodded without hearing.

"For real, man," Lonny added, poking Shea in the chest. "I mean, we had men and women, black and white, every shift pulling together. That's *real*. That's something they can't take from us."

"Yeah, maybe," he said as he followed them into the ship and headed for his worksite. Shea's legs ached to skip down the stairs, to churn past the gates, to breathe in the freedom outside. Instead, he stumbled his way past slaggy mounds of main deck debris toward his gear.

The last whistle blew. Shea flipped the top of his toolbox. He pulled out his shield and the long wire can with its canvas straps. He reached back into the box and extracted a set of leather sleeves pocked with dead black cinders. He tucked the leathers and gloves under the straps on the can and slung the kit over his shoulder. He dropped down a ladder and climbed to his tank.

He raised his shield and looked at the rusted steel seam before him. The gaps of the joint were ridged and encrusted with grit. His nostrils burned with the stink of the sludge, and then with the smoke drifting up from the welders below. He scraped at the joint with his hammer to slough off the grease.

He jerked his head down. His welding shield flipped over his face. Not very loudly he said to no one, "Watch your eyes." He struck an arc with his torch, kept it tight to the steel, trained his eye on the puddle.

A ragged poof of gas blew out from his weld. A molten glob found his left boot, burned its way behind the leather tongue. He felt the ungodly pain. He gritted his teeth and fought to control the puddle.

The surrounding tank faded until all that was left was the comforting shield that echoed his breathing. That, and the sputtering steel that spanned the width of his lens.

He hoped for the will to start over. He wondered who might stand with him at the gate, and if that still mattered. He wanted to know if sunnies still played in the streams down in Lenoir County, or if they'd been driven deep by the unrelenting Carolina summer heat, so much like the love of the woman who lived there.

Sweat trickled and hung at his eyebrows. He worked to the whistle to finish the seam.

ACKNOWLEDGMENTS

I would guess that most first time novelists might have many people to thank. I sure do.

Thank you to Susan Brodkin, my long-time partner and wife, who never once made fun of my efforts to write a story that literary agents didn't want to hear. To early readers Leslie Brelsford, Bill Fletcher Jr., my daughter Emily Rachael Brandow, and William Boggess, whose insightful critiques helped me shape a better book. To Hardball Press Publisher Tim Sheard and editor Matthew Sheard, whose expertise helped me fashion a book from a manuscript, and whose appreciation of the story motivated me to keep at it whenever I imagined there was nothing left to improve. And to my granddaughter Maya Feinberg, whose skill with a pencil and brush created the graphic map at the front of the book. Thanks to David Palmer's *Organizing the Shipyards* which provided historical information on conditions and unions drives at the Bethlehem Steel shipyard in Quincy MA.

Most of all I'm thankful to the many, many shipyard workers I came to know. Their characters and experiences inspired *Goliath At Sunset*.

ABOUT THE AUTHOR

Jonathan Brandow worked for nine years as a welder and elected union officer in a Boston shipyard. His non-fiction book *The Just Market* was published in 2014. He also has written for the *Boston Globe*, *In These Times* and *Tablet*. *Goliath At Sunset* is his first novel.

A DOZEN QUESTIONS FOR DISCUSSION

1. Shea has a sense that his outlook differs from most of his peers even before his entry into the shipyard. How so? Does he primarily identify as white or working class—or both? What are the implications of that for his later activism and leadership?

2. As the first phase of modern industrial decline sparked fear in mid-Seventies Boston, the battle over school desegregation embroiled the city in a virtual race war. Shipyard workers of all colors—including a small number of women—were forced to work side by side at the convergence those upheavals. How did the larger social crises influence the reform movement inside the shipyard? How do the dynamics of deindustrialization and racial conflict spill over into the book's universal themes of respect and dignity as the engines of justice?

3. At several points in the story, the union's old guard is clearly more concerned about securing new work for the shipyard than about safety or racial discrimination. Shea is threatened several times—and then brought up on charges—for allegedly jeopardizing current jobs and future work by pursuing or publicizing grievance issues. How should a union balance all those concerns? (Pp113-114, 241-246, 250-256, 261-263, 304-307)

4. Discuss the initial decision that Shea and Patty made to hide their relationship from the rest of the shipyard (Chapters Pp186-89, 195-98). Did their choice conciliate with racist attitudes or was it just a smart practical move? Similarly, how do you feel about the way(s) that

Shea approached talking to white workers about racism and racial discrimination? (Pp24-25, 42-45, 190-192, 209, 213-215, 233-234, 247-249) About his betrayal of Patty's trust? (Pp282-286)

5. After Shea moves to Dorchester, the troublesome (and violent) émigré bar near his house burns down. In the aftermath, Ramos gives Shea his opinion of the status of minority workers in the yard. What do you think of his analysis? Was the apparent arson of the bar justified? (Pp221-225)

6. Despite the hardhat support for Keefer and the women's pregnancy rights, the union is willing to trade away their gains in the following contract. Rashford doesn't seem worried about blowback from the same broad center that signed the women's petition. How come? (Pp177-182)

7. During the strike, Slidell crosses the picket line, undercutting white and black workers' alike. He is clearly resentful of both the company and the union. Later he protects Magdalena from a racist assault at Wollaston beach. On balance, is he a "good guy" or a "bad guy"? (Pp135-136, 226-231)

8. Cape Verdean welders don't say much in the book, but their actions have an outsize impact on Shea's development and trajectory in the shipyard. How so? (Pp24-25, 42-45, 47-50, 65, 161-162 299, 311-314)

9. Welding superintendent Charley Johnson and General Foreman Pete Rosa are both torn by their belief in "up by the bootstraps". To some extent both also use their positions to help out what they deem to be "their own kind". Are their tribal instincts qualitatively different from those of Rashford, the union president? Why does

Johnson's role infuriate Cotty? (Pp47-50, 137-138, 207-209, 239-240)

10. The Goliath is the shipyard's largest crane. The name is also a metaphor for the company and, in a larger sense, the economic structure within which the hardhats labor. Near the end of the book the author writes that "(t)he hardhats peered up at the god of power and motion they had built and then worshipped. They understood at last, with frightening clarity. It was an idol." (P280) What does that mean?

11. Political scientist Ernst Fraenkel argued that dictatorships come to power by applying special step-by-step restrictions to targeted populations that exist alongside a "normative state" that is privileged by contrast. How were petty privileges like trade categories and job assignments leveraged toward similar ends in the shipyard by both the company and the union's old guard? Does the authoritarian workplace mirror current social and political dynamics? (Pp32-33, 41-42, 153-154, 166-169, 190, 200-201, 210-212, 262-263, 277)

12. What decision do you think Shea makes at the end of the story? Where do you think he goes from there?

MORE TITLES FROM HARD BALL PRESS

A Great Vision: A Militant Family's Journey Through the Twentieth Century, Richard March

A Pandemic Nurse's Journal, Nurse T with Tim Sheard

The Activist Spirit: Toward a Radical Solidarity, Victor Narro

The Art of Organizing, Michael Raysson

Asian Workers Stories, Luka Lei Zhang, editor

Building Unions: Past, Present & Future, Peter Kellman

Care Under Covid: 1199NE Health Care Workers Tell Their Story, Steve Bender, ed.

Good Trouble, Steve Thornton

I Just Got Elected, Now What? Bill Barry

I Still Can't Fly: Confessions of a Lifelong Troublemaker, Kevin John Carroll

Legacy Costs, Richard Hudelson

The Lenny Moss Mysteries, Timothy Sheard

Love Dies, A Thriller, Timothy Sheard

The Man Who Changed Colors, Bill Fletcher

The Man Who Fell From the Sky, Bill Fletcher Jr.

Murder of a Post Office Manager, A Legal Thriller, Paul Felton

New York Hustle: Pool Rooms, School Rooms and Street Corner, Stan Maron

Presente: A Dockworker Story, Herb Mills

Radical Connecticut: People's History In The Constitution State, Steve Thornton & Andy Piascik

Sixteen Tons, A Novel, Kevin Corley

Standing Up: Tales of Struggle, Ellen Bravo & Larry Miller

The Strike That Changed Maryland's Wilderness County

Throw Out the Water, Kevin Corley

Union Made, Ertic Lotke

What Did You Learn at Work Today? The Forbidden Lessons of Labor Education, Helena Worthen

Woman Missing, A Mill Town Mystery, Linda Nordquist